ACCIDENTAL DEATHS

Also by Laurence Gough

THE GOLDFISH BOWL
DEATH ON A NO. 8 HOOK
HOT SHOTS
SANDSTORM
SERIOUS CRIMES

Accidental Deaths

Laurence Gough

VIKING

This one's for Eve

VIKING
Published by the Penguin Group
Penguin Books Canada Ltd, 10 Alcorn Avenue, Toronto, Ontario, Canada M4V 3B2
Penguin Books Ltd, 27 Wrights Lane, London W8 5TZ, England
Viking Penguin, a division of Penguin Books USA Inc., 375 Hudson Street, New York, New York 10014, USA
Penguin Books Australia Ltd, Ringwood, Victoria, Australia
Penguin Books (NZ) Ltd, 182–190 Wairau Road, Auckland 10, New Zealand

Penguin Books Ltd, Registered Offices: Harmondsworth, Middlesex, England

First published 1991

1 3 5 7 9 10 8 6 4 2

Printed and bound in Great Britain on acid free paper

Canadian Cataloguing in Publication Data Available

ISBN 0-670-84469 1

1

Frank borrowed a ballpoint pen with the hotel logo on it from the red-haired guy at the front desk. The guy had an accent. When he spoke, the words seemed to pour out of his mouth, all liquid and silvery, musical. The way he talked, he might've had river rock for teeth, a sandbar for a tongue. Frank figured him for Irish but it turned out the guy was Italian. That was the way it was in Vancouver – everybody in the city seemed to have come from somewhere else.

Frank tried the pen out on a scrap of paper to make sure it worked and made his way to the hotel bar, which was surprisingly busy considering the time of day.

His waitress looked like Heidi gone to seed, but she had a nice warm smile and Frank liked her accent. He ordered a vodka martini on the rocks, twist of lemon. As she was turning away he touched her arm, very lightly, and asked could he have an extra napkin, since he'd left his notebook up in his room. Another smile. No problem. It was that kind of hotel, expensive and friendly.

While he was waiting, Frank drew a happy face on the ball of his thumb. He wasn't a bad artist – maybe it was time to consider a career change. Killing people was a lot different than breaking arms. More permanent. Not as much fun. There were lots of details that had to be worked out. You couldn't just walk up to the job and do it and go home and read the paper. Frank's problem was that he was a novice. He needed to get organized, work out the risks and how to eliminate them.

It wasn't the kind of chore Frank was good at or had any patience with. He wasn't looking forward to the task. When his drink arrived, he asked the waitress to give him five minutes and then bring him a refill. He plucked the lemon out of the glass, popped it in his mouth and chewed it to a pulp. The martini went down like an oyster – one long swallow.

Frank tried his new pen out on the napkin. It worked okay, but he had to be careful not to press too hard or he'd rip the paper. Fine, he could live with that. Now what? He watched the bartender shake his new martini to death. The guy caught his eye and smiled. Frank nibbled on the tip of the pen.

The crime he intended to commit was hit and run. He needed a disposable set of wheels, obviously.

So . . . the first detail that needed to be taken care of was what kind of car to steal.

His instinct was to boost something dependable and common and not at all flashy. Also fairly large. Like maybe a Volvo. But for the moment he wasn't supposed to be thinking like a cautious 38-year-old ex-con. He was a kid on a joyride, and kids didn't think at all. *Go for it!* was what they shouted at each other. Fuck the future, even if it was only ten minutes down the pike.

So Frank decided to steal something loud and fast.

His second martini arrived. He paced himself on this one; took all of five minutes to eat the lemon and drain the glass. Enough thinking! He signed the bill, added his room number and strolled out of the hotel into a wall of heat and bright sunlight, was immediately almost run over by a courier on a mountain bike. He stood there in the middle of the sidewalk, rubbing his elbow where the handlebar had nicked him. Imagine what it must feel like to get whacked by a ton of automobile.

Unbelievably painful. Ouch!

Frank headed east on Georgia towards The Bay, caught the elevator up to the third floor and sauntered through women's fashions and a snack bar and flowershop, made his way across the skywalk and into the parking lot. Another elevator took him up to the lot's top floor. Working his way down towards ground level, Frank hunted for his new car.

Half an hour later he was sitting behind the wheel of a midnight-black Corvette with a tinted windshield and white leather seats and a four-speed gearshift sloppy as a bucket of pigshit. To his mind, the Corvette was so ostentatious and ugly it could give a blind person a migraine. Cops too, unfortunately. Frank pushed the bucket seat back as far as it would go, making room for his legs, and then drove in a long series of straights and spirals down to ground level.

There was a lineup at the ticket booth. He checked the dashboard and sun visor and then the glove box. No ticket. The Vette's owner had apparently taken it with him. Son of a bitch. Frank had to pay the maximum rate. Eight bucks. He gave the attendant a ten and told him to keep the change but give him a receipt for the full amount. The terms on this thing he was doing for Newt were half in advance and the other half, plus expenses, on *completion.* Nice word. What it meant was before Frank got paid in full he had to show Newt a newspaper headline or death notice proving that he'd killed the lady cop, Claire Parker. Frank stuck the receipt in his wallet, put the Corvette in gear and gunned it.

Frank parked the car in an underground lot about six blocks from the hotel, backing it in and then ripping off the front licence plate. Later, he'd lift a set of tags from another vehicle and do a switch. Using the Vette was risky, but the way he saw it, there was an element of risk in everything a person did in his life – people'd choked and died on a piece of steak, right? So what were you gonna do, starve to death? No, what you were going to do was chew your meat more thoroughly, take care not to rush the situation. Exercise caution.

Frank was only going to put about three miles on the car. He'd take it nice and easy. Stop for red lights and everything. Drive every inch like he was somebody's grampa.

He walked down Robson to Burrard, turned right. The hotel was fairly large – three hundred rooms. The front entrance was on Hornby but there was a side entrance on Robson. Frank had been out of town for a few years, but he remembered the street well. Hornby was sunnier and more pleasant than it used to be; the old courthouse – now an art gallery – was set well back from the street and was only a few storeys high. Plus during lunch hour there was usually a bunch of secretaries from the surrounding office towers catching a few rays on the wide granite steps or lying around on the grass. The women were mostly young and attractive. The type that liked to spend their leisure time eating yogurt and smoking and scoping the guys in the crowd, trying to guess their net worth.

There was a white BMW cabrio parked at the bottom of the gallery steps, guarded by a clean-cut type in a folding metal chair behind a plywood table, selling lottery tickets.

Frank walked up to the car, tried the door. Locked. There was a handwritten sign on the table – the proceeds of the lottery were going towards a new clubhouse for a local rugby club. Tickets were thirty-five bucks a pop. The guy behind the table asked Frank was he interested in a ticket?

Frank said, "Why should I pay money when it's so easy to steal one for free."

The guy's smile faltered but didn't die. Frank liked to travel light. He'd breezed into town with nothing but the clothes on his back, walked into a nearby Ralph Lauren outlet and slapped about a grand on Newt's charge card. He wasn't that crazy about the Ralph look; the store was conveniently located, so that's where he'd shopped. But now, because of the way he was dressed, this preppy-type jock wouldn't take him seriously.

Frank said, "You think I'm kidding? Watch this." He used a pick to slip the lock. It took him maybe three seconds. The kid's mouth fell open wider than the door. Frank slid inside the car. His nailclippers scraped a couple of wires bare. He touched the wires together and the BMW's engine caught. He got out of the car. Less than fifteen seconds. He said, "Not bad, huh?"

The kid swallowed. "You a cop?"

"Security biz. Mostly industrial applications. It's a growth industry. Ever been robbed?"

The kid shook his head.

Frank said, "Tough shit, because what you're telling me, whether you know it or not, is you don't own anything worth stealing." He started to walk away. The kid asked him how to turn the engine off. Frank ignored him.

Back at the hotel, he went up to his room and washed the licence plate grit off his hands and lay down on the king-size bed and watched some TV and tried not to think too much about those yogurt-eating secretaries and the way they hiked up their skirts to sun their legs. After a while he drifted off. By the time he woke up, it was past six. Jet lag? From Los Angeles? Doubtful, since the flight only took about three hours and the two cities shared the same time zone. Frank stripped and showered, shaved, blow-dried his hair and dressed in tan slacks and a shirt patterned with what looked like dead leaves, a rust-colored tie and his Bass Weejuns. At a party, you might guess he taught art school for a living, instead of beating people up and making them promise to catch up on their payments, be prompt. He made sure he had his wallet and comb and then locked up and rode the elevator down to the bar.

The piano player was a fat lady with blue hair. She did a pretty fair Billie Holliday, considering the two of them had never dipped into the same gene pool. Frank leaned against the bar and ordered a Paulie Girl. The bartender who'd mixed his eleven o'clock martini had come and gone. This one, night shift, was taller and better looking, wore tight black pants and a crisp white shirt with red suspenders, topped off with a red bow-tie that was left over from Christmas, maybe. A rectangle of gold plastic pinned to his shirt had the name *Jerry* stamped into it in black letters. Geriatric, the way he moved. His shiny black hair was slicked straight back and the gunk he'd put on it had stained his collar pale yellow. He wore a black patch over his left eye and walked with a limp.

But even with only one eye, Jerry had seen enough of Frank to know better than to keep him waiting.

The beer arrived. Frank tilted the bottle to his mouth and delicately sipped.

Jerry used a small white towel to polish the bar in fast, tight circles. Centrifugal force quickly carried him a safe distance away.

Frank sniffed the neck of the bottle. He raised his voice a little and said, "Got a Rolling Rock, Jerry?"

"Sorry."

"Why not?"

A shrug. The name tag glittered under the lights. "Not enough call for it, I guess."

Frank said, "C'mon back here a minute."

Jerry moved reluctantly towards him. The guy had a definite limp, all right.

"Can you score me some dope, Jer?"

The bartender flinched away. "Who told you that?"

"Nobody. I'm just asking." Frank smiled. He had a nice smile, teeth like sugar cubes. "You look like a guy knows his way around, might be able to help."

"I can help if you're thirsty. You got some other kind of problem, there's nothing I can do."

"Nickel bag," said Frank. "Couple of joints . . ." He smiled, "Am I asking for a trunkload of coke? C'mon, be reasonable."

Jerry glanced up and down the bar.

Frank flipped open his wallet, showed Jerry his New York licence made out in the name of Bobby Costello. The bartender gave the licence a quick glance, focused on Frank's fat wad of cash.

"There's a bellhop should be on duty . . . Name's Roger. Short guy, in his fifties. Grey hair, cut real short . . ."

Frank dropped a pair of twenties on the bar.

Jerry shook his head. "No thanks. Roger'll take your money, not me."

"For the beer."

"It's on the house."

Frank shrugged, slipped the money back in his wallet. He went into the lobby and told the desk clerk he wanted to talk to Roger. There was a miniature working steam-engine enclosed in a glass case to the left of the desk. Frank supposed it was a marvel of engineering. He used the glass to study Roger's posture and walk as the guy sneaked up behind him. Frank believed you could tell a lot about a man by the way he held himself, moved. He spun around just as Roger reached out to tap him on the shoulder. Roger was caught by surprise but recovered quickly.

"Something I can help you with, sir?"

Roger was wearing a natty grey suit with dark blue piping but no gold braid. His eyes were dark brown. As he'd spoken he'd backpedalled across the carpet until he was just out of kicking range. Now he waited with his soft hands dangling at his sides. Frank smiled. Roger was smart enough not to smile back.

Frank said, "I was talking to Jerry, in the bar. He thought you might be able to help me."

"Any friend of Jerry is a friend of mine. Are you staying at the hotel?"

Frank nodded.

Roger said, "Then if you'll just give me your room number, she'll be right up."

Frank flicked ash on the carpet, let some smoke leak out of his nose. "I'm not looking for a woman." Frank lifted his arms, as if preparing to be body-searched. "Punch me."

"Excuse me?"

"In the stomach. Hurry up."

Roger glanced quickly around the spacious lobby. He hit Frank with a playful jab.

"No, I mean *hard*."

Roger said, "Should I be getting paid for this?" and delivered a roundhouse right. The sound of the blow made a bellboy turn his head, wondering. He saw Roger nursing his hand, Frank standing there with a cigarette dangling from his smile.

"Jeez!" Roger sucked his knuckes, gingerly rotated his wrist.

"I'm like that all over," Frank said. "Hard as a rock. And you think I'm the kind of guy has to pay for his action, izzat right?"

Roger said, "Hey, the things some people like to do, it wouldn't matter if they were Cary Grant and Mel Gibson all rolled into one, it'd still hurt like hell and cost top dollar."

Frank's broad forehead curdled in thought. "What kind of things?"

"Forget it. If it ain't a dame, exactly what is it that you're after?"

"Drugs," said Frank.

"Coke? I can score a couple lines. Nothing serious. We're not talking more than a gram or two. Although I could probably give you a phone number, put you in touch with the right kind of people."

"Couple of joints is all I'm interested in," Frank said. "A dime bag, whatever." From his point of view, people who got involved with serious drugs were not very serious people.

"I can let you have a quarter-ounce." Roger bent a leg. The way he was standing, his posture, Frank half expected him to unzip and piss on the chair. But all he did was polish the toe of his plain black shoe against his pants leg, study the shine.

Frank said, "Yeah, okay."

"A hundred bucks, courier'd to your room. It'll get there faster'n a Domino's pizza."

Ash fell from Frank's cigarette to the carpet. He said, "Who do I pay?"

"Person knocks on your door. Anything else I can do for you? Sure you don't want a woman? Or something with a little less mileage, maybe?"

Frank said, "Don't be disgusting." He smiled. "I'm in five-eighteen. You can't miss it; it's right next to the ice dispenser and the room with the TV turned up too loud." He started across the lobby towards the bank of elevators forcing Roger to scoot aside to avoid being steam-rollered into the carpet. Frank had been outsized ever since the third grade, and had quickly learned how to wield his bulk so he intimidated and diminished people without ever laying a finger on them or even looking as if he was thinking about it. In fact, it was the unhappy realization that Frank wasn't even *aware* of them that rocked most people, liquefied the marrow in their bones. Frank was six-four and tipped the scales at two hundred and fifty-something pounds. When he took a stroll, the sidewalks were never crowded. When he was thirsty, there was always room at the bar. A few years ago, he'd been up around the three hundred pound mark. Fat, and getting fatter. A stray round from a .45 had steered him into a liquid diet followed by six months of hospital cuisine. Since then, he'd never had any trouble keeping his weight down.

Looking on the bright side, you could say that every cloud had a copper-jacketed lining.

He took the brushed-aluminum elevator up to the fifth floor, slipped the plastic rectangle into his lock and opened the door. He'd left the television on, and all the lights, the air-conditioner and bathroom fan and heat lamp. Two-fifty a night, but that included utilities and, anyway, Newt was paying the bill. Frank loosened his tie and flopped down on the bed. Outside, a siren wailed the only song it knew.

Frank passed the time watching television and honing the fine art of blowing a small smoke ring through a larger smoke ring. After a while there was a discreet knock on the door.

Frank said, "It's open. Come on in."

She was maybe fifteen years old, and had a fifteen-year-old's perfect figure – a little bit tentative but excruciatingly feminine. Her skin where you could see it was white and seamless as a sheet of paper. Her hair was peroxide-blonde and swept up in a French twist. She wore a skintight lycra body suit, electric-blue laced with pink stripes. There was a gold chain with a cross around her neck. A man's chunky diver's watch weighed down her left wrist. Aviator-style mirrored sunglasses dominated her face. Her mouth was wide and sensuous, her lips the color of an overripe cherry.

Frank sat up, interested, wanting a better look. She flicked a wall switch, drawing the curtains. Since the TV was on, there was enough light to see.

Frank said, "Where'd you come from?"

"Roger sent me." She removed her sunglasses with a theatrical gesture. Her eyes were a pale glacial blue. She kicked the door shut with the heel of a size-four white leather Nike with a blue stripe, smiled.

Frank said, "Nothing personal but, like I told Rog, all I'm interested in is scoring a little dope. A roll in the hay don't interest me in the slightest."

"What's your name?"

"Frank."

Rolling her hips, the girl crossed the carpet and sat down on the edge of the king-size bed. She pulled off a Bass Weejun and began to gently massage Frank's foot. Even through his sweaty grey sock, her fingers felt cool, soothing.

She said, "I saw you in the lobby."

Frank waited. Waiting was something he had learned to do well. A prison thing. A working-for-people-like-Newt thing.

The girl said, "I thought you were kind of cute."

"You did, huh."

"Nothing personal. I'm crazy about big men." She smiled, letting him know he was being teased. For what that was worth. The sock came off. She leaned over and kissed his big toe. "How tall are you?"

Frank told her. She took off his other shoe and then his other sock.

She said, "That feels good, doesn't it?"

"It might if I was in the mood."

"Relax, it'll happen."

The phone on the bedside table warbled softly. Frank picked up. Rog said, "Everything okay up there?"

"What's her name?"

"Lulu. Lemme talk to her."

"Not until you say the magic word, Rog."

"Please," said Roger promptly.

Frank handed over the phone. Lulu said hello and then nodded her head and said, "Don't worry about it, you'll wear out your pacemaker." She handed the phone back to Frank. "Roger wants to say a few words." There was lipstick on the mouthpiece. Frank wiped it clean on a pillow.

"What?" he said into the phone.

Roger said, " Be nice to her. Please."

Frank said, "Why should I – you sure that's what she wants?"

There was a slight pause, and then Roger said, "If she tells you she likes you, Frank, you can believe her. She really and truly means it."

"How would you know?"

"The girl happens to be my daughter. As a matter of fact, she's my only child."

Frank said, "Don't bother me again," and slammed the phone down so viciously that, far below him in the lobby, Roger flinched and ducked his head as if to avoid a fatal blow.

2

Seven cream-painted concrete steps led to an open porch about four feet square. The door was off its hinges. The floor of the porch was painted brown, and was littered with chunks of stucco and plaster, wood-splinters, glass, a great deal of blood.

The girl's body lay across the threshold. In the living room, Cherry Ngo sat slumped in a crumbling overstuffed chair in front of a dead fireplace. A Siamese cat lay in Cherry's lap. The cat's huge blue eyes were wide open but saw nothing – a sliver of shrapnel had simultaneously relieved it of all nine lives.

Homicide Detective Jack Willows said, "Hey, Cherry. Wake up. Talk to me."

Willows' partner, Detective Claire Parker, said, "He's in shock, Jack. The ME says we're wasting our time."

"We'll see."

Five minutes earlier, Willows had helped himself to one of Cherry's Players Lights, fired up his Zippo and stuck the cigarette in the corner of the kid's mouth. The glowing tip of the cigarette was only about a quarter of an inch from Cherry's bandit moustache, but he didn't seem worried about it. Smoke had curled up into his eyes for the past five minutes. He had yet to blink.

Thirty seconds later, a quick sizzling sound was accompanied by the sour smell of scorched hair. Parker plucked the cigarette out of Cherry's mouth and tossed it in the fireplace. "Satisfied, Jack? Or should we try something else – maybe give him a hotfoot, or pull his fingernails off with a pair of pliers."

There were only two possible witnesses to the murder – Cherry Ngo and his younger brother, Joey.

Willows and Parker went down into the basement, past the furnace and laundry room, another room containing a set of free weights and a cracked wall-to-ceiling mirror. Joey Ngo's bedroom was just big enough to contain a bureau, a single bed, Joey, and two uniformed cops.

Willows had to duck his head to get through the door. The bedsprings creaked as Joey sat up. He averted his face, wiped tears from his eyes.

Parker said, "We know how you feel, Joey, but we have to talk to you now. It can't wait."

"I didn't see anything." It was hard to say how old Joey was. Twenty, maybe. His hair was cut very short. He was about five foot six, couldn't have weighed more than a hundred-thirty pounds. His face was smooth and round, unformed, a blank. He wore a black T-shirt, faded black jeans. His feet were bare. There was a Band-Aid on the heel of his left foot.

"Just a few questions." Parker smiled. "It won't take long."

"How's my brother?"

Willows said, "He's in shock, but he's going to be okay. Tell us what happened."

Joey blew his nose into a rumpled sheet. Lit a cigarette. Same brand as his big brother. The window was painted black. Willows propped it open with his ballpoint pen.

Joey said, "Like I told the other cops, I was down here when it happened. Sleeping."

"Was the window open, or shut?"

"Shut."

"The heat doesn't bother you?"

"What heat you talking about? The only heat around here is you."

"You heard the shots, is that what happened, the shots woke you up?"

"First thing I remember is Cherry yelling, screaming his head off."

Parker said, "Then what?"

"I got dressed, ran upstairs."

Willows said, "You put on the clothes you're wearing now?"

"Yeah."

"Got a job, Joey?"

"Yeah, I got a job. Speedy Auto Parts, over on East Eighth."

"You Vietnamese, Joey?"

"Canadian."

"When'd you emigrate?"

"Seventy-six."

Parker said, "With your parents?"

"My father, but he died a couple of years ago."

Willows said, "What time you start work?"

"Eight."

"Has Cherry got a job?"

"Not that I know of."

Parker said, "What did your brother say to you when you went upstairs?"

Joey shut his eyes, sucked smoke deep into his lungs. After a moment he opened his eyes and turned his head, exhaled towards the open window.

"He didn't say nothin' at first. He was standing by the door. The door was mostly closed and I couldn't see her. Cherry was trying to shut the door the rest of the way but it wouldn't close. Then I saw it was because her leg was sticking into the living room. That's why the door wouldn't close, because of her leg."

Joey flicked the remains of his cigarette out the window, lit another.

Parker said, "Could you see outside?"

"No, nothing. It was real dark. The porch light was shot."

Willows said, "How'd you get the blood on your feet, Joey?"

"That's her blood, Emily's, most of it. I got cut, but it ain't that bad."

"Emily Chan, that's her name?"

"Yeah."

"She was Cherry's girlfriend?"

"Yeah."

"Tell us how the blood got on your feet."

"I went over and pushed Cherry out of the way and opened the door. You see her?"

"Yeah, we saw her."

"What kind of gun do that?"

"We'll talk about that later."

"Shotgun?"

"Did you touch her?"

"No way."

"But you went out on the porch, didn't you?"

"Cut my foot on the glass."

"Did you see anybody?"

"The woman in the blue house across the street. She don't like us. Makes racist remarks. Was standing in the driveway by her car."

"Did you say anything to her?"

"Never do."

Parker said, "Did you see anybody else?"

"No."

"How long were you outside, out on the porch?"

"I don't know, I couldn't tell you. Maybe a minute. Ask the lady in the blue house. She knows more about me than I do."

"You're sure you didn't touch Emily?"

"Yeah, I'm sure. Fuckin' right I'm sure."

Willows said, "Okay, you went back inside the house. Then what?"

"Cherry was still screaming. I got no idea what to do, how to handle the situation. You see the door? He ripped it right off the hinges. Grabbed it with his bare hands, like he was Superman. Then he grabs *me* and all of a sudden I'm real scared, because he's looking at me but he doesn't see me, know what I mean?"

Parker nodded.

"And he's still yelling, and then he stops, and he shakes me hard and says, 'Cindy's been shot,' so quiet I can hardly hear him. Then he sits down in the chair and kind of goes limp. Is that where he is now, sitting in that chair?"

Willows said, "Cindy is the cat, right?"

Joey started crying again, his slim body shaking with the force of his despair. Willows waited. Joey blew his nose on the sheet and took another drag on his cigarette, fought to get himself under control.

Parker said, "I don't want you to worry about him, but we're taking your brother to the hospital. It's a routine precaution. You have to understand that there's nothing *wrong* with him. They might want him to stay overnight, but probably they'll just take a quick look at him, prescribe a sedative, and send him home. Why don't you come along for the ride – he could use the company."

Joey uttered a long, shuddering sigh. He looked up at Willows and said, "Yeah, you're right. Cindy's the goddamn cat."

3

Lulu took Frank's pack of cigarettes and lighter off the bedside table. She lit up and put the cigarette in Frank's mouth, said, "I guess that was Rog doing his concerned daddy act, huh?"

Frank said, "I've heard of weird scams but this one takes the cake."

"He's my daddy, and I'm an only child. What exactly do you expect from him; callous disregard?"

Frank said, "If I had beef stew for brains, I'd still be smart enough to figure this one out."

"I'll do anything you want, and I'll do it better than you've ever had it done before. But there's one thing you have to understand: I'm not in the life and Rog isn't a pimp."

Frank blew smoke at the ceiling. He stared at her, and she stared right back. He said, "How old are you?"

"Twenty-two."

"Bullshit."

"How old do you think I am?"

"Fifteen, maybe sixteen."

Lulu laughed. It was an interesting experience, kind of. She had perfect teeth. Her tongue was pink and healthy looking. She could've been a ghost, she was so pale. Frank repressed a smile. It had occurred to him that if he tried real hard, he might be able to see right through her.

She said, "I take care of myself. There's no magic to it. Eat plenty of fresh vegetables, exercise. Swim in the hotel pool. Jog." She smiled. "Stay out of the sun, that's *real* important."

"How much?" said Frank.

"For the night, five hundred. Or maybe it won't cost you a dime – who can say?"

"Half an hour?"

She smiled. "Forget about it; you won't want me to leave."

Frank wriggled his feet. He said, "I don't know why it looks so sexy, but it does."

"What's that, lover?"

"Kiss my toe some more."

"Okay. Whatever you want."

"And . . ." Frank blushed.

"No problem," said Lulu.

Frank said, "But first I'm gonna go take a shower, because of the hygienic aspect."

Lulu nodded. "Cleanliness is next to godliness, all right. Especially nowadays, I guess."

"Hey," said Frank, "it's nothing like that. I been walking all over the place, checking out the town. It's hot. I worked up a sweat."

Lulu slipped off the bed. Her movements were fluid and graceful, almost boneless. She was agile as a snake. As she wriggled out of the blue and pink lycra it made a kind of slurping sound, like someone in the far distance using a straw on the bottom of a milkshake.

In the shower, Frank was softly but firmly told to assume the position. He stood with his legs spread wide and the palms of his hands up against the tiles, while Lulu lathered him up and lathered him down. She'd left the heat lamps on but turned off the fluorescents. The bathroom was like a sauna and the lamps turned the steamy air a dusky rose color that was kind of romantic. Frank leaned his head back as Lulu's slick and soapy hands skated in slowly widening circles across the ridged muscles of his belly.

"Like that, do you?"

Frank said, "Yeah." His voice was hoarse. He was having a hard time standing still, keeping his balance.

Lulu got up on her tippy-toes and kissed him in the hollow of his throat, nibbled him gently. "You like that too, don't you?"

"Yeah," said Frank again. He smiled into the spray and then the smile faded, was washed away by the sudden scary thought that the water he stood in was a hell of a lot deeper than it looked.

"Something wrong, baby?"

Frank said, "Your turn. Gimme the soap."

She was like a river, the way her body flowed into its curves, so gentle and sweet, predictable and amazing. Frank tried his best to make his huge, clumsy, calloused hands drift light as feathers down her body. She was so tiny and so perfectly formed, so fragile. Her bones were like the bones of some small bird. He was afraid that if he wasn't careful he might hurt her.

She gasped, moved against him.

Frank said, "You okay?"

"Could I have a little bit more of that, please?"

"Sure thing," said Frank.

After the shower, Lulu asked Frank if he had a clean white shirt. There was a spare in the closet, on one of those hangers you can't steal and take home with you. The suite cost two hundred and fifty bucks a night, and hotel management was worried about being ripped off to the tune of a coat hanger? Modern life. Frank gave her the shirt. It came down to her knees and took a couple more years off her life. Now she looked about twelve. She said, "Where's the key to the room?"

"In my pants pocket."

Lulu slipped on her sunglasses, looked down at him. The big mirrored lenses reflected two naked half-tumescent Franks. She said, "Get it for me, will you."

Frank rooted through his pockets until he found the rectangle of plastic. When he offered her the key she took his hand and led him to the door. He opened the door and followed her out into the corridor. The door swung shut behind them, hydraulics sighing and then the lock making a final small click as if somehow taking an irrevocable bite out of his life. Frank stood there, bare-ass naked and already starting to feel a chill.

What the heck was going on?

A door about fifty feet away opened and an elderly couple came out. The man tried the door to make sure it was locked, and then he and his wife walked arm in arm down the corridor, their backs to Lulu and Frank.

Lulu whispered, "A second honeymoon, I bet. So sweet. Kiss me, Frank."

Frank took her in his arms and kissed her long and passionately.

"Perfect." She leapt up, into his arms, forcing him to take her weight. Frank reflexively assumed the time-honored stance of a groom about to carry his bride across the threshold. Finally it became clear to him why she'd wanted his white shirt – it was the only wedding dress they had. He unlocked the door and carried her back into the room and across to the bed.

"Oh Frank," she said, "I know you're going to have a hard time believing this, but I've been waiting for you all my life."

There seemed to be a million buttons on the shirt. Frank got a few of them out of the way, bent to kiss her breasts.

"I'm crazy about you, Frank." She turned her body slightly towards him, to make herself more accessible.

Frank got ready to say something, and then thought better of it.

Lulu said, "What?"

"Nothing."

"No, you're holding back. I can tell."

Frank kept working at the buttons. There was no sense wasting time. He said, "It isn't that big a deal, but I wish you wouldn't dye your hair." His fingers lightly traced a path across her belly. "Especially down here. It can't be good for you, all those chemicals."

"I don't bleach my hair, Frank." She removed the sunglasses. "Look at me."

Obediently, Frank stared into the cold depths and icy shallows of his lover's pale blue eyes.

"Look at my skin. See the veins? I'm the color of a fucking glacier." She sat up, moved a little away from him. "I'm an albino, Frank."

"An albino?"

"Crows, rhinos, people . . . It's congenital. There's nothing you can do about it. It's caused by an absence of pigmentation in the hair and skin. Notice how pale my eyes are? I'm wearing tinted contacts; my eyes would be even paler without them. It isn't vanity, Frank. The tinted plastic filters out the light. Think about this: light *hurts*."

Frank kissed her on the mouth.

She said, "That's good, Frank. I like that, kiss me just like that. Can we try a little experiment?"

"What?" said Frank.

"Close your eyes. Pretend, just for a moment, that you're blind. Sightless." Lulu's voice was soft as raspberries. Frank shut his eyes.

She said, "Try to remember that you've always been blind, in all your life there's never been anything but darkness." She paused, and then added, "You've lived alone in a room all your life. I'm the first and only woman you've ever touched. You don't know if you'll ever be with me again. Kiss me, Frank. Kiss me and kiss me and kiss me. Memorize me, discover all my secrets. See me as I really am, in darkness."

Frank was thirty-eight years old. For one reason or another, he'd never bothered to fall in love. Maybe it was because he moved around a lot. Also, the kind of women he met tended not to want to get involved. In the past, that suited him just fine. He did care for women, though. During his years in the slammer he'd never once bent over for anyone or made anyone bend over for him. Sex, possibly because he was used to lengthy periods of abstinence, had never been all that big a deal – he thought of it as kind of like kite flying, something you did when the wind was up and you were in the mood.

This time, it was different.

Frank's experience had always been with women who knew how to take, but weren't all that good at giving. Lulu, he was beginning to learn, was unique in that she had an appetite for both pleasures.

Frank decided to go along with her, do the blind-man kissing thing. He paced himself, took his time. After a little while the weirdness of the situation passed away and he forgot all about himself, who he was. It was like he'd shucked his personality, kicked out of it and moved on. Somehow, he stopped being Frank Wright and evolved into somebody else entirely.

But *who* did he turn into? That was the part of it he didn't even vaguely begin to understand.

His butterfly mouth fed on the nectar of her flesh. Because his eyes were shut he couldn't see that wherever he kissed her, she blossomed a delicate pink. But he was acutely aware of the rising heat of her body, the way she warmed to him. He continued to feed on her, began to pick up the pace and then she took his head in her hands and thrashed against him and cried out and pushed him away.

He opened his eyes and found to his dismay that she was crying, tears streaming down her cheeks. He offered her a corner of the sheet. She ignored him. He lit a cigarette. The sun was going down and the window was a rectangle of black randomly dusted with specks of light. Frank pulled smoke into his lungs.

Five hundred bucks. No wonder.

Lulu snuffled, got herself under control. Sighed contentedly. She said, "Tired, honey?"

Frank said, "Maybe a little."

"How long are you staying in town?"

"Just one more night. There's something I got to do."

"What?"

"Don't ask."

Lulu snuggled up against him, rested her head on his chest. He stroked her gossamer hair. She said, "Yeah, that's what I figured you were up to. Something you couldn't talk about. Something bad."

Frank said, "C'mon, really?"

"The minute I saw you, I knew all about you. Didn't you feel that way about me?"

Frank thought about it, watched the smoke from his cigarette curdle the air. When he was confident he had it down right, he said, "When you walked through that door I told myself that if we were together all the rest of our lives, I'd never get to know a thing about you."

Lulu giggled. She said, "Guess what?"

"What?"

"You're right."

She seemed so pleased with him. Frank wondered why. She rolled on top of him, sat up with her long white legs straddling him. She said, "Now it's my turn. But there are some new rules. You can't move, not one little itty-bitty bit. And you can't say anything. No instructions, no requests. And no groaning or any sneaky stuff like that. My *quest* is to figure out what you like. If I do it right, I won't need any hints. You understand what I'm saying, Frank?"

Frank said, "I sure hope so." He took one last drag on his cigarette and stubbed it out in the ashtray.

She kissed him on the mouth.

Frank lay perfectly still. The day's last sunlight streamed through the hotel window, slanting into the room. There were shadows everywhere but her startlingly pale body was bathed in light; it was as if the light passed right through her, pierced her through and through.

Frank tried to let go, fall away from himself, get back to that strange place where he did not know himself and had so much to learn. Her breath on his face was cool and damp.

He might have been a dead man. He floated above himself and looked down. She kissed his eyes. He did not blink.

4

The interrogation room was about the size of an elevator. A cop had once said it was small enough to give a spider claustrophobia, and it was almost true. When two detectives and a suspect squeezed in there, everybody had to breathe at once.

The walls were painted a neutral cream color. The carpet was grey. There were three chrome-legged chairs with beige upholstery arranged around a small table. The table was bare – it held no calendar to remind prisoners of passing time, no ashtray to throw if they got mad. As a matter of fact the whole building, all six floors, was a non-smoking area. But the room was self-regulating in any event – anybody fool enough to light up with the door shut would die of asphyxiation in minutes.

The middle of the three chairs was equipped with a microphone on a flexible stainless steel stalk. A camera mounted high on the opposite wall was permanently focused on the chair.

A door to the left of the main entrance led to an even smaller adjoining room. The door was painted the same color as the walls, so it would blend in and not draw attention to itself.

Cherry Ngo sat slouched in the chair in front of the microphone. He was about five foot eight and very thin, maybe one hundred and ten pounds. He wore a shiny black leather jacket and black jeans, cheap black sneakers, no socks. There were five – count 'em – diamond earrings in the lobe of his left ear. A fat gold chain looped around his ankle. There was a tattoo of a red eagle on the back of his right hand. His hair hung down past his button nose and tight rosebud mouth.

Parker wondered how he could wear his hair like that, why it didn't drive him crazy. In a tussle, it'd be the first thing she went for. She'd grab that long hank of hair and use it to drag him all over the sidewalk. Wipe that sneer off his face.

She said, "Tell me again what time it was when you first heard the car go by?"

"I dunno. Late."

"How late?"

Cherry Ngo shrugged. "Someplace between midnight and maybe three o'clock, half-past three?"

"Then what?"

"Like I already told you. Nothin". So I went back inside."

"No, that wasn't how it happened. Think hard. The car came around again, right?"

"Yeah, yeah."

"And you went out on the front porch again."

Cherry was starting to get a thing for this lady cop who had so much patience, never raised her voice or gave him a hard look. She thought she was tough, but was too good looking to make it work. He liked her hair, black and sleek like his, and her dark-brown eyes, liquid and depthless. The lady cop had a pretty decent body, too, long-legged and slim. Cherry Ngo smiled, flashing the kind of teeth dentists dreamt about – not much enamel but lots and lots of gold. He said, "That's right, lady. The car came back and I went out on the porch."

"Detective."

Ngo frowned.

Claire Parker said, "Not 'lady'. Detective. Was it you who turned the porch light on?"

"I look stupid?"

Parker thought she'd take a pass on that one. "Who turned on the light, Cherry?"

"Emily."

"Emily Chan. Your girlfriend."

Cherry Ngo smiled. His delicate face wrinkled up like a dehydrated apple and his expensive black leather jacket creaked softly as he shifted in the chair. He tilted his head to one side and the constellation of chip diamonds sparkled in the light. "Ex-girlfriend," he said. "I don't go out with dead chicks." He gave Parker a look that clearly said – since there's a vacancy, you interested?

"Okay, Emily turned on the porch light. Then what happened?"

"The car was sitting in the middle of the street. Just sitting there, right in front of the house. Didn't have no lights on, but you could hear the engine. Not throbbing like you see on old movies. More like a kind of whining." Cherry worked his jacket zipper up and down as fast as he could, so it made a shrill ripping sound. The thin waterfall of gleaming black hair danced across his face, into his eyes.

Parker said, "What kind of car was it?"

"Black."

"It was a black car."

"Yeah, black. Or maybe blue, I dunno. See, it was dark out. What I got, X-ray vision?"

"Was it a large car, a small car . . ."

"Somewhere in there. Medium? I really couldn't say for sure." Cherry sat up a little straighter. "Wait a minute. Now I remember. Weird how the picture popped into my mind. I'm lookin' at the lady detective's glossy black hair – my favorite color – and all of a sudden I see a Honda. A black Honda CRX."

"How many people in the car?"

Cherry Ngo shrugged, played with his hair. "Windows was tinted."

"But somebody must have rolled a window down. Or did they shoot through the glass?"

"Window came down real fast. Power-winder. Then all I could see was muzzle flashes." Cherry Ngo made a gun of his hand. He pointed the gun at Parker. "Pow! Pow! Pow! All that noise, bullets all over the fuckin' place. I'm standing there in the light. There's bullet holes in the wall. I say, don't flinch, Cherry. Take it like a man!" He leaned forward, smiling. "Tell me somethin". How come the bad guys run around with automatics and shit like that, and all you cops got is little dinky thirty-eights?"

"Were there any marks on the car? Dents or scrapes, anything at all?"

"Was in showroom condition. Real nice."

"You notice the plates?"

"Not really."

"Okay, Cherry. The gunfire, then what?"

"Emily ducked back inside. At least, I thought she did. We know better now, don't we?"

Cherry's dark eyes searched Parker's face. She gave him nothing, absolutely nothing.

Cherry slouched a little lower in the chair. "So what happened next? Nothin' much. Little black car took off. Cops showed up. Somebody in the neighborhood dial nine-eleven?"

"A concerned citizen."

"Yeah? Thought they was extinct."

Parker said, "Your girlfriend was shot to death and you make jokes."

Cherry Ngo stared up at the ceiling. He crossed his legs, worked the zipper. Parker gritted her teeth. She said, "What's wrong with you; don't you care about her?"

Cherry said, "Laughter's the best medicine. And she took, I heard somebody say, at least three hits. Died on her feet. Man, that's the way I'd like to go. Fast 'n Easy." He grinned. "Sounds like a franchise, don't it."

"How old was Emily?"

"Too young to die, probably. But what if she'd made it? All that scar tissue, she'd of been ugly, miserable, and lonely. So maybe it's better this way, right?"

Parker said, "Her lower abdomen was covered with bruises. Did you beat her?"

Cherry smiled. "Her lower what?"

"Did you beat her?"

"She was always bumping into things. Clumsy. What'd I want to beat her for?"

Parker said, "Stay right where you are. I'll be back in a minute. Don't move an inch."

Cherry Ngo said, "Don't take it personal, *Detective*, but this fuckin' city's already got a big surplus of ugly broads. So I don't think one less is worth making such a big deal about."

Parker went into the adjoining room, shut the door behind her. She was very careful not to slam it. Jack Willows sat in front of a low table that held a Hitachi color TV, a reel-to-reel tape recorder and two Beta format VCRs. The TV screen was split; the big picture was of Ngo's body from the waist up; a closeup of his face was framed in a small box in the screen's upper right-hand corner. The split screen allowed the operator to focus in on a suspect's facial reaction while he was being questioned.

Problem was, Ngo had been about as animated as a brick wall. What Willows had on tape, he could have just as easily captured with a still camera. Ngo had seen a black Honda CRX, and that was it. Nothing else. He had no enemies that he knew of, no one who'd want him dead. Ditto Emily. Why anyone would empty a clip of .45 calibre bullets at either of them, he had no idea. None. And as far as Parker was concerned, if Cherry said the car was small and black, she'd put her money on a white stretch limo.

Parker rested a hip against the table. "Now what?"

"You're doing fine."

"He's laughing at us, the little scumbug."

"But not out loud," said Willows, smiling.

"Got any ideas?"

"Let him walk. Give his bosses a chance to talk to him. Maybe they'll give us something."

"Gangs." Parker said the word as if it was something you had to scrape off your shoe.

Willows ejected a cassette, checked to make sure there was plenty of tape. He didn't trust the counter. It was an attitude problem. He'd been a cop all his adult life. Trust, whether he was dealing with machines or people, wasn't his strong suit.

Parker fiddled with the Hitachi's joystick, adjusting the picture so Cherry Ngo's unlined face and depthless eyes filled the small box in the split screen. Cherry played with his hair, his jacket zipper.

Willows turned the sound down. He said, "The girl, Emily. We keep after him about her, maybe take him down to the morgue to say goodbye . . . think that might help?"

"He doesn't give a damn about her. Probably he's happy he doesn't have to worry about her keeping her mouth shut."

Willows, not wanting to wear out his watch, glanced up at the big electric clock mounted on the wall above the television. It was 4:37. Cherry Ngo reached out and shoved the microphone to one side. He slumped a little lower in his chair and shut his eyes. Willows said, "We might as well let him go home; start patching the bullet holes in his wall."

"And then you can go have dinner somewhere, and still have plenty of time to make it to the game, right?"

"What game?"

"The ball game. Inspector Bradley gave you a couple of free tickets."

"Who told you that?"

"He did."

"Well, you want to go?"

"Maybe."

"Maybe what?"

"Maybe yes, and maybe no. Were you going to ask me if I didn't bring it up?"

Willows smiled. He looked pretty good in his grey suit, crisp white shirt, matching tie. He said, "Yeah, I was going to ask you to the game. But I wasn't going to tell you I got the tickets for free."

"You were going to try to *sell* me one?"

"Suggest you buy dinner."

"Nice, Jack. Very classy." The clock on the wall said 4:39. It would take her an hour to get back to her apartment, shower and dress. Another hour and a half or so to eat, plus about thirty minutes' travel time to get to the game. She said, "Let's work on Cherry until five, then let him go."

"We aren't going to get anything out of him, Claire. You know that as well as I do."

Parker thought it over, shrugged. She went back into the interrogation room to give Cherry the good news. He seemed to have decided to take a nap. She crouched down beside him. His breathing was deep and regular. A vein in his neck surged and fell.

Parker went back into the other room and collected the video tapes and Willows. They locked the door on the video equipment and slipped quietly past Cherry Ngo, leaving the door to the interrogation room wide open behind them.

Cherry wasn't the only one who'd been caught napping.

Detective Eddy Orwell's hand was clamped on a cheese sandwich with a big half-moon out of it. His mouth, as he sprawled in his chair, was wide open. He looked as if he'd fallen asleep getting ready for the next bite.

"Newlyweds," said Farley Spears over the sibilant hiss of Orwell's snoring. Carefully, he used a pair of huge stainless steel scissors to cut a long, thin strip from his brown paper lunch bag.

Parker said, "What about you, Farley. How long have you been married?"

"Long enough so I don't have to worry any more about getting a good night's sleep." The scissors flashed in the light. Spears was concentrating hard, determined to do a good job. He glanced at Dan Oikawa, who stealthily prowled the squadroom windows with an empty styrofoam take-out container held at the ready. Spears said, "How you doing, Danny?"

"Nothing yet."

Parker said, "What're you guys up to now?"

"Dan's hunting for flies." Farley laid several more strips of paper on his desk. Each strip was about half an inch wide and four or five inches long.

Dan Oikawa said, "Why aren't there any flies in this goddamn place?"

Willows said, "Maybe Eddy's already eaten them all."

Oikawa smiled. "You always were a quick study, Jack. How you doing with your star witness?"

"He's cooperative as hell. Unfortunately, it turns out he's deaf and blind."

Spears said, "Keep it down, okay?"

The phone rang. Willows picked up. He cupped his hand over the receiver and said, "It's Judith. She wants to talk to Eddy."

"Wait a minute," said Spears. "Dan, how you doing?"

"Dead or alive, not a fly in the joint. Can't find any spiders, either."

"Okay, I guess we're just gonna have to make do with what we've got." Spears crept over to Orwell's desk, pried open his cheese sandwich and shoved in a dozen strips of brown paper. He gently shook Orwell's broad shoulder. "Eddy, wake up. You got a call."

Willows said, "Line three."

Orwell yawned hugely, rubbed the sleep from his eyes.

Spears snatched up Orwell's phone, punched a button and shoved the phone at him.

"It's your wife, Judith."

"I know who my wife is," said Orwell grumpily. He took a bite of sandwich and chewed slowly. A strand of paper dangled from between his lips. He slurped it up like a wayward strand of spaghetti and said, "Hi baby, it's me."

Oikawa fluttered his eyes at Spears.

Orwell said, "No, I'd *never* do anything like that!" Another huge chunk of sandwich disappeared into his mouth.

"Amazing," said Oikawa

Spears said, "Amazing but true. Ten bucks, Danny Boy. Pay up, pay up."

Orwell stuffed the last of the sandwich into his mouth, licked his fingers.

Willows leaned back in his chair. Judith was yelling so loud he could almost make out what she was saying.

Parker said, "There's a place on Cambie, just below sixteenth. Romero's."

"Italian? White paint, green trim?"

Parker nodded. "How's this sound – lasagna, a salad, bottle of red."

"Great, perfect."

"Six-thirty, is that too early?"

"No, fine."

Willows cleaned up his desk, made sure the drawers were locked.

Spears said, "Stick around. Soon's Eddy gets off the phone, we're gonna let him know about the extra roughage in his diet."

"I'm going to pass, Farley." Willows jerked a thumb at the interrogation room. "When you leave, wake up the punk and send him home, will you?"

"Sure thing, Jack." Spears turned his attention to Parker. "I got five bucks says Vancouver by three runs. Interested?"

"How'd you know I was going to the game?"

"Same way I knew Eddy'd eat a brown paper bag, and salivate over every bite."

Parker waited.

"Because I'm a *detective*," Spears explained as Dan Oikawa handed him a ten dollar bill. Spears slipped the money in his wallet and pulled out a five, which he gave to Orwell.

Orwell, still listening to Judith, folded the five in half without looking at it, stuffed the money in his pants pocket.

"Hey," said Oikawa. "Wait a minute!"

"The bet was whether or not Eddy'd eat a paper-bag sandwich," said Spears. "Well, he did it. And the fact that he knew what he was doing hasn't got a thing to do with it. Case closed."

Oikawa glared down at Spears. "Don't go all legal on me, old man. You guys set me up."

Orwell hung up. "Damn right," he said, and burped loudly. He glanced up at Parker, smiling broadly, and then looked past her, the smile fading, his eyes turning cold. "What the fuck you want, kid?"

Cherry said, "To use the phone, please."

"Got a quarter?"

Cherry Ngo fumbled in his pants pocket, offered him a shiny new coin.

"Put it on the desk."

The quarter spun on the metal surface, wobbled and lay still.

Orwell pushed the phone across the desk. "Make it fast, kid."

Cherry punched seven numbers, spoke rapidly in Vietnamese.

Orwell turned to Oikawa, raised an eyebrow. Oikawa shrugged. Chinese, Japanese, and Vietnamese. Orwell persisted in assuming that all those languages were more or less the same.

Cherry listened for a moment, spoke briefly but with heat, and then slammed down the phone.

Orwell said, "Break my phone, I'll break your bones."

"May I go now?" Cherry said to Parker.

Parker said, "Give me a few minutes to get out of here, Dan, and then take him down to the lobby and show him the way out, will you?"

Oikawa nodded. "You outta here?"

"Long gone," said Parker, already heading for the door.

Parker lived on the top floor of a three-storey block on West Eleventh, off Burrard. The street was narrow and, to avoid blocking traffic, parking was allowed only on the south side. Parker eased her battered Volkswagen into a tight spot half-way down the block, locked up, slung her purse across her shoulder and hurried across the street.

Her apartment was hot, stuffy. She hadn't drawn the curtains, and the late July sun had streamed into the apartment all day long, turning the place into a furnace. She had her hand on the latch to open the window and let in a little fresh air when a maroon Ford cruised past, a little too slowly. The driver was hunched down behind the wheel but she was high enough up so she got a fairly good look at him. He wore sunglasses but it seemed to Parker that his eyes locked on hers for a fraction of a second. Then the Ford accelerated hard, passed out of view. Parker caught a glimpse of a red and white sticker on the back bumper. She pushed open the window as far as it would go, took a breath of fresh air and then went into the apartment's single bedroom and undressed. She wore a plain white blouse and conservatively-cut dark-blue jacket and matching skirt. Hidden beneath her work clothes was a silky black camisole, lacy black bra and matching panties. Why did she wear such feminine things? Why did she *bother*?

She did it for herself, obviously, since there was no one else. Naked, she made her way towards the bathroom, and the long hot shower she'd been thinking about all day long.

An hour later, sitting at a prime window table at Romero's, watching the crowds go by and toying with her wine, Parker found herself telling Jack Willows about the maroon Ford, describing how the driver was slouched down low behind the wheel, his sunglasses and long hair and the bushy moustache that looked like it'd been glued in place.

Willows said, "You didn't recognize him, but his bad posture rang a bell, is that it?"

Parker shrugged. She wasn't at all sure what the problem was, if there *was* a problem.

She was a cop, had been a cop for five long years. During that time she'd put a lot of people away, and most of them hadn't been too happy about it. Threats had been made. It was part of the life. You couldn't afford to waste time thinking about it, not if you wanted to keep your head on straight. But there were times the paranoia crept up on you. Probably what she was feeling was just a little residual creepiness from spending the afternoon with a scumbug like Cherry Ngo.

Probably.

She held her glass up to the window. The wine turned a woman passing by on the sidewalk blood red.

Willows broke a crusty roll, reached for the butter and decided against it.

Parker said, "You heard from the kids?"

Willows topped up Parker's glass, and his. The way things were going, if the lasagna didn't show up pretty soon, they were going to need a second bottle, miss two or maybe even the first three innings. He said, "They're fine. A little worried about flying all the way out from Toronto on their own, but they'll be okay."

Parker nodded, sipped at her wine, tried to think of something intelligent to say. But if she had any brains, she wouldn't have brought the subject up in the first place, would she?

Willows' wife had left him a little under a year ago, taking their two children, Sean and Annie, on a one-way flight to Toronto. Three thousand five hundred miles away. Made it kind of tough to work out the custody, arrange weekend visits. As part of the agreement, Willows was supposed to have the children every summer for the month of July or August, his choice. This year it was supposed to be July, but Sheila had thrown him a high hard one, switched the visit to August at the last moment, knowing full well that Willows would have court dates and a million other problems, hoping he wouldn't be able to make the adjustment.

The waitress arrived with the salads. A garden for Parker, Caesar for Willows. Parker noticed Willows also got a cute little bunny-dip, a quick flash of cleavage, if he cared to look. A handsome boy, Jack.

Willows said, "What're you thinking about, Claire?"

Parker started, drew back. Hiding her blush behind her glass, she said, "Dessert, Jack. What else?"

5

As soon as Frank caught Parker's Volkswagen in his rear-view mirror, he checked the rental's dashboard clock. 5:37. He made a note on the back of an envelope. The woman worked pretty regular hours, for a cop. Maybe it was a quiet week.

He had it figured now, how to do the job.

The street was lined on both sides with three-storey apartments. There was plenty of parking until around five, maybe a little earlier, and then the street started to fill up, people getting home from work.

If he got there early, slotted the stolen Corvette in opposite her apartment and then pulled out when he saw her coming, drove about a hundred feet up the block and made a U-turn in one of the driveways, the timing would be just about right. She'd park in the spot he'd just vacated, right where he wanted her. If she was slow, he'd take his time. If she was quick, he'd goose it. Either way, it'd be easy enough to adjust the timing so he could swat her as she crossed the street to her apartment.

He could've done her this time, if he'd been driving the Corvette. But even though he'd paid a hefty premium for collision insurance, the Hertz guy – fat, a crooked tie, lots of nose hair – wasn't too likely to waive damage caused by a hit-and-run situation.

No, best to use the Corvette. Park the Hertz maybe a block or two away. Hit her and ditch the sleek, shiny black look-at-me car in an alley and switch to the Ford.

Then what? Back to the hotel, or should he check out before he went to work, put his new luggage in the Ford's trunk and drive straight to the airport after he bumped the lady cop?

One of the things Frank had learned during his life was that being hit by a car hurt like hell. He'd do his best to do it right, but it was a shame he had to do it at all. Parker was a lovely woman – a real looker. That shiny black hair framing the delicate, heart-shaped face. Terrific complexion. Great legs, a nice package. Her eyes, seen through the Bushnells, were probably her best feature. But mostly what attracted Frank was the way she carried herself, her posture and every step she took, the confident but feminine way she strode forward into her life.

Back in California, Newt had gabbled away for hours about her, asked Frank a million questions about how he got shot in the stomach. Parker had been there at the time. And, of course, years earlier she'd shot Newt. It was weird, how selective Frank's memory was about the night he'd been shot. Some parts of it he recalled with vivid clarity. Other bits and pieces of it he remembered not at all. Parker had been there when it counted, though. When the shooting started, she'd jumped right in. She was about all he and Newt had in common, when you came down to it.

Too bad about her. Like they said, a waste.

Vancouver was a big city. Reasonably big. One point four million, including the suburbs. The Hertz guy had told him that the airport handled about three hundred flights a day, eighty thousand people or more; that planes came in from all over the continent, Europe, the Middle East.

There was no way the local cops could check everybody flying out of the city.

But he'd never smacked a homicide detective before, so he had no idea how much they'd put into it. And there was the fact that she was a woman, the only female in homicide.

Frank lit a cigarette. They'd put everything they had into nailing his ass to the wall. Bet on it. Count on it, or pay the price. He blew out the match and let it drop. There were two things he liked about rentals – you could drive the hell out of the car; if the thing fell apart, tough shit. Plus you could turn the car into a garbage can and not have to worry about cleaning up after yourself.

Frank scanned Parker's third-floor windows with the binoculars. The sunlight on the sheets of glass turned them burnt orange. Nothing. He turned the key, put the Ford in gear. There was no point in hanging around, drawing attention to himself. He pulled away from the curb. Behind him, a rust-acned rag top black Cadillac came around the corner on two wheels. The car had fins on it that would make a whale envious. A vapor trail of blue smoke hung in the air. The brakes shrieked as the ugly car nosed into the space Frank had vacated only moments before. Well, so much for plan A.

Frank drove the Ford back to the hotel, parked and locked – people'd steal just about anything, nowadays – and went back up to his suite. His tiny white hope was waiting for him at the door with a freshly poured beer in a frosted glass.

She said, "Surprised to see me?"

Frank drained the glass. "What makes you want to know?"

Lulu shrugged. "I dunno." She was wearing lycra again, a flashy skintight gold number with bold diagonal slashes of black that were straight lines on the flat parts of her, but arced in gentle rainbows of doom across her breasts, hips. Frank stared at the slash of black in her hair.

"It washes out, Frank. I can do it right this very minute, if you want."

"No, it's great . . ." Kind of dark, really. But she was a woman. Entitled to her moods.

There was a big plastic tub of ice and bottled beer on the table by the window. Frank had a choice of Asahi Super Dry, Becks, Heineken, Tsingtao, Steinlager, and half a dozen local beers. He grabbed a can of Kokanee Glacier Light and popped the tab. He liked the TV ads, that cute little white dog they took camping that'd cock his head at his owner when the guy realized he'd left the beer at home, then charge through the woods all day and night, dodge city traffic and find a way into the house through an open window or whatever, yank open the fridge door and snag a six-pack in his teeth, hot foot it all the way back to camp and get told off for taking so long, then give the camera a good-natured look that wanted to know how he'd got stuck with such a dummy.

Frank burped, apologized.

Lulu said, "You like lobster? A crate just got flown in fresh from Halifax. Guy in the kitchen told me about it, I asked him to put aside six big ones, send them up at seven. Is that okay?"

Frank drank some more beer. Lobsters were a mystery to him, mainly because he wasn't too sure how to go about getting at the meat and hadn't yet been prepared to risk making a fool of himself in public. Now the decision was being forced upon him. What parts were edible and what parts would make him toss his cookies all over his new Ralph Laurens? He decided he'd follow Lulu's lead, do what she did, but let her do it first. He grinned. That was pretty much the way he'd handled the lovemaking, and that seemed to have worked out pretty well.

Lulu said, "What's so funny?"

"Life," said Frank, "when it's going well."

Lulu checked her watch; a thin, dark-blue and gold disk studded with diamonds. "The food'll be here in about three-quarters of an hour. Just enough time for a shower and . . ."

"What?" said Frank.

"Use your imagination, and let's see what you can come up with, okay?"

As he stood in the shower, the water beating down on him, slowly washing away some of the tension he'd built up stalking Claire Parker, Frank wondered how much longer it could last. He'd knocked around a fair amount during the past twenty years. Never stayed in one place long enough to strike up a serious acquaintance. But Lulu was considerably different than what he was used to. She really seemed to like him. He didn't care to dwell on why that might be. There'd be something she wanted from him, no doubt about that. If he was lucky, it'd be as simple and uncomplicated as a wad of cash. He tilted his face to the blast of water. It was all he could hope for, really – that her needs were predictable and easily met.

He jumped as Lulu pulled back the shower curtain and stepped into the tub.

She said, "Scare you?"

"I scare easy."

"You work out, Frank?"

"Yeah, a little."

"Where? In a gym?"

"Wherever I happen to be," said Frank.

"Lift your arms." She turned her head to the shower and filled her mouth, hosed him down, rinsing him off with a goofy smile that faltered when her eyes travelled down his body to the puckered scar tissue in the middle of his stomach. The wound obviously distressed her but, if she was going to play twenty questions, she'd have started by now. Frank liked that about her; that she could be curious and still keep her mouth shut. Women were better at that sort of thing than men, maybe. They couldn't be worse. He bent and turned off the shower. A few last drops splattered down.

They ate in bed, sitting cross-legged on the sheets, using their fingers and teeth on the Nova Scotia lobster and wild rice, baby carrots and a spicy green vegetable that Frank didn't much care for but chewed and swallowed with feigned enthusiasm because he didn't want to make a fuss, washing whatever it was down with quick mouthfuls of icy-cold champagne.

After dinner, Lulu showed Frank her family album; it was bound in scuffed red leather, with a brass lock and hinges. The book was the size of a small suitcase. She lugged it over to the bed and thumped it down.

Frank had to move his knee so there was room. Lulu had lost the key so had to use a hotel corkscrew to pick the lock. There were six tiny black and white photographs on the first page, the edges scalloped, corners fixed in place with triangles of black paper.

The first picture was of a naked infant lying on a rug in front of a fireplace.

The second was of the baby in a wicker baby carriage with big overlapping wheels.

In the third picture, the baby was sitting up in a crib, crying.

The fourth snapshot was of the baby being baptized.

In the fifth shot, the baby was nestled in the arms of a gigantic snowman with lumps of coal for eyes and a carrot for a nose, a rosebud mouth carved out of a slice of beet.

In the last shot she was sprawled out in diapers on the hood of a ragtop TR4.

"That's you?"

"Sexy, huh?"

"What is that, a seventy-two Triumph?"

"Daddy won it in a raffle. He had it a week and then the kid next door, Trevor Whyte his name was, he stole it right out of the garage. Took his girlfriend for a joyride down to the docks and lost control and drove into the side of a freight train at about a hundred miles an hour. They both burned to death. What a tragedy."

Frank nodded, but he wasn't really listening because his mind was busy working out how old she was.

"Trevor's parents hired some fatcat lawyer and sued. So did the train company. They said Daddy shouldn't have left the keys in the ignition. He was innocent but the legal fees ate up everything we had. I was four months old when he ran away. I haven't seen him since and don't expect I ever will."

Frank said, "Hold on a minute. You told me *Roger* was your father."

"My step-father. Sort of. Number six. Mommy chewed men up like they were potato chips. Couldn't find the right one, I guess." Lulu gave Frank a look so bold and direct it seemed to squeeze the air right out of his lungs. "Not like me," she said softly, and turned the page.

A guy on a BSA. One leg hooked over the gas tank, arms folded across his black leather chest.

"Daddy number two," said Lulu. "Joseph. He was a self-employed thrill-seeker. He'd find a small town on a river, set up a portable ramp and folding bleachers and fly his bike over the water to the other side. You could watch for free, or spend a couple of dollars on a seat and get an autographed picture thrown in. He crashed about once a week, on purpose. He said it was to keep the crowds up, but mom believed he wiped out for the pure joy of it. He was my first real dad, the first one I ever remembered anything about, I mean. Mom told me that stuff about Trevor and the train. I was five years old and working the bleachers selling motorcycle key chains the day Walter broke his neck.

"Killed, was he?"

Lulu nodded, and turned the page. Marriage in the House of Mirrors.

Frank said, "What's the deal?"

"That's my mother. Beautiful, wasn't she? But kind of philosophical. Oh well, nobody's perfect."

Frank didn't get it.

"All those reflected images," said Lulu, "which one is real? Who can tell? Let's say you go out to dinner. You're with the person, and she's with you. But maybe both of you are somewhere else."

Frank nodded. Now he understood. Mostly, wherever he happened to be, he wasn't there at all. For example, when he was waiting for the Hertz guy with the nose hair to process his rental, he was thinking about a movie he'd recently seen, reliving a scene. Gene Hackman was in a parking lot with a pretty girl and her boyfriend. Hoods were after them. Gene was scuffling around, yelling at the chick and her date, trying to find out why the hoods were shooting at them. It wasn't the way Frank would've played it. At a time like that, who cared about motive? People were shooting at you, take a hike. At as little as twenty feet, a pistol in the hands of the average shooter was almost useless. This he knew from personal experience, and from sharing Kodak moments with cops and guys in the joint. Frank knew a black guy from Toronto someone had tried to take out in a toilet stall. Barely room in there to pull the trigger, they'd fired six shots at the guy and all the damage done was he got singed by the muzzle blast.

On the other hand . . .

It was as if she'd been reading his mind. Or maybe his hand had come up . . . the scar tissue had become like a medallion to him, a Saint Christopher's medal, something he turned to in moments of crisis.

"That's a bullet wound, isn't it?"

Frank shrugged. "No bullet was ever recovered – it was what they call a through and through. But a guy took a shot at me, pointed a gun and pulled the trigger and down I went. So, yeah, it's fair to say that's what it is, a bullet wound."

"And there's one in your back." She stroked the hard ridges of his belly. "And another in your stomach. You were shot three times and left for dead, is that what happened?"

It was strange, the way he didn't mind that he was wrong about her, that she was asking about his scars after all.

Frank told Lulu about the shootings, the three separate and extremely distinct times in his life people had pulled a trigger on him. The chest wound had been a cop doing his job. Case closed. No hard feelings. The one in the small of his back he remembered best of all, even though it'd gone down a long time ago and of course he hadn't even seen it happen. He was at a friendly high stakes cribbage game, couple of jerks decided to make some easy money. First night of his life Frank'd gotten along with the cards. Almost eight grand sitting in front of him and he'd lost every dime. Not that he said a word. Put his hands on his head and froze, just like they told him. Problem was his size, how big and tough he looked. Freaked out the punks and they drilled him just to make sure.

"What about this one?" She touched his stomach.

"My innocent bystander story. Happened a few years ago. A woman shot me." Frank smiled. "If you want to know was it an act of passion, the answer is no. She was aiming at the hot-shot asshole I worked for at the time, guy named Gary Silk. Made a forty-five calibre mistake, and hit me instead."

Frank sketched out his life in servitude, told Lulu all about Gary and how he treated women, what happened to the poor sap in the end.

"How could you work for a creep like that?"

"I needed the money." Frank turned the page. There was a black and white shot of Lulu's mother in sequins and parasol, balanced on a high-wire. He grinned and said, "So that's where you got your agility, huh?"

Lulu blushed. Frank'd never had to deal with an embarrassed albino before. It was a unique experience. Reminded him of a weird thing his own mother used to do – cut white long-stemmed geraniums from a neighbor's garden where they grew through the fence and arrange them in a vase filled with fresh water, add food coloring until the water was stained red. Over a period of several days the white flowers would turn pink. This was exactly what happened to Lulu, except remarkably speeded up.

Lulu turned the page, kept turning pages. There were lots of dead step-fathers. They were on number five when the bedside phone warbled like a heavily sedated canary. Frank got there first but Lulu said, "It's for me," and snatched the phone out of his hand, flipped her ghostly white hair out of her ear and said, "What is it *now*?" in a voice suitable for grating cheese.

Frank sipped at his champagne, inhaled a noseful of bubbles. He viciously pinched his nostrils shut to stop himself from sneezing.

Lulu said, "Are you sure?" There was a pause and then she added, "No, I'm not in the least bit interested. And I don't think I ever will be, either."

She handed the phone to Frank. "It's for you; hope you're in the mood to chat with a California slimeball."

Frank said, "Hello, Newt."

Junior Newton said, "Frank, it's my dime. Put your fuckin' hand over the phone if you can't stop the bimbo from making insulting remarks."

"Nice of you to call, Newt."

Frank could hear traffic sounds in the background. The blare of horns, screech of tires. Newt was calling from a payphone, which meant he was worried again about his lines being tapped.

Newt said, "So, how's it going?"

Frank said, "Not bad. Had Nova Scotia lobster for supper. Tastes kind of like chicken."

"That your waitress, picked up the phone?"

Frank said, "I should be back tomorrow night, if it goes okay."

"Tomorrow night?"

"Assuming no problems."

"I want receipts for everything, Frank. Don't think you can bill me a hundred bucks for a lobster dinner and then sneak over to McDonalds for a burger and fries. I'm not as old as I look, but on the other hand, I wasn't born yesterday. Know what I mean?"

"I doubt it."

The operator broke in. Newt said he didn't *have* any more fuckin' change, baby. The line went dead.

Frank tossed the phone on the bed.

Lulu said, “I’m not going to hang up, just in case he decides to call back.”

“What’d he say to you?”

“Nothing you’d want me to have to listen to a second time.”

Frank said, “Want to look at some more pictures?”

Lulu backhanded the remains of their meal off the bed and stretched out on the bed.

“Like this pose?”

“Nice,” said Frank.

“How about this one?”

“Even better.”

Frank said, “Roll over.” The Lycra was seamless, impenetrable. So tight and slippery smooth you couldn’t get a grip on it. There had to be a zipper, but where was it?

6

Newt loved the endless sunshine and the easy money and easy women, the way the ocean looked at certain times of the day. But that was about it – everything else in Southern California could shrivel up and die for all he cared. The smog was killing him. All those hundreds of thousands of people on the freeways burning up millions of gallons of gas, polluting the atmosphere. They even made jokes about it; how they didn't feel comfortable if they couldn't see what they were breathing. Crazy. He downshifted into second, gunned the Porsche's engine and pulled up against the curb.

He checked the payphone first, to make sure it was in working order, then trotted across the street to a liquor store for some quarters. The clerk said he didn't have any change to spare. Newt squinted at him and snatched a bottle of Wild Turkey Kentucky bourbon off the shelf. The tab was nineteen dollars eighty-five cents. He threw a fifty down on the counter. The clerk gave him three tens and a dime and a nickel in change.

Newt said, "Okay, I'm a legitimate customer, you made a sale, now gimme five bucks worth of fuckin' quarters, you asshole."

The clerk stared at him.

Newt thrust a ten dollar bill in the clerk's face. "Hurry up, move it, I gotta make a phone call!"

The clerk pointed out the door. "There's a Bank of America three blocks down. Or maybe it's five or six, or eight, or even more. You'll see it on the left. Or the right. You can't miss it. Or maybe you could."

Newt scooped his ten and the brown paper bag full of Wild Turkey off the counter. He held the bottle low, by the neck.

The clerk crouched slightly and reached below the counter, grasped the .45 and thumbed back the hammer. He'd shoot right through the counter's cheap fiberboard kickwall. It'd take him no more than half an hour to sweep up the blood and splinters, slap a little masking tape and a fresh coat of paint over the holes. Half an hour, and nobody would ever know the difference.

Newt saw the look in the clerk's close-set eyes and recognized he was in deep trouble, up against a guy who made six bucks an hour and bought his clothes at Sears and figured he was in control of the situation. Now, why would that be, unless the dude happened to be a trigger-happy psycho with a gun. But what were the odds, how many trigger-happy psychos could there be? In a Los Angeles liquor store, one hundred per cent. Newt backed out of the doorway, into smog-raddled sunlight and off the premises. He grinned, and gave the clerk the finger.

The clerk sighed. Skinny little bastard knew the law. He popped him now, cops'd kick his ass all the way to court. He eased the safety back on, dropped the gun and grabbed a pen.

Newt's satan-black Porsche Cabriolet was parked by the pay phone. He climbed in and red-lined it and popped the clutch. The car leapt away from the curb. The clerk ran out on the sidewalk and wrote down the licence number on the back of his hand, used the payphone to dial 911.

"There's a black Porsche on Mulholland, heading east. A ragtop. Vanity plate is NEWT. Yeah, that's what I said. NEWT. Asshole's whacked out of his gourd, a boozer. He waved a gun at me."

A disembodied voice requested his name and number.

The clerk knew the drill.

Hang up fast.

7

Willows scooped beans into the grinder, gritted his teeth and pressed the button. The stainless steel blades chopped the mix of Colombian and Dark French into a fine powder. He dumped the coffee into the filter, inserted the filter into the machine and turned it on. The toast popped. He lightly buttered both slices and sprinkled on a mix of cinnamon and sugar, poured a dollop of milk into his coffee mug – it saved dirtying a spoon.

Bachelor habits. He took his breakfast out on to the sundeck, eased into an old-fashioned deck chair with a maple frame and a canvas seat in faded stripes of yellow, red and green. He balanced the mug on the rail and the plate of cinnamon toast in his lap. The sky was bright and clear, but it was early; the sun was low on the horizon and it was still cool, in the high sixties. At this time of year, mid-summer, it might hit ninety before the day was done. Willows bit into the toast.

The neighbor's Siamese cat skulked in the unmowed lawn. A Stellar's Jay shrieked horribly at the cat from its perch high up on a branch of a plum tree, and a fat black squirrel, it's fluffy tail held low for balance, trotted confidently along the high tension wires running parallel to the lane.

His neighbor's dog wandered down the lane, sniffed the base of a telephone pole and then continued on his way.

Urban wildlife.

Willows wished he was working a creek somewhere in the interior of the Province or on Vancouver Island, hip-deep in clean water, stalking a two-pound rainbow. It was late July and his holidays were scheduled for the last three weeks of August. No chance of any fishing, though. His children were flying in from Toronto; it'd be the first time he'd seen them since Christmas. Sean was an outdoor fan, but Annie was a city girl through and through.

Willows sipped his coffee. The squirrel crouched and then leapt from the power line across three feet of air and vanished in the thick greenery of a plane tree.

Seven o'clock in the morning, a beautiful day, the only blemish in the pale-blue sweep of sky a baby cloud the sun would quickly burn off.

Willows finished his toast and drank the last of his coffee and went inside to pour himself another cup. The newspaper thudded against the front door.

When he came back out on to the deck, the cat saw the rolled-up newspaper in his hand and scooted between the fence pickets into the safety of home ground. Willows tossed a crust of bread into the yard. The jay tilted its shiny blue-black head and then swooped low, snatched the crust into its beak and was back in the plum tree so fast it was almost as if it had never moved.

The front page story was about the death of a local hooker – the eighteenth unsolved murder of a prostitute in the city during the past eight years. Another hooker, a friend of the dead woman, seemed to think that if it was doctors who were getting bumped off, the police would work harder to solve the crimes.

Well, maybe. But on the other hand, doctors tended not to wander the streets selling their bodies, mixing it up with violence-prone types like drug dealers and pimps, the kind of scum who had to pay cash to fall in love.

The phone rang.

Willows had left his watch in the bathroom, but if he leaned back in his chair he could see the electric clock on the kitchen stove through the open door. Quarter-past seven. The phone rang again, strident and demanding. It was odd how the sound of the ringing changed according to the time of day.

It occurred to him that it could be his wife, Sheila, calling from Toronto, where it was already quarter-past ten. He went into the kitchen and picked up.

Parker said, "Jack, I've got a flat. Can you give me a ride downtown?"

"You've got a flat tire and you want me to change it for you. If that's what you're saying, Claire, speak up."

"That's *not* what I'm saying, Jack. What I'm saying is that I've got a flat tire. And yes, the spare's flat too."

Willows said, "I'll be there in about three-quarters of an hour. A little past eight."

"I've got some paperwork to catch up on. Tell you the truth, I was hoping to get in a bit sooner."

"If you're in a hurry, maybe you better call a cab."

"A taxi'll cost me ten dollars, Jack, and you drive right by me on the way to work!"

"A little past eight," said Willows. "Meet me at Burrard and Eleventh."

Parker often thought that female detectives and bank employees and maybe lawyers must shop at the same stores, because the narrow range of clothing that was considered suitable for women in the three professions was virtually identical.

Today she was wearing a lightweight dark-blue poplin suit, the skirt cut full so she could stretch her legs, in the event she had to pursue a criminal at full gallop. White blouse. Dark-blue shoes with sturdy heels. A black purse. She kept her gun, a snubnose .38 Special, in a low-profile clamshell holster clipped to her skirt in the small of her back.

Parker was sitting by the kitchen window, drinking coffee, idly looking out at the streetscape, when she saw Willows' Oldsmobile waiting for traffic to clear before he made the turn at the end of the block. She emptied her cup into the sink grabbed her purse and hurried out of the apartment. Part of the reason she and Willows got along as well as they did was because they were both always in a hurry; neither of them liked to be kept waiting.

Willows had installed seat belts in the Olds; Parker buckled up and then turned down the radio, which was tuned to an all-news station. She said, "I got a phone call this morning."

"Somebody wants to clean your carpets."

Parker smiled, shook her head.

"Chimney?"

"Cherry Ngo. At least, it sounded like Cherry. I'm pretty sure it was him."

Willows braked for a stop sign, shifted into first gear. A cop on a Harley cruised through the intersection. Willows watched him go by. Never catch him riding one of those beasts. He hit the gas, turned after the bike. The motorcycle was moving at a steady twenty-eight miles per hour. Willows signalled, pulled into the next lane and swept past. The cop ignored him.

"Terry O'Brien," said Parker. "He recognized the car, probably figured you were trying to sucker him into pulling you over."

"Tell me about the call."

"I was in the shower. The answering machine picked up. He didn't identify himself; all he said was that he had something he wanted to talk about and he'd try me again at work."

"Interesting."

Parker nodded. "Yeah, isn't it." Like virtually all cops, she had an unlisted phone number.

Farley Spears was the only homicide detective at his desk when they arrived at the third floor squadroom. A red light was flashing on Eddy Orwell's phone and Farley was staring at it but making no move to answer.

"Problem?" said Willows.

"It's Judith. Must have an automatic redial; she's driving me crazy."

"Take a message."

"Good advice, Jack, but I already took it. She won't quit, she's ruthless. I look up, the light's flashing, I gotta answer it."

"Where's Eddy?"

"Half-way to Mexico, probably. The honeymoon's over, that's for sure. The roses died and the champagne went flat." Spears glanced at Parker. "I don't know what he did to her, but whatever it was, I bet he never does it again."

"Any calls for me?"

"Just one. Young guy. Wouldn't leave his name, said he'd get back." Spears smiled at Parker. "Nice outfit."

"Thanks."

"I was down at the bank at the weekend. Had to speak to the manager about a little problem with my account, a clerical error, nothing serious. Anyhow, the point is, I swear to God she was wearing the exact same suit you're wearing now, Claire."

"You think I loaned it to her, is that it?"

Spears caught the menace in Parker's voice. "Hey, no, of course not."

"Well, what are you saying, Farley? That she loaned it to me?"

Spears frowned. He didn't understand what Parker was so upset about. Women. The phone rang. He snatched it up, punched a pulsing red button and said, "Detective Spears." His face sagged. "Like I already told you, Mrs Orwell, I'll have him call you the minute he gets in."

Willows, sitting at his desk, picked up a pencil and sketched the outline of a telephone, added a rotary dial, worked in a little shading to give the drawing dimension.

Parker's desk butted up against Willows'. Both desks were metal with a dull grey enamelled finish. But since he had a lot more seniority than Parker, his desk faced the window, with its view across the lane to the brick walls of the remand center. All Parker had was a view of Willows. Sometimes that wasn't so bad. She pulled back her chair and sat down, glanced up to find him watching her. He said, "How did Cherry get your number?"

"Jealous?"

"If it makes you happy."

Willows filled in the numbers on the telephone dial, nine through zero. A lifetime of possibilities.

Parker said, "I didn't give it to him."

"Somebody did. Either that, or he broke into your apartment."

"No way. I would've noticed."

"Maybe you better change your locks, Claire."

"Forget it."

One of the civilian clerks down at the far end of the major crimes section yelled a warning, and Willows turned in time to see Orwell vault the waist-high counter.

Farley Spears said, "Whyn't you use the fucking door like everybody else, Eddy?"

"Forgot my keys."

"Bullshit, your pants are so tight, you couldn't get 'em in your pocket."

"What're you doing looking at my pants, Farley? Think I'm kinda *cute*, is that it?"

"No, but somebody does."

Orwell smiled. "Who's that?"

"Your wife."

The smile faded. "I told her a million times not to phone me at work. She calls again, tell her you haven't seen me, okay?"

"You want protection, it's gonna cost you."

"*What?*" Orwell's face turned the color of a radish with varicose veins.

"Five bucks," said Spears calmly. "Cash in advance, no checks."

Orwell turned to Parker. "I can't believe this is happening to me. It's like a nightmare, except worse."

"You're getting a bargain, Eddy."

"Yeah?"

Parker smiled sweetly. "I wouldn't do it for less than ten."

Willows' phone rang. He picked up, listened for a moment and then clamped his hand over the receiver and said, "Hey, Eddy."

"Yeah, what?"

"Relax, it isn't for you."

Spears roared with laughter.

Willows pointed at Parker. "Your new boyfriend. Line three."

Cherry Ngo arranged to meet Parker and Willows at a Vietnamese restaurant on Commercial, just off Hastings. The restaurant was called Pale Green Shoots. It wasn't listed in the phone book. Willows had wondered out loud if Cherry was playing games with them. Parker said she didn't think so. He could call it intuition, if he liked, but she expected Cherry to be there. Willows balled up his sketch of a telephone, bounced it off his desk and into his wastebasket.

Women's intuition. He'd learned a long time ago not to mess with that one.

They arrived at the restaurant at quarter to ten. A sign on the door said that the restaurant was open from 4:00 p.m. until 2:00 a.m. Willows tried the door. It was locked.

Parker checked her watch. "Think Cherry expects us to hang around until they open?"

"And then buy him dinner and a couple of beers to wash it down, probably." Willows peered inside. The transparent reflections of passing traffic obscured his vision. He pressed his hand up against the dusty glass. The restaurant was small – seven or eight tables, a couple of dozen chairs. Willows couldn't find two chairs that matched.

The cash register drawer was open.

Behind the cash register there was a travel poster, thumb-tacked to the wall, of a water buffalo standing in a rice paddy.

To the left of the cash register a bead-curtained doorway led to a back room. Parallel lines of light lay upon the floor between alternating rows of red and blue and green.

There was a break in the traffic. Willows heard a snatch of music, thin and reedy.

"Let's check the back."

Parker nodded.

The two detectives walked briskly down to the end of the block, turned the corner and followed a crumbling sidewalk to the mouth of the alley. There was a bakery a few doors away from the restaurant and the air was heavy with the warm, sweet smell of fresh bread.

Willows clipped his badge to the breast pocket of his jacket. He drew his revolver and held the gun nestled in the palm of his hand so his extended trigger and second fingers concealed the weapon's stubby two-inch barrel.

Parker drew her pistol.

The restaurant was located near the middle of the block, squeezed in between a drycleaner's and a florist. There was a parking lot behind the building with unoccupied spaces for three vehicles.

The rear door was off the latch, open about a foot. Willows leaned against the wall, listened to the music and then the voice of a woman singing. He had no desire to get up and dance. A gust of wind made the door swing towards him a fraction of an inch. A hinge squeaked.

The music died.

Willows' .38 was out in the open now. He braced himself and kicked hard. The door crashed against an inside wall and stayed put.

Parker covered Willows as he risked a quick glimpse inside, ducked back.

Willows yelled, "Cherry, you in there?"

The music started up again, the whine of stringed instruments leaking through the bead curtain.

Parker said, "We need a warrant?"

"No, I don't think so. We're supposed to meet him here. The door's open . . ."

Inside, there was an empty storage room on the left, a locked door on the right. The beads rattled as Willows pushed through. Cherry Ngo lay on his back on the floor behind the counter. His hands were folded against his skinny chest.

Parker felt the blood drain from her face. She began to tremble.

Willows grasped her arm. "Claire."

"Yeah, what?"

"Call it in for me, will you?"

Parker took a deep breath, nodded, holstered her gun. On the way out, she saw that Willows had kicked the back door so hard that the doorknob had penetrated the lathe and plaster wall.

When the smell of the bakery hit her, she fell to her knees and was sick.

Willows knelt in the confined space beside the body. Cherry Ngo's eyes were wide open. Willows braced himself against the counter, crouched over the body. Miniatures of the water buffalo filled Ngo's eyes.

Willows drew back. A shiny brass .45-calibre casing lay on the floor beside Ngo's feet, and there was a .45-calibre hole in the middle of his forehead.

Ngo's open mouth and empty face were splattered with glistening wet chunks of a sticky, brownish-orange pulp. There was a second gunshot wound in his right hand, which was scorched and stippled with powderburns. He had been holding something in that hand when he was shot. A piece of fruit?

No, a sweet potato.

Willows heard approaching footsteps. He glanced over his shoulder. Parker. He realized he was still gripping his gun, and put it away.

She said, "The coroner and crime scene unit's on the way." She pointed at the cassette player. "Mind if I turn that off?"

"Go ahead."

Parker followed the electrical cord to the socket, pulled the plug.

The cassette stopped turning and the music died. Now they could hear the hum and throb of the traffic again, through the dusty plate glass windows.

Willows said, "What time did he phone?"

"Twenty-past eight. On the button, I'd just checked my watch. What's that in his hand?"

"A sweet potato."

"They used it for a silencer?"

"Yeah."

"Made him hold it, and shot him."

Willows didn't say anything. The adrenalin rush had left him feeling a little weak in the knees. Suddenly, the world was full of possibilities. He felt like a man with a brand-new lover. He could hardly wait to start running his hands over the crime scene, gain intimate knowledge of every bloody nook and cranny.

Cherry Ngo's body was still warm, the chunks of sweet potato splattered across his smooth young face so fresh that they were still wet and glistening.

A siren wailed up Commercial, closing rapidly in on them. Willows took another long, slow look at the poster of the water buffalo standing placidly in a rice paddy half a world away and more.

"Claire?"

"Yeah, what?"

"Maybe we better put a tap on your line."

"Why's that, Jack?"

"You weren't sure it was Cherry who phoned. Maybe it was somebody else."

"And what about round-the-clock police protection – you going to volunteer, Jack?" Parker was working hard to look sardonic and unconcerned, but Willows could see the fear lurking in her eyes.

The siren howled into the alley.

Now the crime scene had to be photographed, sketched, powdered and painted. Cherry's corpse chauffeured to the morgue, where they'd gut him and saw off the top of his skull, subject him to indignities far worse than a bullet in the head.

All in aid of Jack's pleasure, Jack's pursuit. All for Jack, all for Jack.

8

All that stuff she'd showed him last night, the family album. How much of it was real? She was a very strange woman, and not just because she happened to be an albino, either. She was strange inside, as well as out. Maybe the one followed from the other. Why did she keep all those pictures; why had she showed them to him? He didn't believe any of that stuff about circus freaks and motorcycle stunt men. But why would she make it all up, what was the *purpose* of it all?

Not that it made any difference. At five hundred a night, she was out of his league. He'd already gone at least a grand over budget. Newt was gonna have a class three tantrum, for sure.

A shaft of reflected sunlight splashed across the street as the glass front door of Parker's apartment block swung open. Frank slouched a little lower in the white leather bucket seat. Plan A had been a flop so he'd moved on to plan B, a first-thing-in-the-morning bump-and-run. The pie fork with the bent tine that he'd borrowed from the hotel to let the air out of Parker's tire dug into his belly.

Parker stepped into the light. Yeah, nice looking woman. Tall, slim.

Frank tossed the fork on the floor and turned the key. The Vette's big V-8 coughed and roared. Plenty of room in front of him. He checked the rear-view mirror, cranked the wheel, eased cautiously out of the parking slot, lining her up.

Parker began to walk away from him, in absolutely the wrong direction. Frank couldn't believe his eyes. He leaned forward, peered through cigarette smoke and green-tinted glass and across the long sloping hood of the Corvette. What the hell was going on? Had she forgotten where she'd left her car?

Then he saw the Oldsmobile, bulgy fenders and a high, rounded back. Split windshield. The car dated from the forties but, despite it's age, the black paint was waxed and shiny, the chrome gleamed.

The Olds pulled up against the curb. Parker slipped inside. The door thudded shut.

Frank lit a fresh cigarette as the car cruised past him, close enough to reach out and touch.

Sweating every inch of the way, he drove the redhot look-at-me Corvette back to his underground hidy-hole and then walked down Robson to the hotel.

Lulu was waiting for him in his room, in exactly the same position she'd been in when he'd left. It was almost as if she existed only in the landscape of Frank's imagination, had no life of her own, only took breath when he was there to witness the event.

She smiled at him as he shut the door. "How'd it go, Frank? Everything turn out okay?"

Frank said, "I let the air out of her tire and a guy came by and picked her up. Thought she was the liberated type. Guess I was wrong."

"Work up an appetite?"

Frank shrugged, somewhat dispirited by the unexpected turn of events.

Lulu dialled room service. Scrambled eggs and croissants with English marmalade, a chrome pot of strong black coffee.

"Hawaiian and chocolate spice. My own blend. Like it?"

"Sure," said Frank. The croissants were crumbly as hell, getting all over the sheets.

After breakfast, they watched race cars on TSN and then, in a sporting mood, went down to the mini-mall in the lounge. Lulu picked out a black Speedo number so tiny Frank was able to crush it up and hide it in his fist. He said, "You crazy – I'm not going to wear that in public."

"It expands. One size fits all."

"Like hell," said Frank, and paid thirty dollars plus tax for something he felt comfortable in; a boxer-type swimsuit, pale blue with dark-green palm trees, that did the job without being too revealing.

The pool was up on the third floor, under a canopy of glass. It was deserted except for a guy doing laps with his girlfriend, who hauled her out of there the minute he got a look at Frank's shoulder span, his washboard belly and narrow hips, the ropy veins and hard bulge of muscle on his arms and thighs, the puck and whorl of scar tissue left by the few large-calibre bullets that hadn't bounced off him and, most of all, those bright uncaring killer's eyes.

Lulu used an elastic band to tuck her hair into place. She was wearing a snazzy little two-piece number that exactly matched her skin tone, and made her look naked. When she dove into the bright blue water she left scarcely a ripple.

Frank lunged after her, creating a miniature tsunami that rolled the length of the pool and splashed over the lip, nipping at the heels of the retreating swimmers. He dove deep, stayed down until his lungs ached, then pushed off the tiled bottom and came up rolling his eyeballs and spewing quarts of chlorinated water. Lulu pinwheeled around him like a sprite in a Disney film. He started to go under again, kicked hard and lurched across the water, churning the surface into a froth. He made the lip of the pool and held on tight, gasping and spitting.

"Where'd you learn to swim, Frank, in a thimble?"

Frank caught his breath. He said, "It's deeper than it looks."

"No kidding. Jeez, with your talent, you could drown in a kitchen sink. I'm gonna do some laps. Go relax in the whirlpool, so I don't have to worry about you, and I'll be there in a few minutes, okay?"

Frank hauled himself out of the water and made his way down to the whirlpool at the far end of the glass-enclosed room. The whirlpool was more his speed. The water was nice and warm, and only waist-deep. He lowered himself into a sitting position. It wasn't much worse than a bathtub. He began to relax, enjoy the spectacle of his albino sweetheart gliding back and forth in her element. Probably during her circus days she did a high-dive act into a bucket of icewater. He'd have to ask.

A shadow darkened the water. Frank looked up. He said, "Hi there, Rog."

"Brought you some towels."

"So I see."

"And a bottle of champagne. French. Cold."

Frank nodded, didn't say anything.

Lulu eased out of the pool, her movements smooth and silky. She padded across the tiles, kissed Rog on the cheek and stepped into the whirlpool.

Frank openly admired the curve of her hip, all that smooth white skin, the strength and grace of her lines. Lulu stared at Rog, maintained eye contact as she made herself nice and comfortable in Frank's muscled lap, snuggled up against him like a child.

"Champagne, Daddy? How nice!"

Rog said, "A going-away present."

Frank said, "What makes you think I'm leaving?"

"Your reservation was only for two nights."

"So?"

"Checkout's at eleven. It's half-past. Your bags are at the front desk."

Lulu smiled at Frank, her pale eyes full of light, a fireworks display of pure love.

Frank said, "Can we have our champagne now, please?"

"Sure." Rog crouched, placed the tray on the tiles. He unwrapped the gold foil and popped the cork. Strong hands for a guy that old. He poured both glasses past the brim and handed one to his daughter and the other to Frank.

Frank raised his glass. He looked carefully into Lulu's eyes. "Here's to you and me."

"Check."

The glasses coming together made a sound like a tiny icicle breaking.

Frank drained his glass, placed it on the tray and reached out and grabbed Rog by his maroon tie, pulled him slowly but inexorably into the whirlpool.

Rog, windmilling on the edge, started yelling.

Frank yanked him into the water and turned him face down, held him steady.

Lulu waited for a reasonably long time and then said, "Frank? He's my dad, sort of. Frank?"

"Be right with you." Frank kept counting, reached sixty, and flipped Rog over and held his weary grey head clear of the burbling water. Rog lay quietly in Frank's arms, unresisting. For the moment, he was content merely to be alive.

Frank said, "I want my room back."

"Fuck you," said Rog weakly.

"I mean right this minute," said Frank. "Long as I'm staying in this wonderful hotel, I don't want nobody but me and your beautiful daughter sleeping in our bed. You might even think about sealing the room after we leave. Making it into a kind of shrine."

Rog struggled to sit up. Frank let him. Rog said, "You think she's *beautiful*?"

"Don't you?"

"Unusual," said Rog. "Or maybe *interesting* . . ."

Frank pushed him away. "Beat it. Go clean up the mess you made; get me back my room."

Rog scrambled out of the pool. Splashing and dripping, he made his getaway.

Frank said, "Sorry. Lost my temper."

"Don't apologize. It doesn't suit you."

Frank grinned, tilted his head and shook some water out of his ear. "Rog doesn't want you getting mixed up with a guy lives out of a suitcase. Can't say I blame him."

"That's not exactly the worst thing about you."

Frank nodded. True enough. He said, "Want some more champagne?"

"No thanks. I'm going to go take a shower." Marble stairs led out of the water. Lulu paused with a foot on the top step, looking down at him.

What a pose. Frank was glad he'd decided against the Speedo. He said, "You mad at me?"

"Chlorine's murder on my skin. If I don't rinse myself off, I'll get a rash like you wouldn't believe." She held out her hand. "Come with me. I wouldn't want daddy to see me alone and think we'd had a fight."

The red message light was flashing when they got back to the suite. There were dark footprints on the carpet. Frank checked the closet. More wet carpet. His suitcase had been put back exactly where he'd left it, his shirts and the grey sports jacket neatly rehung. Good old Rog had done what he was told without even taking the time to get changed.

Lulu peeled out of her bikini, sat down on the bed and dialled the operator. She listened for a moment and then hung up and turned to Frank. "Newt's left half a dozen messages. He wants you to call him at home."

Frank said, "Yeah, okay."

Lulu stretched out on the bed. She smiled at him and said, "Why are you looking at me like that?"

"Lust."

"That's your lust look?"

"I got two or three of them. This one's been my most successful, over the years."

"Irresistible, is it?"

"So far."

Lulu smiled. "Well, it certainly seems to be working on me. C'mere a minute, Frank."

"What about the chlorine?"

"We'll think of something."

Afterwards, Frank made the call. Home for Newt could be any one of several addresses, but the house at Laguna Beach was the best bet, so Frank tried there first.

Newt answered on the third ring. Without preamble, he said, "You're surprised you got through to me, right? My answering machine broke. A new one's on the way, but it ain't here yet, so what can I do?"

Frank said, "You been watching George Raft movies again?"

"Maybe. Why?"

"You called me, remember?"

Newt had to think about that one. Frank could hear the waves pounding the beach. Or maybe it was the sound of his boss's brain in high gear. Newt was a wealthy man but not particularly powerful or smart. Inherited money. Sometimes it was a blessing, sometimes it was a curse. Without it, Newt'd probably have a job at a car wash somewhere, if he was lucky.

Newt said, "I expected to hear from you by now. You got a problem?"

"Nothing serious."

Lulu had left the bathroom door open. She turned on the shower.

Newt said, "What's that noise, Frank?"

"It's raining."

"In the middle of the summer?"

"Hey, this is Vancouver. People go down to the beach to grab some tan, they take two things – a paperback and an umbrella."

Lulu began to sing. *Mack the Knife.* She had a real nice voice, even better than Bobby Darin.

Newt said, "Somebody singing?"

"Right across the street," said Frank. "Listen, I'm out of quarters, gotta run."

"Be there much longer?"

"What, here at the phone booth?"

Newt shouted, "Fuck!" into Frank's ear. Frank heard a grunt and then glass shattering. Newt yelled, "Lemme tell you this, Frankie! Your sense of humor is the only sense you got, and you ain't quite funny enough to make a living!" Newt breathed raggedly into the phone as he struggled to get himself under control. After a moment he said, "You gonna be staying in Vancouver much longer?"

"No way. It's been raining ever since I got here. A regular flood. There's people drowning on the sidewalks, it don't even make the papers." Frank let his voice get serious. "Couple more days, maybe three."

"That's an expensive hotel, Frank. I checked it out. Cheapest room they got is a hundred-twenty a night."

Frank didn't see the point of getting into another argument.

"Gotta be running up a tab," said Newt.

"I'm a professional. What you wanted, remember? A guy who could get the job done nice and quiet. Jeez, I'm cruising around town in a *Ford*. A two-door. No sun roof or nothing. Gimme a break."

Newt sighed wearily, an exhalation of noxious gases that Frank knew all too well. Stale Marlboro cigarette smoke. Scope mouthwash. Mexican beer. Frank recoiled, reflexively jerked the telephone receiver away from his mouth.

Newt said, "You give *me* a fuckin' break, Frank. Stop spending my hard-earned money and get it over with and come home."

Frank said, "Listen, it ain't . . ."

Newt hung up.

Click.

Just like that, the miserly little twerp.

Frank gripped the receiver in both hands and rotated his wrists in opposite directions. Chunks of plastic hit the walls and ceiling, ricocheted off the window.

"How're we going to call room service to tell them we need a new phone?" said Lulu, from the bathroom doorway.

"It's okay, I think I can fix it or we can get a new one."

Lulu giggled. "You're a funny guy, Frank. Want to go shopping?"

"Yeah, sure."

"You do?"

"Is something terrible gonna happen?"

"Maybe."

He watched her dress. She put on a pink blouse with a high neck, a full-length white summer skirt of a material light and frothy and translucent as the champagne they'd had in the whirlpool. White panties. No bra. She made up her face as if it were a mask; when she was finished Frank didn't know what to think. It was her but wasn't her, it was weird. She looked as if she were terribly sunburnt, *raw.* She used something like a pencil to draw a pair of dark eyebrows across her skin. Glued on dark eyelashes that were like tiny pushbrooms without handles. Added lipstick that turned her mouth into a bruise. The way she worked, so slow and deliberate, it was like she was an artist drawing a self-portrait on the paper-white canvas of her body. Frank was bewitched. He watched her add mirror sunglasses, a mauve wig and wide-brimmed pink straw hat.

When she was finished, she turned to him and said, "How do I look?"

"Good, good."

Frank was pretty sure he could see the shape of her breasts through the thin silk of her blouse. It made him feel restless and cranky, to think that any fool could look, any fool could see.

"Something wrong?"

"The shirt . . ."

"Blouse."

"It's kind of . . ."

"Revealing?"

"Yeah."

"That's the idea."

Frank said, "To be blunt, I got to tell you I don't like it."

"Don't worry. Remember, anybody can look, but only you can touch."

Frank decided to let it go. He said, "I happened to pass you on the street, I doubt I'd recognize you."

"That's the idea, honey-pie."

They took the elevator down to the lobby, strolled past the front desk and model steam-engine. Frank looked for Rog but didn't see him. As they stepped through the automatic doors and on to Robson Street, Lulu handed Frank a white parasol. He popped it open and held it up to shield her from the corrosive sun. They crossed Howe and walked up Georgia past the skateboarders, fountain and the pair of big stone lions flanking wide granite stairs that led to a cul-de-sac; huge doors that would not open. Legions of sweaty tourists risked a gallery of frisky pigeons to climb those steps, try the doors and find them forever welded shut. It was an architectural joke not even the locals understood.

The light on the street, reflected off a thousand car windshields, was dazzling. Lulu guided him through the glare towards Eaton's Mall. She wanted to get him a watch. Frank said he didn't need a watch – he already had one.

Lulu said, "When you wear a Rolex, people look at you and know that you're a success."

"What do I care what people think?"

Lulu stared solemnly up at him. "Sometime soon, let's buy a book on outer space. One with lots of pictures, so you can show me what planet you were born on."

"Fine," said Frank, smiling.

They took an escalator up to the mall's second level, strolled through the shiny brass portals of a jewelry store, the name over the door, Wexler's, scrawled in brass letters two feet high. The man behind the counter was in his late-fifties or early-sixties, chubby and balding, dressed in a dark-grey suit, grey shirt with button-down collar, a tie in wide dark-blue and maroon stripes. He smiled and said, "May I help you?"

Lulu adjusted her mirror-lensed glasses. "We're looking for a Rolex. Gold, no diamonds. You Mr Wexler?"

"Paul Wexler." The guy produced a tiny brass key, unlocked a glass display case. Frank glanced casually around. Polished glass display cases took up most of the floor space. The carpet was pale-bronze. Everything in the store was gold, or gold-colored. The walls were covered in paper that looked like sheets of gold. The glass display cases reflected slivers of gold light. A piano played waterfall music from hidden speakers. The air was still and cold. Wexler's icy fingers helped Frank with the lizard strap of his Seiko, slipped the Rolex over his wrist.

"It looks very good on you, don't you think?"

"How much?" said Lulu.

"Thirteen-five."

Thirteen thousand dollars for a watch? Frank's wrist stung.

Lulu's credit card fluttered across the counter and dropped to the floor at Wexler's feet.

Lulu said, "I *am* sorry."

Wexler bent to retrieve the card. Lulu winked at Frank. Wexler came up frowning.

"Excuse me, this . . ."

Lulu snatched the card out of his hand and punched him on the nose. The jeweler staggered back, eyes wide with shock. There was a smear of blood on his upper lip. He reached for his handkerchief. Lulu turned to Frank. "Better deck him before he hits the alarm."

Frank caught Wexler on the chin with a hard right. The jeweler folded like a cheap accordion and vanished behind the counter. For a moment his handkerchief marked the spot where he had stood. Lulu plucked it out of the air, used it to wipe stray fingerprints from the glass counter. She scooped up Frank's Seiko.

Frank leaned over the counter. Wexler's mouth was open. His chest rose and fell steadily.

Frank said, "He's gonna be okay."

"Good for him."

As they rode the crowded escalator down to the lower level, Lulu said, "How long is he going to be out?"

"Five minutes, somewhere in there."

"Is that all?"

"Maybe less. It's a nice watch, but you can pick one up on the street for five hundred bucks. I mean, I sure ain't gonna *kill* anybody for it."

"We better get out of here."

"I'm glad you got a plan," said Frank. "For a minute there, I thought we were gonna have to take it one step at a time."

"Think we can get back to the hotel in five minutes?"

"Easy," said Frank, "but there's no hurry. Wexler's gonna be groggy as hell, probably have a mild concussion. It takes a lot out of a guy, getting kayo'ed. By the time he gets his act together, dials nine-eleven . . ."

"We should've ripped the phone out of the wall, is that what you're telling me?"

"The operator'll ask him if it's an emergency. He'll start yelling at her. Lose his temper. It'll take at least ten minutes for the cops to show up, maybe longer. From their point of view, what's the rush? There's no chance they're gonna catch anybody. We're long gone, and they know it. Besides, they don't *care* if they get us."

There was a security guard near the Georgia Street exit, but he had his back to them, his eye on a Japanese girl in skintight jeans and a halter top.

Lulu pushed the door open. Frank wished she'd let him do that for her. He kind of enjoyed it. She said, "The cops don't care if they catch us? How can that be?"

Frank had to back up a little. "Yeah, they care. But not as much as they ought to. See, there's nothing to motivate them, no sympathy factor. *They'll* never be able to afford to buy one of Wexler's thirteen thousand dollar watches, and they know it."

He moved around to Lulu's left and popped open the parasol. She smiled at him, snuggled up close.

"And also," Frank continued, "they'd never say it out loud but they gotta be thinking that if a guy carries a million-dollar inventory and is too dumb and too cheap to hire a minimum-wage clerk for backup or even spend a few bucks on a security camera, then he deserves everything he gets."

"How do you know there wasn't a camera?"

"First thing I looked for."

There was a tourist bus parked in front of the hotel, diesel engine pushing black smoke across the sidewalk. Frank folded the parasol. If this was his hotel, he'd tell the dumb-ass drivers to turn off their engines or park somewhere else.

The automatic doors snapped open with a flourish of glass and polished mahogany. The restaurant was to their right, and then the bar. Frank was thirsty, but guided Lulu towards the bank of elevators because he figured it was probably a good idea to get her out of those deep-South clothes and wig. He jabbed at a button with his thumb. The elevator opened wide to receive them.

Frank held Lulu in his arms as they were carried imperceptibly upward. Her wig was askew and her eyes overflowed with tears.

Post-robbery syndrome. Frank had seen it many times before.

Despite the crooked wig, swollen eyes and scarlet cheeks, nose full of mucus, banshee wail of distress and flood of salty tears that drenched his new shirt, Frank thought she was absolutely stunning.

Why in hell would Rog grudgingly acknowledge that his step-daughter was *unusual* or *interesting* looking but refuse to admit the obvious – that she was beautiful, a stunner?

There was no room in Frank's heart for that old saw about beauty being in the eye of the beholder.

It never occurred to him that for the first time in his rough-and-tumble life, he wasn't spending every last minute looking out for himself. He'd fallen head-over-heels in love, but due to his complete lack of previous experience, failed to recognize the symptoms.

9

Mel Dutton exchanged the 50-mil for the 35-mil wide-angle, shot half a dozen frames and then took out his pen and noted the case number, date, subject, type of camera, lens, film used and shutter speed and *f*-stop in his photo log.

Willows stood there, waiting patiently for him to get the job done. He'd shared enough crime scenes with Mel to know that there was no point in trying to hurry things along. Dutton didn't react well to pressure. He had a tendency when pushed to push back or, if rank made that impossible, to turn surly, slow down to the point where people were gritting their teeth. He considered himself an artist, and over the years had slowly cultivated what he conceived to be an artistic temperament. Willows had visited Dutton's home, had a beer with him and admired the beautifully framed color photographs that covered his walls. Dutton had talent, all right. Especially if you got a kick out of looking at gruesome closeups of people who'd died violently and bloodily.

Dutton exchanged the Nikon for a 4 × 5 format Pentax. He loaded the camera with Kodak Plus-X, a fine-grained black and white film, then attached it to a small wooden tripod. He adjusted the length of the legs and placed the tripod so the camera was directly above a footprint etched in blood. He placed two folding wooden rulers next to the footprint, the first ruler parallel to the long axis of the impression, and the second adjacent to the heel print, at right angles to the first ruler. He was the only photographer he knew who didn't use a metal tripod. Metal was cheaper and much less heavy; a major consideration when you were packing fifty or more pounds of equipment to a fifth-floor walkup. But Dutton always used a wooden tripod and never intended to change. If you asked him why, he'd tell you it was because wood was less subject to vibration. But the truth was he believed wood to be *artistic*.

Kneeling, he peered through the Pentax's viewfinder. Light from the restaurant's window fell on the footprint at a sharp angle, creating a pleasing pattern of shadows and highlights.

Dutton moved the tripod six inches to the left. He said, "Would you mind holding that pose for maybe another twenty minutes or so, kid?"

Parker glared at him. He ignored her, bracketed the *f*-stop as he power-wound through a dozen frames. He straightened and his knees creaked ominously. He said, "Handsome, wasn't he?"

Parker said, "Why don't you ask him out, Mel. He probably wouldn't say no."

Dutton laughed, took a couple more shots.

"You going to be much longer?" said Willows.

"Gimme another five minutes. Maybe ten. Now that the sun's moved around, I can get some better shots of the splash pattern on the wall. Hot stuff, Jack. Lemme tell you, the tabloids'd pay a month's wages for this. Not that I'd consider moonlighting. It's just I've been looking down the road lately – to the retirement years."

"Mel . . ."

"What I'm gonna do is publish a book. Coffee table thing, twice the size of an encyclopedia. Crime scene pictures. I was thinking of calling it *Dead Bodies* or maybe *Scene of Crime*."

"Sounds terrific," said Willows without a trace of enthusiasm.

Dutton folded the two wooden rulers, stuffed them in his shirt pocket and turned his attention to the blood-spattered wall. Cherry Ngo was about five-eight. The angle of impact indicated that whoever'd shot him was at least a few inches shorter. The narrow end of teardrop-shaped blood stains always pointed in the direction of travel. Well, from what he knew about Cherry, the kid's direction of travel was basically a straight line to hell. The weapon used was a .45-calibre semi-auto. Two rounds had been fired and both spent casings had been recovered, as well as a single unfired cartridge. Only one bullet had struck Cherry. It had passed through his hand, the sweet potato, his skull and three-quarters of an inch of sturdy lathe-and-plaster wall. Now it was in an evidence bag in Willows' pocket.

Dutton moved along the wall, shooting a series of overlapping photographs of the blood and bone-chips and chunks of brain and gore and sweet potato that stippled the smooth white paint. He wondered if there'd ever been an artist who created his work by lining up cans of paint in front of his canvas and then blasting the cans full of bullet holes. Might be worth looking into. Be a real unique effect. He finished the role of film and clipped the lens cap back on his Pentax.

"Anything else, Jack?"

"That'll do it, Mel."

Dutton avoided eye contact as he slipped past Parker and out the door.

Willows knelt beside the body. Ngo's wide open eyes stared right through him.

Parker said, "Somebody found out he was down at 312 Main, that we questioned him. He was killed because of something he told us, or something he *might've* told us, but didn't."

Willows shook his head, no. "Whoever shot Cherry tried to gun him down *before* he talked to us. Emily was a mistake."

Cherry Ngo was wearing a plain white shirt, charcoal pants held up with a thin red belt and scuffed white leather basketweave shoes. He wasn't wearing socks. The shoes were laceless.

The body removal services employee loitering in the doorway said, "You gonna be much longer?"

Willows ignored him.

The guy said, "Mind if I smoke?"

Parker said, "Out in the alley."

A crime scene technician named Willy Talbot stepped into the room. Talbot was tall, thin enough to qualify as anorexic. He had a terrible complexion, his dark, oily skin pitted and cratered by childhood acne. There was a story Willows had heard about Talbot – that he'd been down in the basement of 312 Main, getting into his uniform, when a wise-ass vice cop named Lewis Brandon told him he looked as if he shaved with a cheese grater. Talbot had knocked Brandon cold with a single punch and handcuffed him to a locker door, pulled down his pants and kicked him in the ass so hard they heard it upstairs and thought there'd been a traffic accident out on Main Street.

When Brandon regained consciousness, there was a huge purple bruise on his ass and a note taped to his locker door advising him that if he wanted the key to his cuffs, he'd need a mirror and a pair of rubber gloves.

Talbot nodded to Parker, crooked a finger at Willows and said, "C'mere and take a look at this."

Willows and Parker followed Talbot into the staff washroom at the back of the building. Despite health laws to the contrary, the bathroom was located directly off the kitchen.

The two detectives and Talbot squeezed into the tiny bathroom. There was a toilet against the far wall, and next to it a sink with a mirror above it. An unpainted plywood shelf held a stack of paper towels and a water glass containing a toothbrush and wrinkled tube of Crest toothpaste. Several crumpled paper towels lay like dead flowers in a rusty metal wastebasket beneath the sink. The wall in the area of the sink and within arm's reach of the toilet was covered with crudely drawn artwork, but the scrawled captions were unreadable because they were in Vietnamese.

Talbot shut the door and said, "Get the light, will you?" The bathroom had already been dusted. Parker hit the switch. Talbot had a flashlight. He aimed the narrow beam at the sink. Willows and Parker moved closer. He switched off the flash. In the darkness, the sink glowed with a faint, pale-green luminescence. Talbot turned the flashlight back on, produced an aerosol can and sprayed the wastebasket and paper towels. He switched off the flashlight. The paper towels glowed pale green.

"Weird, huh?" Talbot turned the bathroom light back on. He shook the can. "Luminol."

Parker said, "I've seen it before."

"It's a reagent. Blood reacts to it by luminescing."

Parker glanced at Willows. Talbot was one of those guys – a born lecturer.

Talbot said, "Don't ask me how it works, because I got no idea. Normally, in a situation like this, I'd use the laser. But somebody dropped it out a window last week and smashed it all to hell." He waved the aerosol can at the sink. "Pretty obvious your perp washed up in here after he did the job. The quantity of blood in there is very small, minute. Best bet's the wastebasket. The question is, whose blood was the perp getting rid of, the victim's or his own?"

Willows said, "How long's it going to take?"

"I dunno, Jack. We're snowed, as usual. This time tomorrow, maybe."

"Push it. You need some weight, give me a call and I'll see what I can do."

The body removal services employee – what some of the cops called the ghoul patrol – was asleep in his vehicle. The guy's name was Harvey McArdle. Parker knew him from other cases. He was okay. Quiet. Not like some of them, always cracking jokes. Parker made a fist and rapped on the windshield. McArdle came awake instantly, got out of the car and pushed his gurney through the back door of the restaurant. He unrolled a rubberized bodybag on the floor next to Ngo's body. Willows helped lift the corpse into the bag. Ngo didn't weigh much. Willows held his head steady while McArdle worked the zipper. Together, they lifted Ngo on to the gurney.

The gurney's rubber wheels rolled across the chalked outline of the corpse, smudging the lines.

Willows looked away. The smudged chalk irritated him. It was a minor form of degradation, in a way – like turning over a gravestone.

Parker said, "There's no family except for Joey – the parents are both dead. We better talk to Joey, and do it fast. There's a mobile unit from Channel Eleven down at the end of the alley."

Willows zipped up his leather jacket. He stepped carefully over the chalked lines. "Okay, let's get it over with. He's got a job, hasn't he?"

Parker nodded. "At a wholesale auto parts supplier over on East Eighth."

Willows said, "My car could use a new set of wipers. Maybe I can get a discount."

In the car, crawling down Broadway through the snarl of mid-morning traffic, Parker said, "Four years now, since I was rotated to homicide. You ever get tired of it, Jack? Feel worn out and used up?"

Willows shrugged. A delivery van cut in front of the unmarked Ford, forcing him to stab at the brakes. He grinned at Parker and said, "Cynical, too, and world-weary."

They weren't going to make the light; it was going to be close but they weren't going to make it . . . The light went from green to amber. Willows braked. There was a shriek of tortured rubber behind him. He glanced in the rear-view mirror. A red Miata convertible. The driver waved his fist in the air, gave Willows the finger and leaned on the horn.

Parker glanced behind her. "What's his problem?"

"Me. I've just been tried and convicted of driving with due care and attention."

"Sentenced to deafness."

"What was the address on Eighth?"

"Five twenty-seven."

The instant the light turned green, the Miata's horn started up again.

Willows said, "Okay, that does it." He put the Ford in gear and yanked open the door.

"Don't do anything crazy, Jack."

"Why not?" Willows got out of the car. He walked slowly back to the Miata. The driver was in his fifties, wearing a suit and tie. Willows took out his wallet and flipped it open. The driver stared straight ahead, as if hypnotized. He had both hands on the wheel and his knuckles were white, the blood squeezed out of them by the pressure of his grip. Willows slapped his badge against the windshield. Metal on glass. The man glared at him and then registered the badge.

It was a pleasure, watching the color drain out of his face.

Willows said, "Follow me, please." He walked back to the Ford, climbed in, put the car in gear and pulled away.

"What'd you say to him?"

Willows reached up, made an unnecessary adjustment to the rearview mirror. The Miata was in a holding pattern, keeping a respectful distance.

"I asked him if he wanted to play a little game of follow the leader."

"Where are we going?"

"Five twenty-seven East Eighth, to talk to Joey Ngo. It's about what, a fifteen minute trip?"

"Somewhere in there," said Parker, smiling.

Speedy Auto Parts was housed in a crumbling stucco building squeezed in between a tiny lunch-hour cafe and a print shop.

Willows parked in a towaway zone in front of the building. The Miata pulled up behind him. Willows flipped down the Ford's sun visor so the "Police Vehicle" card was visible. He and Parker got out of the car. Parker waited at the curb as Willows went around to the Miata.

Willows held out his hand. "May I see your licence and vehicle registration, please."

The driver – Peter Reikerman, was the registered owner of the Miata.

Willows waved the licence in his face. "This your current address?"

Reikerman nodded. "Yes, Officer."

"Detective."

Willows walked slowly around to the rear of the car. The licence plate decal was valid. He told Reikerman to turn on his lights, signal a left and then a right-hand turn, hit the brakes and put the transmission in reverse.

Willows walked slowly back to Reikerman. He still had Reikerman's licence in his hand. He said, "Everything works – not just the horn. Lucky you. Your driving improved considerably on the way over here. Think you can maintain that standard?"

"Yes, sir." According to the licence, Reikerman was fifty-two years old. Half a dozen cassette tapes lay on the passenger seat. The Band, Lovin' Spoonful, Grateful Dead, Bob Dylan . . .

The guy was half a century old, drove a sports car that had been marketed for his children, liked music from the sixties. Willows smiled. He could bust Reikerman, but what was the point – his development had already been arrested. But at the same time, the guy pissed him off. An adult, acting like a kid.

"Wait here, Peter."

The first thing Willows saw as he walked into Speedy Auto Parts was the Corvette coming right at him, bursting through the cinder-block wall with headlights blazing, the driver and the girl in his lap looking startled but not dismayed.

The man lounging behind the counter was short but not fat. He was about as bald as he was ever going to get, but to compensate wore his blue coveralls unbuttoned half-way down his hairy chest. He scratched himself, gave Parker an appreciative look and fashioned a carnivorous grin around the stub of his cheap cigar. "First time, am I right?"

Parker nodded.

The man winked at Willows. "The first time a person walks through that door, don't matter how much of a hurry he thought he was in, he's gotta stop and take a look at the wall. And the look on the guy's face – it took me a while to figure out what he's thinking. Why can't I *hear* anything?" Bob was stitched in red thread on the blue overalls. "And maybe they was gonna ask something like do I got a rear fender for a fifty-six Chev. But the first question's always . . ." Bob aimed the juicy stub of his cigar at Parker. "Go on, take a guess."

"They want to know what happened to the Corvette's rear end."

"And you know what I always tell them?"

Willows said, "That you're sitting on it."

Bob leaned his belly against the counter. "What are you guys, psychic?"

Willows showed him his badge.

"Cops. I mighta guessed. It's about the eighty-two Caddy I bought last week, right? Kid told me it was an estate vehicle, his grampa died and . . . I knew goddamn well I shoulda checked the paper on that baby. Look, if there's anything . . ."

Willows said, "Don't say it."

Bob lifted both hands, palms out. "Never crossed my mind, believe me."

"We're from Homicide, not Auto. We want to talk to Joey Ngo."

"What about?"

"That's between him and us."

"Yeah, sure. But you wanna talk to him on my time, right? I mean, who's paying the shot here, if it isn't me?"

Parker said, "Maybe you better show us the Caddy after all."

Bob sucked on his cigar and pondered his limited options. The cigar was dead. And, judging from the look on the cop's face, he was too, unless he cooperated.

There was a swing gate at the far end of the counter. Bob pointed at it. "Joey's out back. Whatever time you spend with him, he's gotta take off his lunch."

They found Joey Ngo sitting in front of a computer terminal, punching at the keyboard with two stiff fingers while he talked into a telephone wedged between his cheek and shoulder. He glanced at Willows, nodded, and went back to work. "No, we're out of stock." Pause. "Three working days, if I fax the order to Toronto and you don't mind paying air freight." Another pause. "Well, that's the best I can do. Otherwise, all you can do is phone around, try the wreckers for a used one." Pause. "Yeah, sure." Pause. "Five, but Toronto won't start to process your order until tomorrow morning unless we fax them by two 'clock." Another pause. "Right, because of the time difference."

Joey Ngo rolled his eyes, sighed, and hung up. He looked Willows straight in the eye and said, "Like I told you, I didn't see anything. All I heard was the shots. No voices. The car was long gone by the time I made it to the door. And my brother's friends are no friends of mine."

Willows said, "The reason we're here is somebody took another shot at Cherry."

"Surprise, surprise."

"From a lot closer range this time."

Joey Ngo became very still. His eyes seemed to go out of focus. He fished a pack of Export cigarettes from the back pocket of his jeans, lit up with a disposable lighter.

"He hurt bad?"

Willows said, "It couldn't be much worse."

Joey Ngo sucked deeply on his cigarette, pulled the smoke down to the very bottom of his lungs. He held his breath a long time, and then shrugged and said, "The way he played, I guess he got what he wanted."

Parker said, "You don't really believe that."

"I knew he was in trouble."

"What kind of trouble – gangs?"

Joey said, "Hey, look at me. I got a job. I pay my bills, keep my nose clean. Don't mess around with drugs. Cherry was my brother, but that's it. We didn't hang out with the same crowd."

"You lived in the same house."

"It was a temporary arrangement. He was staying with me 'cause he had no place else to go."

"He never talked about his friends?"

"I didn't want to hear it. He'd start to tell me what a tough dude he was, I'd shut him right down. I'm telling you right now what I said to him lots of times – I ain't interested. I don't want to get involved. But he didn't run with a gang, I know that much. He was too smart, too independent."

Parker said, "Joey, the impression you're giving me is that you aren't too concerned about finding out who shot your brother."

"The way he was headed, somebody was gonna do it sooner or later. What difference does it make who pulled the trigger?"

Willows said, "I heard Cherry was dealing."

"Yeah? Who told you that?"

"A friend of mine in narcotics."

Joey shrugged. "Yeah, he sold a little dope, now and then. It wasn't his main thing; just a way of picking up a few extra bucks."

"So how did he make a living?"

"Stealing cars. There's a chop shop out in Delta he worked for. But I think he quit; almost got busted once and decided there had to be easier ways of getting rich."

"What else was he into?"

"That's it, far as I know."

"There must've been something else. If he quit boosting cars . . ."

"Look, I got to get back to work. Bob's gonna fry my ass, I spend too much time talking to you."

"Still at the same address, Joey?"

"Fuckin' landlord's trying to get me evicted, but the rent's paid till the end of the month, so I guess I'm good until then, at least."

Parker said, "Did Emily have any friends who might have wanted Cherry dead, because of what happened to her?"

"I didn't know her that well."

"You sure about that?"

Joey Ngo's face darkened. The kid was five-six tops and might weigh a hundred and thirty pounds after a full meal, but for a moment there, Parker thought Joey was going to take a run at her.

Then the phone rang, and Joey snatched at it, and the moment had passed.

Outside, Willows returned Reikerman's licence. "I decided I'm going to give you a break. Beat it."

"Hold it just a minute, now. You made me wait all this time and you're not gonna even give me a ticket?"

"I'm going to give you some free advice instead. Drive less aggressively, Peter. Otherwise, despite your impeccable taste in music and dinky cars, people are going to think you're *immature.*"

Reikerman flushed.

Willows said, "Oh, and one more thing . . ."

Reikerman stared at him.

Willows smiled. *"Don't look back."*

10

Frank was amazed to discover what a jar of creamy white paste and handful of Kleenex could do for a girl's complexion. By the time she came out of the shower, less than half an hour after the big heist, Lulu's pale flesh was a whitish vapor, hardly more substantial than compacted fog, and her hair was the shimmering silvery color of bleached candy floss.

There was a darkening patch of skin in the hollow of her throat, though, where Frank had smooched with a little too much passion.

She caught him staring and said, "I bruise easily, don't I?"

Frank nodded. He was conscious of the gold Rolex on his wrist; the weight made him feel a little off balance.

Lulu finished toweling herself off and wriggled into a midnight-blue lycra bodysuit, the space-age stretch material spangled with dozens of glossy five-pointed gold stars. She turned her back on Frank and lifted her hair out of the way. "Zip me up."

Frank did as he was told.

Lulu turned to face him. She held his hands and looked him in the eye. "Are you mad at me?"

Frank shrugged. "Not exactly."

"I'm a spontaneous sort of person, Frank. But I've always been willing to learn from my mistakes. Tell me what you think I did wrong, okay? Let's talk it over, clear the air."

Frank said, "Never shit in your own backyard."

Lulu's eyes widened. She lifted a hand to her mouth. Mock shock. Or maybe it was the real thing. She said, "Excuse me?"

Frank said, "There's jewelry stores all over town. It wasn't smart to pick one so close. What if the guy finishes talking to the cops and decides to stroll over here to the hotel and have a drink in the bar, try to wash away the shakes?"

"He'd probably go to the bar in the Georgia, it's closer and cheaper."

"That ain't the point. The point is, he could come in for lunch. Or maybe to make a deposit in the bank down in the lobby."

Lulu shook her head. "No, he'd do his business at the Commerce in the mall. That'd be a lot safer, he wouldn't have to go outside at night, risk the streets."

Frank rubbed his jaw. He said, "We ain't on the same wavelength. What I'm trying to get across to you is that Wexler was too close. Like a neighbor. He could bump into you at any time. Then what?"

"You tell me." Lulu let go of Frank's hands. He couldn't tell if she was pouting or getting ready to have a good cry.

There was a purple tub chair on castors by the window. Frank went over and sat down in it and put his feet up on the window ledge. "Probably he'd trot over to the nearest phone and call the cops. And the cop's would arrest us and throw us in jail."

"They'd have to catch us first."

"I doubt that'd be much of a problem for them. What d'you think, they're gonna give us advance warning? 'Hi, we got a warrant we're on our way over.' Is that how you think it works; they call ahead, give you time to tidy up the apartment?"

Lulu said, "Please don't be sarcastic. It's mean and it isn't fair."

"What happens," said Frank, "is the door caves in and all of a sudden the room's full of cops pointing guns at you. And that's it. Game over."

He looked out the window at what he could see of the city. He wondered how many crimes were going down right that minute. Not just big stuff, armed robbery and so on, but even teeny-weeny crimes like stealing a pen from the office, or taking an extra ten minutes at lunch. Hundreds of thousands of people, hundreds of thousands of scams. It was something he believed, a truth he held tight. Everybody was a thief. Everybody.

Frank tore the filter off a cigarette, cranked his Zippo and inhaled deeply. He said, "Know what'd happen next, after they booked us and got our fingers inky and told us not to say cheese and snapped our pictures?"

"No, Frank. What happens next?"

"Rog would spend some of his dope money on a lawyer, arrange your bail."

"That doesn't sound so terrible."

Frank said, "You weren't listening. I said Rog would bail *you* out. Me, he'd leave right where I was."

"He would *not.*"

"Maybe you don't think so, but you're wrong. He'd leave me to rot, and he'd do it for two good reasons. First, he'd blame me for the robbery, figure it was my fault."

Lulu said, "I'd tell him what happened. That it was my idea, not yours."

"He wouldn't believe you, not for a minute. And I wouldn't blame him."

There was a noise out in the corridor. Shouting. A door slammed shut. Frank saw Lulu's body stiffen, the leap of fear in her eyes.

He said, "Second, Rog'd figure that if he paid my bail, I'd skip town and he'd forfeit, lose his five grand or whatever. Which means I'd be stuck in remand until I went to trial, unless Newt took pity on me, which is very unlikely."

"How long would that take, to go to trial?"

Frank said, "Six months, if I was lucky."

"Six months – you'd miss Christmas!"

Frank said, "With my record, I'd miss a couple of Christmases, at least. You wore a disguise, but Wexler'd pick me out of a lineup like a maraschino cherry off a fudge sundae."

"You're a good man, Frank."

Frank said, "Huh?"

"So patient with me." She smiled. Her teeth were translucent, her gums the soft pink of bubble gum. "I guess it was pretty irresponsible, what I did. Next time we'll get it right. *Case* the joint, and all that stuff."

"There isn't gonna be a next time." Frank squashed his cigarette butt out in the ashtray for emphasis.

Lulu sat down in his lap, snuggled up, put her arms around him and held him tight. "I just loved the way you leaned over the counter and punched him on the nose. Like it was all in a day's work. You were so casual, so *relaxed.*"

"Chin," said Frank. "I hit him on the chin."

"He was out on his feet, wasn't he? I saw his eyes roll up in his head. It must be a weird feeling to get knocked unconscious."

Frank said, "What if he'd bashed his head against the floor and got brain damage, couldn't talk right, slurred his words or whatever? What if I'd killed the poor guy? That'd be pretty ironic, wouldn't it – doing twenty-five years for stealing a watch."

"God, they probably wouldn't even let you keep it, would they?"

Frank said, "A long time ago, when I was hardly more than a kid, I had a short career as a pro boxer."

"What did they call you?"

"They called me Frank Wilder."

"The *Wild One*!"

A lucky guess, but it struck home. Frank ducked his head. "Yeah, they called me that for a while."

Excited, Lulu bounced up and down in his lap. "What happened? Tell me about it!"

"I had eight fights. The first five times I climbed in the ring, my opponent went down in the first minute of the first round, the first time I hit 'em."

"You're kidding me."

"First punch. A roundhouse right. Pow!" Frank made a fist and demonstrated his style. "Five fights, and then my contract was picked up by a guy named Herb Munsch. Herb figured he had a hot property. He spent some money on me, invested in sparring partners and steaks. The next two fights it was just the same. First round, first punch. Pow! and down they went."

"Were you ever on TV?"

"Herb pulled some strings, got me a bout on TSN. If I did okay, they were gonna broadcast the fight in the States. Big time."

"God, how exciting!"

"For the big fight, Herb bought me a new outfit. Green trunks with white stripes and a pair of matching shoes, white with green tassels."

"You must have looked incredibly handsome. The women were all over you, weren't they?"

Frank shook his head. "Herb wouldn't let 'em near me."

"Good for Herb."

Frank smiled, a slow remembering. Some of the women had been a lot smarter than Herb, as it happened.

"What's so funny?"

Frank said, "I go in against the guy and right away I know I'm in trouble. I'm throwing everything I got at him but I can't get through his defense. Meantime, he seems happy enough to just sit back, let me wear myself out. The crowd's booing and tossing stuff in the ring. I'm mad, confused. Five seconds into the fourth round, I wind up for a punch and he hits me with a right jab and down I go. That's it."

"What? You lost the fight, you let him beat you?"

Frank said, "I was too slow. I was strong, but not fast enough, not for the pros. You wondered what it felt like to get knocked out. Did I see stars, or a bunch of bluebirds flying around in circles, going tweet tweet? What there is, is nothing. I was out cold for almost three minutes. The crowd went nuts. A lot of guys lost a lot of money on me, and weren't too happy about it. But that was Herb's problem, not mine. I spent the night in emergency. They thought my jaw was broken. I had X-rays, they even gimme a CAT scan. The next morning, Herb comes around to pick me up, takes me out to lunch at a real nice restaurant. While we're eating he tells me that right after the count, as I'm lying there out cold on the apron, he jumped into the ring with a gun in his hand. He'd dropped fifty grand on me, and all he could see was red. Figured I'd thrown the fight. If I'd been faking it, he told me, he'd have shot me right there in front of everybody." Frank shrugged. "And that was that."

"The end of your career."

"Yeah. I worked for years as a bouncer, and got by because people mostly left me alone because of my size, and I usually got in the first punch. I still had the old magic – if I did have to hit a guy, down he went. But the jaw, it looks good, but it's solid glass."

Lulu said, "They don't have any bouncers here in the hotel. Not what they call bouncers, anyway. There's security, though. Mr Phil Estrada's the man in charge. Maybe you've seen him around. He wears three-piece suits and is always smiling and looks as if he just came from the barber's, which he probably did, because Daddy told me one of Mr Estrada's perks is unlimited free haircuts at the shop in the mezzanine, and he gets a trim three times a week, Saturdays and Mondays and Wednesdays. So I guess if the hotel had a problem, he'd be the one to take care of it."

"It don't matter where you go," said Frank, "there's always a guy who specializes in problem solving, quieting things down."

"Phil gets complimentary manicures, too. But Sheila refuses to do him more than once a week."

Frank said, "It's a handy skill to have, the ability to make people cool down and behave reasonably. There's always work to be had. You can make a decent living, and it ain't all that dangerous, most of the time."

"I like danger. It's good for the soul."

"But bad for the heart," said Frank, who'd been there and back, and knew the territory all too well.

Lulu's instinct was to argue with him, but she made an effort and managed to hold her tongue. Frank had a melancholy look on his face. She wondered what he was thinking. It never did much good to dwell on the past – it couldn't be changed no matter how strong your needs. Part of the reason she'd been attracted to Frank was because he seemed like a man with his feet on the ground and his eyes on the horizon.

But what was his reason for spending time with her?

She knew what she looked like. People, men and women alike, couldn't take their eyes off her. But it wasn't because she was exotic, an endangered species, fragile and beautiful and rare. It was because she was strange, because she was weird, a circus freak, *different.*

She said, "Let's get out of here, go downstairs and have a drink."

The phone rang. Frank stared at it for a moment as if he'd never seen a phone before and had no idea what it did or why it would make such a strange sound.

Lulu said, "You going to answer it?"

Frank said, "It might be somebody I know." He moved, and Lulu slipped off his lap. He said, "Yeah, let's go down to the bar, get a drink."

The soundproofing was excellent. When Frank shut the door to the room, the noise of the phone was immediately cut off. But Lulu somehow knew it was still ringing, silently pursuing them, and she felt that as long as she and Frank were in the hotel, the unknown caller would let the phone ring on and on, that the ringing would never stop.

In the bar, they found an empty booth with a clear view of the lobby. Lulu wanted them to drink vodka martinis. Frank usually tried to keep his distance from hard liquor, due to the stormy effect it had on his head and stomach. But since he'd given her such a hard time about the jewelry store, he decided not to argue.

The martinis arrived, and then a waiter drifted by with a tray loaded down with deep-fried chicken wings. The chicken looked good and it was free and Frank was hungry. He told the waiter to leave the tray. The guy said he couldn't do that, it wasn't allowed. He had an accent. Italian, maybe. Frank grabbed the tray away from him. Nobody seemed to notice except the bartender. Frank tried to remember his name. Jerry. Frank waved at him and signalled for a fresh round of drinks. The waiter said something in Italian, and minced off to the kitchen. Frank offered the chicken to Lulu. She wasn't hungry. He gnawed the meat off a wing, dropped the bones in his empty martini glass.

The fresh drinks arrived. Doubles, with five olives in each glass.

Frank ate an olive and then a chicken wing and then another olive and another wing. He was just getting into the rhythm of olives and wings when Lulu said his name in a way that made him break stride, pause in his chewing and swallowing and glance up.

The guy standing there was about five-eleven, no more than a hundred fifty pounds. He was wearing a black silk suit over a crisp white shirt and black silk tie. There was a black silk handkerchief in the breast pocket of his jacket. Frank glanced down. The guy's socks were black silk. There were no tassels on his shoes. Frank looked up, mildly curious. The guy's mouth was a little too small and his nose was a little too straight. He wore a gold ring with a blood-red stone on the pinky finger of his left hand. His hair was black, with a faint bluish sheen along the sides, and he wore it short except at the back, where it was long enough to reach his shirt collar.

Frank wondered about that, the streak of blue hair that merged into the black. It was so shiny, slippery looking. It reminded him of a fish. The guy was kind of fish-like, if you thought about it. So thin, so sleek. Frank leaned forward in his chair, offered his hand. Just for a moment, a fraction of a second, the guy looked a little startled. Recovering, he reached out to shake. It came as no surprise that his nails were perfectly cut, glistening with lacquer. Frank said, "How ya doing, Phil."

Phil Estrada glanced at Lulu. It was clear he didn't much care for the fact that she'd obviously told Frank about him before they'd had a chance to meet, *described* him to the guy. Phil wondered what words Lulu had used. One time when she'd had a few, she'd told him he looked like a hairdresser for dead people. The words would come back to haunt him on his deathbed, he was sure.

Frank said, "Sit down, have a piece of chicken."

"I can't stay. I only got a minute."

Frank said, "The waiter complain about me?"

"Yeah."

"You guys related?"

Estrada shook his head.

"But you're Italian, right?"

"Of Italian descent."

"How long you been with the hotel?"

"Longer than you, Frank." Smiling, Estrada flicked an invisible speck of lint from the sleeve of his jacket. The way his hand moved, it might have been Frank he was getting rid of, not the lint. He rested his manicured hand on Lulu's shoulder. "Frank, I been talking to Rog and he says you seem like a real nice guy. That don't give you a licence to make trouble. *Capice?*"

Frank didn't like Estrada's hand on her, didn't like him resting any part of his weight on her. And he didn't like the way Estrada kept looking at her, either, with his fish-eyes shiny and black and dead as olives.

Frank wiped his hands on the tablecloth and stood up.

Phil Estrada shot his cuff, checked the watch that glittered like a golden egg in the nest of coarse black hairs on his wrist. Lifting his heavy eyebrows in mock astonishment, he said, "Later than I thought, gotta run," and turned his back on Frank and slowly walked away.

Lulu finished her martini in one long gulp. She said, "How much longer are you going to have to stay in town, Frank?"

Frank shrugged. "Couple of days, maybe three. It depends."

"There's a Travelodge a couple of blocks away. Or we could stay at the Meridian or wherever you like."

Frank said, "I like it here." He lit a cigarette and dropped the match on the carpet.

Lulu said, "Why go looking for trouble, Frank?"

Frank smiled, "Because if you're gonna get your fair share, sometimes that's what you have to do."

11

The closest grocery store was two blocks south of the restaurant, squeezed in between an Italian restaurant and a shoe repair. A bright green and white awning protected sidewalk shoppers while they browsed over wooden boxes filled to overflowing with rows of cucumbers and celery, pyramids of tomatoes, half a dozen different varieties of apples from the Okanogan and Washington State, oranges trucked in from California, mounds of bright green snow peas, clumps of yellow bananas that lay like misshapen fists . . .

Parker said, "Lettuce, apples and grapes . . . What else do we grow around here; can you think of anything?"

"Cranberries," said Willows.

"*Cranberries?*"

"There was a thing on the news a few months ago. I'd fallen asleep during the sports report. When I woke up, they were in the middle of a piece on bogs. Cranberry bogs."

"So when the big quake hits, and all those Californian farms we're dependent on slide into the ocean, we won't necessarily starve to death. We'll feast on apples and lettuce and cranberries."

"And spuds from the Fraser Valley."

"But not sweet potatoes?"

"Not that I know of," said Willows. He was in the mood for an apple. The frisky red of the Macintoshes appealed to him, but after a moment's reflection he decided in favor of the tongue-shrinking tartness of a Granny Smith. Polishing the apple on his sleeve, he followed Parker into the store.

There were two people behind the counter; a man and a woman Willows immediately assumed were man and wife. They were in their late-forties or early-fifties, and had the hunched posture of an avant-garde chess set. She'd washed the grey out of her hair with a blonde rinse. It didn't suit her. Willows flipped open his wallet, let them have a look at his badge.

The man smiled at him. "What is this, an old movie? – You show me your badge and help yourself to an apple? Want a bag?"

Willows shook his head.

"It comes in its own bag, am I right? Some people like to eat the whole thing, gobble it down seeds and all. Not me. Know why? Because when I was a kid my dear sweet mother told me I'd grow an apple tree in my gut, the branches would rise up and fill my throat and choke me to death." He glanced at Parker. "You both cops?"

Parker nodded.

"So what's the problem – more parking tickets Elaine forgot to mention?"

Willows introduced himself, and Parker. The owner's name was Tony Minotti. Elaine was his wife.

Parker said, "Do you sell sweet potatoes, Mr Minotti?"

"Yeah, sure. Thanksgiving. Christmas. That's the best time."

"Do you have any in stock now, today?"

"We got a few pounds." He grinned at Parker. "You want to take a look at them?"

"If you don't mind."

The Minottis exchanged a quick look. Mrs Minotti shrugged and said, "Over here, follow me."

The sweet potatoes were on the far side of the store, directly opposite the cash register. Willows picked one up, hefted the weight of it in his hand.

Parker said, "Do you sell some of these every day, Mrs Minotti?"

"No. Three or four days could go by. Sometimes we throw them out, or maybe I take them home and cook them. Like you can see, we only got a few pounds. It's just to provide variety for our customers. So they don't go someplace else. The potatoes are cheap and if you take care of them they got a good shelf life."

Mrs Minotti was wearing a green apron over a white sweater and black dress. She wiped her hands nervously on the apron, glanced over her shoulder at her husband, who was watching them closely as he continued to man the cash register. "Is there anything else I can do for you?"

Willows took a bite out of his apple, chewed and swallowed. "Claire, why don't you explain the situation to Mrs Minotti while I have a talk with her husband."

Parker nodded. She turned to Mrs Minotti and said, "Do you know a restaurant a couple of blocks from here, called Pale Green Shoots?"

Willows made his way back to the cash register. He waited until Tony Minotti had finished with a customer and then asked him the same question.

Minotti nodded. "Yeah, sure. They don't buy from us. Never. They been closed a long time, since before the spring. I walk down that way at night; there's a place I go for coffee."

"Did you ever eat in the restaurant?"

Minotti shook his head. "No, never." He thumped his chest, grinning. "I'm Italian, you can see it? So I eat in Italian restaurants. If I was Greek, that would be a different situation. But I'm Italian."

Willows showed him one of Dutton's gory Polaroids of Cherry Ngo. "Do you know this man?"

The color drained from Minotti's face. He averted his eyes. "No, absolutely not, I'm sure of it."

Willows tried another of Dutton's snapshots. "You never saw him in the restaurant as you were walking by?"

"Like I told you, it's been closed for a long time, two or three months, maybe more."

"Before it was closed."

"I don't look in there. I make a point of it, you know what I mean? Punks. They stare at you. One time I'm looking and one of them makes a pistol of his hand, like this. He points it at me. His eyes laugh at me and his mouth shapes the sound of a gun. *Bang!*"

Willows held the photo up at eye level. "But you're sure it wasn't this man?"

Minotti stared at the picture. "If I saw this man, I would remember him, for sure. Wouldn't you?"

"You sold a sweet potato. Maybe yesterday or the day before. Only one. Not to this man, but probably to a friend of his. Mr Minotti, this is very important."

"I didn't sell no sweet potatoes to nobody."

Willows thrust out his hand so the photo of Cherry Ngo was inches from Minotti's face. "This man is dead." Willows took a bite of his apple. Crunch. "Somebody shot him. Murdered him." He watched Minotti's face.

Nothing.

Willows placed the photograph carefully down on the counter. "The shooting took place early this morning, at the restaurant. We found the body on the floor, behind the cash register. Right about where you're standing now."

Tony Minotti glanced involuntarily down at his feet.

Willows said, "The killer used a sweet potato for a silencer."

"I don't know anything about this . . ."

"He pushed the barrel of the gun into the potato, and then pulled the trigger." Willows shifted his grip on the apple, took another bite. "The potato absorbed part of the sound of the explosion, cut down the risk of the shot being heard." He turned away from Minotti and said, "Claire, toss me a spud, the biggest one you can find."

Parker dug a sweet potato out of the box, threw it underhand to Willows.

Willows pulled out his Smith .38-calibre snubnose. He held the potato up to his face, pressed the barrel of the gun hard against the potato and said, "This is what they made him do."

Tony Minotti stared at him, his mouth open.

Willows said, "They made him hold the sweet potato, Tony, that we think was bought here, in your store. They made him hold the sweet potato like this, in his hand, up against his face. Can you imagine what the boy must have felt, what he might've been thinking about? The killer shoved the barrel right into the soft flesh of the potato and pulled the trigger. The bullet passed through the boy's hand, and your sweet potato, and blew out his brains." Willows slipped the Smith back in the clamshell holster on his hip. He handed Tony Minotti the sweet potato. "What time do you open for business?"

"Seven o'clock."

"Were you open at seven this morning?"

"Yeah, sure."

"We think the murder occurred sometime between eight-thirty and nine-forty."

"I didn't sell no sweet potatoes."

"Would it help jog your memory if I took you down to the morgue and showed you the body?"

"I don't wanna see no body! What kind of person you take me for?"

A man passing by on the sidewalk paused to stare at them.

Willows said, "What about your wife, Elaine. Would *she* like to see the corpse?"

Tony Minotti reached for the phone on the wall behind him. "I'm gonna call a lawyer."

Willows turned and glanced behind him. Parker and Mrs Minotti were talking quietly. Parker had her spiral-bound notebook in hand. Willows said, "Put the phone down, Tony. You don't need a lawyer. Not yet, anyway." He put the Granny Smith gently down on the scale. The apple weighed in at 62 grams. At eighty-nine cents a pound, that was about ten cents. Willows fished in his pocket for a dime, offered the coin to Minotti.

"You kidding me – you ate everything but the core!"

Willows nodded. Good point. He went over to the bin and chose an apple slightly smaller than the one he'd eaten, came back and dropped it on the scale. 180 grams.

"Fifty cents."

Willows frowned. "You sure about that?"

"For one apple, a guy comes in off the street, I always charge the same thing. Fifty cents. Don't matter if the apple's a big one or a small one. All the same. It's simple that way, quick."

"Profitable, too."

"That's why I'm in business. To make money."

A watertight philosophy. Willows couldn't argue with it. Willows fished in his pants pocket, came up with two quarters. He handed the money to the greengrocer.

"Ever see any fifty cent pieces, Tony?"

"Once in a while. Not often."

"They're useless in vending machines, I guess. And I read somewhere that pennies cost more to make than their face value. You do your banking nearby?"

Minotti led with his chin. "Bank of Montreal. On the other side of the block, at the corner."

"How late do you stay open?"

"Eleven o'clock."

"You do a night deposit?"

"Yeah, sure. Otherwise, somebody's gonna throw a rock through the door, come in and rob you."

"Have you ever been robbed, Tony?"

"Only once. Years ago. Not since then."

"Mind if I use the phone?"

"What for?"

Willows stared at Minotti as if the man had suddenly begun speaking in tongues. After a long moment, he said, "To make a call, Tony." He began to walk around to the far end of the counter. "That's all I want to use your phone for. Just to make a call."

Willows had expected a machete or maybe a baseball bat or tire iron, but Tony Minotti's weapon of choice was a cheap sawn-off shotgun. Willows broke open the barrel and the extractor shucked a single 20-gauge shell into his hand.

Minotti stood there, helpless, defiant and ashamed.

Willows didn't need to ask him if he had a licence – the answer was written all over his face. He said, "If this is a first offense, I doubt you'll do any time."

"You're gonna arrest me? All I wanna do is protect myself, and you gonna *arrest* me?"

"Ring up the sale, Tony."

Minotti rang up the fifty cent sale. The cash register popped open. Several shotgun shells lay in the slot reserved for one dollar bills.

Willows said, "What happens if some kid comes in here and tries to steal a banana – you blow him away, or just use this thing to threaten him?"

"No, no! I don't use the gun for that. It's only for self-defense. If my life is threatened."

"So, if some kid wandered in here and stole a sweet potato . . ."

"I'll chase him down the street, catch him and beat him bloody. But I ain't gonna shoot him, that's for sure. And anyhow, it never happened."

Willows said, "Give me the shells."

Minotti scooped the shotgun shells out of the cash drawer. They were made of brass and red plastic. He gave the shells to Willows and Willows slipped them into his jacket pocket. He handed Minotti the empty shotgun. "Come with me, Tony."

Minotti followed Willows out on to the crowded street. Willows unlocked the unmarked Ford's trunk. "Put it in there."

Minotti put the shotgun in the trunk and Willows shut it and made sure it was locked. He unlocked the car and opened the back door. "Get in."

The greengrocer glanced up and down the street. He was being watched. Everyone was watching him. People who happened to be passing by. His friends. What must they be thinking? He got into the car.

Willows shut the door and went back into the grocery store.

Tony Minotti sat in the car with his head in his hands. A kid from the neighborhood pressed his face up against the car window and waved at him and yelled his name, kept waving as he was dragged away by his mother.

Parker waited for Willows and then said, "Okay, tell my partner what you told me."

Elaine Minotti said, "He was maybe twenty years old. He had a friend, but he stayed outside, on the sidewalk. The one who came in, he saw I was alone. My husband was in the back, taking a delivery."

Willows said, "This was yesterday?"

"No, early this morning."

"Okay, what happened next?"

"He went straight to the sweet potatoes, took one and tossed it high in the air and caught it with both hands. Then he smiled at me. His eyes were cold, and I was very much afraid of him. He put a finger to his lips, warning me to stay quiet. All this took less than a minute. He was here and then he was gone."

"Did you tell your husband?"

"No, never."

Parker said, "Apparently he's got quite a temper. He used to keep a bat behind the counter. Waved it at a kid last summer and the next day the kid and a bunch of his friends came back with *their* bats. A month later a store in the next block was robbed and the owner was stabbed in the leg with a butcher knife. That's when Tony bought the shotgun."

"Gotta protect those mangos," said Willows, "gotta protect those pears." He turned and looked out the open door. Tony Minotti was sitting in the back of the police car, watching them. "Could you identify the man if you saw him again?"

"I think so, yes."

"Was he from the neighborhood – had you ever seen him before?"

"No, never."

Parker said, "Mrs Minotti's already said she's willing to come downtown and look at the mug books. But to do that she'd hate to have to close up shop, which would result in a substantial loss of business."

Willows, staring hard at Mrs Minotti, nodded slowly. "If we let Tony off the hook, he can mind the store while his wife helps us solve the murder, is that the idea?"

"That's the idea," said Parker, smiling despite herself.

12

Newt Junior sat at his desk in the den of his Laguna Beach house. The den was on the ground floor at the far end of the south wing. It was Newt's favorite place when he was feeling muddled because it was quiet, the only sane room in the house. Everywhere else, Opra or Donahue or somebody was yakking away on a portable TV, or there was salsa music blaring out of a portable radio the size of a refrigerator. Newt employed anywhere up to a dozen Mexican houseboys and each and every one of them was crazy about music, liked to play it *loud*.

But not in the den. The den was soundproofed and strictly off limits. Not even the maids came in there unless Newt told them to.

Newt leaned back in his upholstered leather chair. He made a sound deep in this throat, a karate kind of noise, and kicked out. The heel of his shoe knocked a bright splinter of rosewood off the corner of his desk. *Son of a bitch!* Fortunately the force of the blow spun his swivel chair around two hundred and seventy degrees. With his back to the damage, Newt could forget about it.

He let his eyes wander over the deluxe custom-made floor-to-ceiling oak shelves that lined three walls out of four. The shelves, sturdy though they were, sagged under the terrible moral weight of more than a thousand Gideon bibles.

Each bible had been stolen from a hotel or motel. It wasn't that Newt was a kleptomaniac – just a way for him to keep score. If he'd had a babe with him, he'd get her to write the date and name and location of the hotel in the bible's fly-leaf, and then add her autograph. If she cared to mention something about having had a wonderful time, real unforgettable, well, that was fine too.

Occasionally Newt found himself in a situation where his date had a fairly decent grasp of the spoken language but hadn't yet mastered the art of the written word. In these circumstances he settled for a signature, skip the adulation. If this too was impossible, Newt's absolute bottom line was a lipsticked kiss and awkwardly scrawled "X".

Newt also kept a memento in the form of a Polaroid photograph, which he also filed in the bibles. Some of the pics were kind of borderline tasteless, but most of them were harmless Fredericks of Hollywood-type lingerie shots or candids of the girls having loads of fun in the motel pool or maybe leaning against the Coke machine or checkout counter or the Porsche or wherever he could get them to hold still for a minute.

Not that there was a picture or even an autograph in every bible. Before his father died, Newt had worked hard in the family business, spent a lot of lonely nights on the road. Now that Felix was finally dead and buried, Newt's road trips had pretty much come to an end. He'd grown up in Los Angeles and felt safe and at ease in the city. Palm Springs was okay, and Vegas. Miami Beach, in a pinch. But the rest of the country, as far as Newt was concerned, was just waste space. So when there were out-of-town chores to be done, he usually sent somebody like Frank, rather than taking care of the work himself.

Yeah, Frank.

Newt swivelled his chair around through the remaining ninety degrees, so he was once again facing the picture window with it's flawless unimpeded view of the dunes and beach, the restless ocean, empty blue sky and the smudged black triangles squatting on the horizon that were oil rigs.

Frank, Frank. Hello, Frank. Earth to Frank, where are you, Frank? Come in, Frank.

He leaned forward in his chair and stabbed with his index finger at the speakerphone's redial button. A red light flickered as the instrument's electronic innards digested the eleven-digit number, and spat it out.

The phone rang twice and then the hotel switchboard picked up.

Newt said, "Gimme room five-eighteen."

"One moment, sir."

There was a pause, and then the connection was made and Frank's phone began to ring. Newt lit a Marlboro. Where in hell was Frank? He adjusted the volume control on the speakerphone, turned it all the way down and then all the way back up, very slowly. And as he turned the volume up, Newt began to shout Frank's name.

"Frank? *Frank!* Where the hell are you, Frank!"

Newt kept turning up the volume, kept yelling louder and louder, until the shrill ringing of the unanswered telephone filled the room and his voice cracked and he couldn't shout any louder.

The operator came on the line and tried to tell Newt that Frank wasn't answering and would he care to leave a message?

Newt slammed down the phone, stared bitterly out at the million-dollar view and saw to his consternation and surprise that a small black dot was hurtling towards him from the other side of the picture window. The dot was moving at a high rate of speed and it was coming straight at him, unwavering in its course. Newt's heart pounded in his chest so hard it seemed as if it was trying to flee his doomed body. Some rotten bastard had launched a missile at him! God, but it was quick. He jerked to his feet. Cigarette ash spilled across his rosewood desk. Then time ran out. The missile crashed into his window, and the sheet of pale-green bulletproof plate glass vibrated crazily. But it didn't shatter, and there was no explosion.

A dud?

Newt went over to the window. A large brown bird lay on the gravel in the shadow of the house. It definitely wasn't a seagull and probably wasn't a robin. Other than that, who could say? Newt was a major player in the drug and film rackets, not an amateur ornithologist.

He got down on his hands and knees for a better look. The bird's wings were tucked up tight against its body and its head lolled to one side. Its tiny, glossy black eyes didn't seem to be looking at anything. Maybe the creature was stunned. It's beak was open and a thin black tongue hung out. Newt had never seen a bird's tongue before. It wasn't very sexy. He tapped his pinky ring against the glass. No reaction. The bird looked dead and probably was, but how could you tell for sure?

Newt went back to the desk and used the intercom to locate Rikki, his *numero uno* houseboy.

"Hey, Rikki, I'm in the den. Yeah, the small room where I keep my bible collection. Rikki, there's a bird flew into the window, crashed into the window. Yeah, it is a crazy world, isn't it. Look, I want you to go and get it and bring it inside the house. See if you can do anything for it, okay?"

Newt noticed the spill of ash on his desk, made a face and wiped the polished surface clean with the palm of his hand, briskly rubbing his hands together. Rikki was having a major problem with the concept of Newt being concerned about a bird when he had never before in his life shown the slightest compassion for any living thing.

"*Pajaro?*" said Rikki.

Newt said, "Yeah, right, you got it. *Pajaro*. With the wings and feathers, the whole outfit. It's right outside the window. Yeah. *La ventana*."

"*Es muerte?*"

Dead. Now there was a word Newt knew very well. He said, "Check it out, Rikki. *Es el pajaro muerte?* That's the question I want answered."

Rikki said, "You tellin' me you wan' me find out is our featha" compadre wasted?"

"Yeah, yeah!"

"Okay, sure 'ting. I do eet." Rikki made a high, keening noise. "*Nueve uno uno!* The ambulance ees on its fokin' way!"

Newt hung up. Rikki had slipped into LA via the underside of the border and the slums of Mexico City. He was a cute kid but not too quick between the ears. A few books missing outta his library, you might say. The kid was superfast with his hands, though. An artist with a knife. *Artista de joja*. During his job interview Rikki had bragged he could slice a steak off a heifer, do it so sweet and clean the cow wouldn't even say moo. Newt had laughed at the bullshit, and hired him. A couple of months later he was in a club downtown and got in a tussle with a guy in the washroom, a real loud argument over who was next in line to use the toilet. Rikki was lounging out in the hall. He heard the racket and came in and stepped between Newt and the two hundred fifty pound meatball and told the meatball to wait his turn, said, "You the world's biggest asshole, no contest. But that don't mean you can jump the line." The meatball ignored him, stared right over his head, held his killer look on Newt.

Rikki had said, "You ain' listen to me. Thas a bad choice. Use 'em or lose 'em, what they say."

The meatball was still trying to figure out what the hell Rikki was talking about when the Mexican reached up and sliced off his left ear, stuck it in the meatball's jacket pocket like a limp pink hankie.

Newt had been pretty drunk when the skirmish went down. So drunk in fact that he assumed it had been a mirage or whatever. The next day, however, he read all about it in the *LA Times*. A quick-thinking bartender had slipped the ear into a martini glass full of shaved ice, wrapped a towel around the guy's head and called a cab. The cabby refused to accept the fare because he thought the guy was an Arab. Eventually the cops showed up and gave the meatball a ride to emergency, where a doctor with nothing better to do sewed the ear back on.

A happy ending. Oh well, these things happened.

Newt dialled the hotel in Vancouver again and got the same response. He looked up and there was Rikki in front of the window, smiling at him through the glass. Rikki'd thrown a white lab coat over his cream suit, and was wearing a false nose and glasses. He went over to the bird and picked it up in both hands, very gently.

Newt leaned back in his chair. A movie. The picture window was like a big screen and it was like watching a movie, a movie that had been made just for him.

Rikki held the bird's breast up against his ear. His face was very serious. He looked at Newt and solemnly shook his head.

Newt wished he had some popcorn.

Rikki tried to revive the bird with little one-finger slaps to its feathered cheeks. When that didn't work he applied mouth-to-beak respiration. No joy. Desperate, he pulled a 9-volt battery out of his pocket and mimed giving the victim shock treatment, making the bird twitch and jerk spasmodically in the palm of his hand as he applied the current. Newt laughed so hard he fell off his chair. By the time he'd finished wiping the tears from his eyes, Rikki and the dead *pajaro* were long gone.

That evening, Newt had a lady friend over for dinner. They went out on the deck afterwards, for a glass of wine and so Newt could enjoy his cigar without stinking up his date's fancy silk dress, and spoiling the mood, queering his romance.

Rikki drifted by, on his appointed rounds. He was wearing his night clothes; a matt black shirt and baggy black cotton pants, no shoes. He was standing less than five feet away, but Newt would never have noticed him if he hadn't smiled.

In his soft voice, Rikki asked Newt did he enjoy his dinner.

"Real good," said Newt tersely. It was well known that he didn't much appreciate the help socializing when he had a broad on the premises.

Rikki apparently didn't notice that Newt's close-set eyes were glowing red as his cigar. He said, "I am glad to hear the food was good, Senor." He grinned again, teeth flashing white. "How do they say it – the patient died, but the operation was a success."

Newt said, "How's that?" He leaned over the sundeck railing, peered down into the darkness.

Rikki said, "*El pajaro*, Senor!" and drifted off into the darkness, flapping his arms like wings.

Newt broke open another bottle of champagne and told the story to his date, a girl named Annette who worked in the stockroom at a Toys 'R Us over in Glendale. Annette didn't think the story was very funny at all. When she'd finished being sick to her stomach all over the deck she washed her mouth out with at least hundred dollars worth of Newt's Dom Perignon and then told him in no uncertain terms she wanted a ride home right this minute or she was going to call the SPCA.

Newt let Rikki take care of it. Serve him right. He watched the Caddy's tail-lights dwindle down the road and then got a fresh bottle and made his way down through the dunes to the beach.

There was no moon, and all was blackness except for the thin line of the surf; a frothy smear of white that growled and snarled and worried at the beach like a long, strung-out pack of rabid dogs. Newt listened to the music and nipped at the bubbly. The dogs fell back and regrouped, attacked again.

His daddy's sodden ashes were out there, somewhere. Endlessly drifting on the currents. Newt never would've believed it, but there were times – mostly when his blood alcohol reading was into double digits – when he almost missed the old bastard.

He grabbed a fresh bottle and kicked off his shoes and walked down the pathway of sun-bleached planks, past the dunes and long gritty slope of the beach and into the cold black water. When he was deep enough to start thinking about sharks, he held the bottle of champagne high above his head with both hands and shook hard and then pulled the cork. A long jet of foam shot out of the bottle and curved down through the blackness and merged with the surf.

Newt said, "Here's looking at you, Daddy." He tilted his head back and put the neck of the bottle to his lips, drank deeply and belched.

The dogs howled along miles of beach. The silvery air was thick with salt. Newt finished the champagne and threw the bottle at those unruly hounds – as sincere a gesture of defiance he was ever likely to risk.

Trudging back across the dunes towards the house, he thought about Annette and what she had said, the truth of it. That only a seriously demented person would pluck and gut and pan-fry and serve with mixed vegetables and wild rice some poor bird that had flown into his picture window.

What *was* the matter with him? She was only eighteen or nineteen years old and her date with him was probably the first time she ever got out of Glendale, but she was *right*. He should've *buried* that poor bird, not *eaten* it, even though it melted in his mouth.

She'd told him in her silky-sweet heartbreaker voice that she hoped he never darkened the doors of Toys 'R Us again, *ever*, and Newt couldn't say he blamed her.

He was going crazy. He needed a break, a chance to get away and clear his mind.

In the kitchen, the dishes had been cleared and the pots were soaking in the sink. Newt checked the garbage but there was no sign of the bird's remains. Probably they were being used in some kind of weird Aztec ritual. The houseboys were always stealing candles, taking them out to the toolshed, running around chanting. He had no idea what they were up to. As long as they were happy; that was the main thing.

Newt used the wall phone by the microwave to try the hotel again. Still no Frank. On impulse, he dialled the cellular in the Caddy.

No answer from Rikki, either. Newt's mind skittered from one unrelated thought to the next.

Maybe Frank wasn't answering his phone because he'd screwed up real bad, and didn't want Newt to find out about it.

Goddamn that Rikki. The guy was only about five feet tall but he had that smooth skin and those big brown eyes and teeth like pearls. Newt knew *exactly* what he was up to. In a fit of pique, he decided to drag his little Mex Lothario along to Vancouver – assuming, of course, that loverboy ever made it back from Glendale.

It was July, but chances were still pretty good that when they got to Vancouver it'd be raining like a bitch.

With luck, maybe Mr Stud would catch pneumonia, and die.

13

Willows helped Elaine Minotti with her coat, pulled back a chair.

Mrs Minotti sat down.

Parker said, "Can I get you something to drink, a cup of coffee, tea . . ."

Mrs Minotti smiled a quick, nervous smile. "I'm fine, thank you."

Willows said, "If you need anything, just give us a shout."

Mrs Minotti gave him a startled look.

"Call us," Parker explained. "If you see anybody you recognize, or have any questions, call us."

"Yes, I will do that."

There were three mug books, each of them about twice the size of an encyclopedia. Parker put one in front of Mrs Minotti and opened it to the first page. The police photographs were in color, about three inches square. There were six ranks of four per page. Each book held about one hundred pages.

Parker smiled and said, "After a little while your eyes are going to get tired. All the pictures will start to blur into one another. It won't take long, believe me. When it happens, take a break. You can get up and walk around if you want to. Do you smoke?"

"Sometimes. Not too much."

"This is a public building. Smoking isn't allowed. And I have to ask you, please don't leave the squadroom without letting me or Jack know about it. Do you have any questions?"

"No, I understand."

Mrs Minotti was sitting at Parker's desk. Willows borrowed Eddy Orwell's phone and dialled Walt Fisher, in ballistics. Fisher picked up on the third ring. His voice was slow, clogged.

Willows said, "Got a cold, Walt?"

Fisher laughed. "Tunafish sandwich, Jack. You detective-type guys who live on adrenalin and fresh blood tend to forget that the rest of us mortals march to a different diet."

Willows was no fan, but the word *tunafish* had made him salivate. He glanced at his watch. It was quarter-past one. No wonder he was hungry. He said, "What have you got for me on the Cherry Ngo thing?"

"Not much, Jack." Willows could almost hear Fisher shrug. "We've got a make on the calibre. Forty-five ACP. It was a very well-behaved bullet. Expanded exactly according to design."

"What kind of shape's it in?"

Fisher'd been fed that line before, and he jumped on it with both feet. "Not bad, considering everything it's been through."

"You're a funny guy, Walt. Have you got enough to make a comparison?"

"No problem. Why? You and the pin-up girl recover the weapon?"

"Pin-up girl? Parker's gonna love that one, Walt."

"Jack, no, please . . ."

Inspector Homer Bradley marched briskly through the squad-room. He caught Willows' eye and pointed at him and Parker, then towards his office.

Willows said, "Enjoy the tuna, Walt," and hung up and followed Parker into Bradley's tiny cubicle.

"Shut the door, Jack." Bradley indicated the two plain wooden chairs lined up against the wall opposite his battered cherrywood desk. "Take a load off your feet. Make yourself comfy."

Willows said, "We've got a possible witness on the Cherry Ngo thing."

"No flies on you."

Parker said, "Her name's Elaine Minotti. She and her husband run a greengrocer's a couple of blocks from where the shooting took place."

"The sweet potato, right?"

"No flies on you, either, Inspector."

"She sold the spud to the dude?"

Parker said, "He bought the tuber on the long-term installment plan." Bradley's eyebrows came together. "Five-finger discount," Parker explained.

"Your witness, that's the lady presently sitting at your desk working her way through the mug books?"

Willows nodded. "Yeah, that's her."

"Cute."

Parker said, "She's married, Inspector."

Bradley flushed. "It was an innocent observation, Claire. I wasn't going to *pounce* on the poor woman, if that's what you're worried about."

Willows, stepping into the breach, said, "If she doesn't come up with anything, we're going to try an artist's sketch."

"Probably not a bad idea," said Bradley gruffly. He leaned forward in his chair. The worn burgundy leather creaked like an old man's bones. He flipped open the lid of the carved cedar box his wife had given him so many years ago. The box had been carved by a Haida Indian, and his wife had given it to him on the courthouse steps only a few minutes after their twenty-three year marriage was officially declared null and void. She'd always been on his back about his smoking. The cigar box was her way of saying she didn't care any more, about his health or anything else.

Bradley selected a cigar, held it up to his ear and rolled it between his index finger and thumb. It made a pleasant crackling sound. *Autumnal.* A drift of fallen leaves scurried through his brain. He used his gold-plated clippers on the cigar and fished a wooden kitchen match out of his vest pocket. Parker eyed him warily.

Bradley said, "That new guy, Stoller. He's pretty good with a pencil, isn't he?"

Willows nodded.

"I'd always meant to ask Bailey to draw me, but I never got around to it. Don't get me wrong. I didn't want to *pose* for him. I wanted Bailey to sketch me from memory, or even better, get a cop to describe me to him without saying who I was. It'd be nice to have something like that, frame it and have it on the wall to look at when I retire."

Bradley leaned back in his chair. He stuck the cigar in his mouth at a jaunty angle and looked out his tiny window at a fluffy white cloud, the first cloud he'd seen in days. "But now it's too late. Bailey's gone."

There was an awkward silence. Parker said, "Orwell told me he won a lottery."

"Yeah? I heard he came into some money. An uncle died; somebody back East."

Willows said, "Why don't you ask Stoller to draw you?"

"Don't know him well enough. Crazy idea, anyhow. If the chief heard about it . . ."

"He'd want one, too," said Willows.

"Maybe. How'd Joey take it when you told him his big brother bought the farm?"

"Bad."

"Sure, why not. What's next?"

"Mrs Minotti identifies the guy who pinched her sweet potato. We pick him up and he confesses, pleads guilty and goes down for life."

"Sounds promising. Got a backup plan, just in case that one doesn't work?"

Willows said, "Emily Chan's family, friends. Maybe one of them can point us in the right direction."

"What about the restaurant – the people who own it. Talk to them yet?"

"We don't even know who they are. The building's owned by a numbered company. If we can find out who's behind the numbers, who the owner is, we should be able to get some names out of him."

Bradley twirled the wooden match in his fingers as if it was a miniature baton. "Okay, I guess that's it for now. Stay in touch. If anything develops . . ."

"You'll be the first to know, Inspector."

Mrs Minotti was still industriously working her way through the first mug book. Parker rested a hand lightly on her shoulder. "Jack and I are going out for a late lunch. Would you like to join us?"

Mrs Minotti smiled up at her. "No, I think I better stay here and keep looking at these handsome men."

"You sure?"

"Yes, thank you."

Parker said, "We won't be long. If you see someone you recognize, tell a detective or one of civilian staff, and they'll beep us. Okay?"

"Yes, fine. Thank you."

Parker and Willows rode the elevator down to the main floor. The doors slid open and they walked across the lobby past the reception area. Willows nodded to one of the cops behind the desk, a rookie who was the son of a guy who'd graduated in his class.

Parker said, "What's on your mind, Jack? You look depressed, all of a sudden."

"Old age."

"Bradley?"

"No, me. Where do you want to eat?"

"How about that Japanese restaurant on Water Street, with the bamboo plants in the window?"

"Kubiko's."

"Right," said Parker, "Kubiko's."

Outside, the sky above them was cloudless; a deep, flawless blue. The streets were thick with traffic and the sidewalks were crowded with shoppers. Half a dozen drunks lounged in the shade of the Carnegie Library. The situation had been a lot worse before a nearby liquor store had been shut down. Parker remembered going out to her patrol car and finding a thin smear of vomit across the windshield and a derelict sleeping it off on the hood, soaking up residual warmth from the engine as if he was a stray cat. She'd heard a story several years ago about a cop named Rafferty who'd found a drunk curled up on the hood of *his* car and started the engine and driven down the alley. He'd hit twenty miles an hour before the drunk woke up and, terrified, bailed out and flattened himself against a brick wall. Final score: one fractured skull and one severely reprimanded cop. But after that, for a little while at least, the drunks had abandoned the alley behind 312 Main.

Willows said, "What's so funny?"

"Nothing, really. In fact it isn't funny at all, but I was thinking about the drunk who fell asleep on a squad car a few years ago."

"A cop named Rafferty bounced him off a wall?"

"Yeah, that's the one."

"Never happened. Cop bullshit, that's all. Wishful thinking." Willows looked down Main Street towards the harbour. There was a haze of exhaust fumes in the air. On the far side of the harbour, two or three hundred feet up the slope of the North Shore mountains, a faint line of bluish grey marked the level to which the pollution had ascended.

There was a short line-up at the restaurant, but Parker had phoned ahead and made reservations. As they were led to their table, Willows said, "Asking me where I wanted to eat was just a formality, wasn't it?"

"You're slow, but you're learning."

They both opted for the daily special; a noodle soup and steamed rice spiked with artistically cut medallions of steam-fried vegetables and tiny chunks of deep-fried chicken. Parker ordered Perrier. Willows settled for a local beer.

Parker checked her watch. She said, "It's late. We shouldn't stay too long."

Willows smiled. "What's the rush? Mrs Minotti's in no hurry to get back to work. How'd you like to spend your life weighing vegetables? The way I see it, we ought to give her a break, take the rest of the day off."

The soup arrived, and the bottled water and Willows' beer. Kubiko's was only a few blocks from 312 Main. The restaurant's wooden floor was unfinished and splintery, the chairs didn't match and the napkins were paper – but the prices were still a bit steep for uniformed cops. The restaurant was a favorite of the force's detectives, though, because of its convenient location and quick service. And of course detectives spent considerably more time in court and consequently earned roughly twice as much money as their uniformed brethren.

Willows drank some beer. He said, "How long have we been working together?"

Parker had to think about it. "Four years, pushing five."

Willows said, "A long time."

Parker said, "Sometimes it's sure seemed like it."

"We've had our share of arguments."

"No argument there."

Willows wasn't about to be put off. He said, "But it's never been anything we couldn't work out, right? I mean, we've always found a way around our differences."

The chicken dish arrived. Parker stripped the paper wrapper off her chopsticks. The food smelled delicious and she was very hungry.

Willows said, "How often do you hear about a couple of cops splitting up because they can't get along on the job?"

"Almost never."

"That's right – but look at the divorce rate in the department."

"You're asking me why cops can tough it out on the job, but can't keep it together at home?"

"I'm not asking you anything. I'm just making an observation."

"Small talk."

"Right."

Parker toyed with her food. "It bothers you that the two of us get along like peaches and cream and your wife left you; is that what this is all about?"

"No, it isn't. Christ. I was *generalizing*, that's all."

Parker said, "The first time I saved your miserable life, we weren't even on a first-name basis."

"*Possibly* saved my miserable life."

"That scumbug Junior Newton would've fried your bacon if I hadn't shot him."

"You'd have shot him anyway, the mood you were in."

Parker said, "The point I'm trying to make is that we depend on each other, you and I. Sometimes in situations of extreme stress."

Willows reached across to snatch a choice piece of chicken, and Parker batted him on the knuckles with her chopsticks. "Maybe what's wrong with married life is that it isn't dangerous enough."

"Or there isn't enough paperwork."

Parker adjusted her chopsticks and managed to pluck the chicken Willows had tried to steal out of its bed of rice. "No, I like my theory better."

"Which is, if you really care about your marriage, try getting shot at."

"Because it's a wonderfully bonding experience."

"Exactly."

Willows said, "Has Sheila been in touch with you?"

"Your wife?" It was a stupid question, but Parker had been caught by surprise.

"Last time I talked to her, she said she wanted to see you next time she came to Vancouver." Willows made a show of studying his watch. "Soon, Claire."

"Why would she want to talk to me? You didn't . . ."

"*Involve* you?"

Parker blushed and Willows smiled and said, "No, not in any way."

"Good," said Parker firmly.

Willows said, "I'm only guessing, but I think she hopes you're going to reassure her that I'm getting along okay without her."

"Why would I do that?"

"To put her mind at ease."

"No, I mean, why would she be under the impression that I'd have any idea how your personal life was going?"

"Don't ask me."

"Well then, who in hell should I ask?"

"Claire, are you *angry* with me?"

"Yes!"

The waiter arrived with their check. He knew Parker and Willows well enough not to enquire about dessert, and didn't bother to ask them about coffee because at least a thousand cops had smugly told him that they could get all the coffee they wanted back at the office for twenty-five cents a cup. And, they'd usually added, they didn't even have to pay the quarter unless someone was watching.

*

When they got back to the third floor of 312 Main, Mrs Minotti was nowhere to be seen. Parker asked a clerk where she'd gone and was told she was out in the alley, taking a smoke break.

Parker turned to Willows. "You want to get her?"

Willows said, "I got the tip."

Parker gave Willows a look that showed him another tip – the tip of the iceberg.

Behind Parker, the squadroom door swung open and Eddy Orwell, red-eyed and hunch-shouldered, made an entrance that would have rung Lon Chaney's bell.

Willows said, "On second thoughts, maybe a little fresh air is exactly what I need."

He found his witness in the alley, standing downwind of Inspector Homer Bradley, who seemed to be enjoying her company almost as much as he relished his cigar.

Bradley smiled and waved. "Jack, there you are. We were just starting to wonder what happened to you."

Mrs Minotti stubbed out her cigarette. She said, "It's been a pleasure talking to you, Inspector."

Bradley's smile was as wide as the alley. "Elaine, the pleasure has been all mine, I assure you."

Judging from the look Mrs Minotti gave Willows as she turned her back on the Inspector, she was in no mood to disagree.

Mrs Minotti had worked her way through all three mug books. Half-way through the third book, she'd stumbled across a photograph of the young man who had stolen a sweet potato from her store that morning.

Her index finger came down hard, striking the suspect right between the eyes.

Parker said, "You're sure?"

"Yes, him. He's the one who took the potato. The other one, his friend, I couldn't find."

Willows and Parker exchanged a look. Mrs Minotti said, "What is it, is something wrong?"

Parker said, "I'm afraid we're going to have to ask you to go with us to the city morgue, to identify a body."

"*His* body?"

Parker nodded. Elaine Minotti had fingered Cherry Ngo, the boy they'd found murdered that morning at the Pale Green Shoots restaurant.

14

There was no way Newt was going to leave his Porsche or the Jag or even the BMW at LAX. Unless you drove a ten-year-old Ford Pinto, airport security was a bad joke. The only way you could protect your car against thieves was by letting all the air out of the tires and leaving a ripe corpse in the trunk.

And even that was no guarantee.

So Newt had Rikki phone one of the limo services and order a black stretch.

Newt wanted the car at the house at one 'clock sharp, and it arrived right on time. The driver was a skinny black guy, wearing a cheap tuxedo with lumpy padded shoulders, a glossy yellow bow-tie. The guy'd shaved fairly recently, and his fingernails were clean, but his shoes were badly scuffed, the toes scraped down to raw leather.

Newt said, "You like to hang around the schoolyard, shoot baskets in your spare time, right?"

The guy stared at him, finally nodded. He had a military haircut, no beads or razor-cut advertising his neighborhood gang or favorite brand of beer or the name of his girlfriend. Amazing. He introduced himself but Newt didn't catch his name.

Rikki, standing in the shade of the house with his macho black leather suitcases wedged between his stumpy legs and his passport clenched firmly between his teeth, stared at the limo guy as if he expected him to suddenly double in size and grow fangs, or maybe metamorph into a giant insect – somehow change in such a way as to require Rikki to fetch his gun and riddle him with bullets. The killer look didn't mean anything, however. It was just Rikki being abrasive, Rikki being Rikki.

The chauffeur opened the trunk and started to stuff it full of Newt's Louis Vuitton suitcases. The work caused beads of sweat to bubble up on his face. Was it that he was unaccustomed to physical labor or terrified of Rikki?

Idle minds, thought Newt. He lit a bootleg Cuban cigar and watched the shiny-faced black man load gleaming black luggage into the polished black car.

The limo guy noticed he was being watched. Smiling, he said wasn't it just a wonderful day and was Mr Newton aware that there were upwards of *fifty thousand* stretch limos prowling the mean streets of the city. Wasn't that incredible?

Newt tilted his head at the washed-out sky and let Cuban smoke leak out of his mouth and nostrils.

The limo guy wouldn't stop, told Newt probably it was the music biz and film industry combined, but there were more limos in LA than any other city in the whole darn world, including London and Paris and Marrakesh. Newt gave him a sideways look. The guy continued to ramble on. His point was that with all them sets of wheels to choose from, he felt real privileged that Newt picked his. Slam went the trunk. If there was anything at all he could do to make the ride more pleasant, all Newt had to do was let him know.

Newt jabbed at him with the hot end of the cigar and said, "Cut the minstrel hall shtick, bud. Just shut the fuck up and get behind the wheel and drive."

The guy's mouth opened wide in surprise. Newt said, "Rikki does whatever I tell him to do. *Anything*. It's his job, unnerstand what I'm saying to you?"

"Yessuh."

Newt slid into the back of the car. Soft leather. Chrome. Polished wood. It was like being inside a high-tech cave. He said, "Rikki, we got a long drive ahead of us. Maybe you should take a leak before we get going."

Rikki said, "Where?"

The black turned from Newt to Rikki and back again. Was this a joke? If he didn't figure it out pretty soon, he was going to pop a disc.

Newt said, "Front tire."

"Right side, or left?"

"Whatever's closest."

So Rikki walked up to the nose of the car and lifted a leg and pissed on the limo's Goodyear tire, splattered the hubcap pretty good and then gave himself a shake and zipped up.

The limo guy said, "Hey now . . ."

Rikki climbed into the back of the car. He was so short he hardly had to bend over to get in. Newt said, "He'd of pissed all over *you*, if I told him."

The black guy said, "Well, I'm grateful, naturally."

Newt said, "Hold on to that attitude – it's a good one. Now shut the door and hit the gas, we got a plane to catch and stews to goose."

On the ride out to the airport, Rikki was no fun at all. He kept staring at his bootleg passport, flipping through the stiff new pages and then working his way back to the photograph, mumbling something about the pic not doing him justice, what a badass handsome dude he really was, if he was professionally lit.

Man, he was *absorbed.*

Newt whacked him on the side of the head to get his attention, told him to open a bottle of champagne. Rikki did what he was told, poured Newt a tulip glass. Newt politely asked did he care to join in? Rikki shook his head, continued studying his passport. The official statistics – the stats regarding his height and weight and hair color and so on, seemed to mesmerize him. Newt was on his second glass of champagne when Rikki noticed that his height had been listed at five foot four.

"Looka dat!"

"What?" said Newt, who'd been watching a blonde in a silver Mercedes cruising along in the next lane, who could've been Kim Basinger, maybe.

Rikki showed him the passport. "Wha" they fok with me? Got me at five foot four inch when I'm at least five-seven."

"Jeez, is that right?" Newt grabbed a large hit of bubbly to give himself time to work out a translation. He'd never seen Rikki so worked up. The guy was usually more cucumber than human being. It was amazing, the way all those ESL classes went straight to hell the minute he got stressed out. He was harder to understand than Sly Stallone, in *Rocky V*. Unbelievable.

Height, height. Yeah, he was bitching about how tall he was. Newt said, "When you got measured, did they make you take your boots off?"

"Yeah, but so what?" Rikki reminded Newt that he *never* took his Frye boots off except to take a bath or hit the sack. And sometimes not even then. He'd told as much to the fake passport guy. What da fok was the *matter* with him?

Newt said, "You tip-toe around the yard in your bare feet every night, what about that?"

"That's a different thing altogether." A sly grin, all teeth and saliva. "I worry about you. Bad guy's sneakin' up. Is part of my fokin' job to save your ass. How'm I gonna do any serious creepin' around wearin' big old thumpy boots, huh?"

Newt said, "Good point, Rikki."

"Fokin' right." Rikki turned the passport upside down. He sniffed the glue that held his picture in place.

"Nice?" said Newt, grinning.

"Man, always I want this. But I never dreamed I'd get one looked so right."

"Feels pretty good, I bet." Rikki was starting to calm down, and Newt had an idea. He remembered the time Rikki had sliced off the ear. Afterwards, his English had been so good it was almost like listening to Winston Churchill. Newt said, "Remember the guy couldn't wait his turn for the toilet?"

"Nah . . ."

"Fat guy. You cut off his ear to teach him some manners."

"Yeah?" Rikki was interested. "When was that?" But even as he spoke, Newt could see the pages of Rikki's calendar turning over in his brain.

After a moment, Rikki's eyes cleared. His pupils expanded. The artery in his neck stopped trying to jump out of his skin.

"Yeah, I remember the guy. Why'd you ask?"

"Nothing, forget it. Check the babe in the Merc."

"*Muy picante*," said Rikki automatically. He frowned. "What're we talkin' about?"

"Passports."

Rikki nodded. "I took one offa Puerto Rican once, when I was livin' in Tijuana. Bein' a lowlife pimp and lookin' for a way out. This Rican guy, just like me he looks. So I take his passport."

"That easy, huh. What, the guy liked you so much he wanted to give you a present?"

"Was a trade. I had a real nice switchblade knife, was stainless steel 'cause I keep it hid under my armpit and don' want it gettin' rusty. Guy don' wanna gimme his passport so I do him a trade for the knife. Know what I'm sayin' to you, Mr Newton?"

"A pimp with a rusty knife looks like a fool, that it?"

"Close, but not close enough."

"You stabbed him."

"I guess so. An' then I mesmerize my new name and how old I am and where I was born and all the details of my new life."

Newt said, "Hard work, huh?"

"Waste of time, too. At the border they grab me and gonna charge me with murder. Said I look more like Santa Claus than this Puerto dude. Wanna know where he gone, what I done with him."

"What'd you say?"

"Tell 'em I buy the passport off a guy onna street, I never seen him no more. That's it."

"They let you go?"

"No fokin' way. Turn me back, Mexicops hold me in a stinkin' pisspot jail for six months, I lost my pimp job, all my hopes and dreams. But the Rican guy never show up so they gotta lemme go. But first they beat me up, hurt me real bad. So I decide what I gotta do. Emigrate to America."

"And here you are, safe and sound. Prosperous and healthy."

"Took me a while, but I done it."

"You oughtta be proud of yourself. Know something, Rikki?"

"What?"

"This country was founded by men like you."

"Guys onna run?"

Newt got a chuckle out of that one. He laughed so hard he almost – but not quite – spilled his drink. "No," he said, "I'm talking about men of vision. Courageous, daring men who were willing to take desperate chances in order to make a new and better life for themselves."

"No shi'."

"Want some champagne?"

"Yeah, okay. All this chat-chat makes me dry inna throat."

"We're gonna have fun in Vancouver, you and me."

"Yeah, okay." But Rikki had already forgotten about the champagne, was immersed in his new passport, the tiny book of wonders that gave him the freedom to create havoc and commit murder all over the world, almost.

Newt squinted through his champagne glass at the back of the limo driver's head, which looked remarkably like a smaller-than-average bowling ball covered with a coarse, fuzzy black mold.

He flicked the intercom and said, "Limo guy, who cuts your hair?"

"My wife."

"You're married; a dude like you?"

"Three years, almost."

"Got any kids?"

"Not yet."

"Smart woman," said Newt, and settled back to enjoy the ride.

Kim Basinger turned out not to be Kim Basinger after all – she was one of the flight attendants working the Delta 727 to Vancouver. Newt made a special trip all the way from the first class cabin to the rear of the plane, to introduce himself and hit on her to the very best of his ability. She turned him down flat.

"What is it," he said to Rikki as he slid back into his seat, "I got a wart on my nose, or something?"

Rikki said, "Probably she already got somethin' lined up."

"Yeah?" said Newt, eyeing his pint-sized companion suspiciously.

They touched down at Vancouver International at ten minutes past five. Rikki wanted to adjust his watch but Newt explained there was no time-zone difference. Rikki didn't believe him, had to ask Kim Basinger about it, except he called her Jessica.

Newt got the last laugh, though, as he watched Rikki yank a pair of thick woolen mittens, a down parka, wool toque and insulated gumboots almost big enough to qualify as hip waders out of his carry-on.

Newt said, "Where'd you get this stuff?" He tried on the toque. One size fits most. He pulled the weird itchy thing down over his head, all the way past his nose. "Planning to rob a bank?"

"Rodeo Drive," said Rikki. "Cost me fifty bucks. It was the last one they had."

"It was the only one they had, dummy." The toque was decorated with a winter motif of evergreen trees and snowflakes. Rikki shrugged awkwardly into the down parka and was immediately bathed in sweat. Newt handed him the toque and Rikki put that on, too. The guy was a bear for punishment.

Somebody in the jostling crowd behind them giggled through his nose. Rikki kicked off a shoe and reached for a gumboot.

Newt said, "It's almost a miracle, but if you take a peek out the window, you'll see it ain't raining. You'll also see a lot of people walking around in shirtsleeves. Must be a high-pressure front or something, Rikki. Looks like we really lucked out."

Rikki bent and peered out the window, squinted into bright sunlight. The sweat pouring into his eyes made it hard to see anything. He wiped his face with a Delta pillow the size of a roll of toilet paper. It didn't happen all that often, but this time Newt was right.

Weatherwise, it didn't seem as if he was going to need his snowshoes after all.

15

Arthur and Betty Chan lived in a False Creek Co-op with a view of Coal Harbour, two bridges, the downtown core, bits and pieces of the mountains.

The apartment occupied all three floors of the building. Access was via the north-facing sundeck on the second floor. A glass slider led directly to the living room. Mrs Chan was sitting on the couch reading a copy of *TV Guide*. Pastels splashed across the screen of a 28-inch color television against the far wall.

"*Santa Barbara*," said Parker.

"I don't believe it."

"Believe what?" Parker continued to peer through the plate glass.

"That you watch the soaps," said Willows. He sounded a little surprised, maybe even a bit dismayed.

"Why not?"

"Because I didn't think you were that kind of – "

Parker held up a warning hand, cutting him off before he went too far. "Careful, Jack."

Willows said, "What do you do, tape them on your VCR so you can watch them when you come home from work?"

"What d'you mean, *them*? I watch *Santa Barbara* and *Guiding Light*. Two programs, and they both happen to be on at the same time so, unless I've got a day off in the middle of the week, I have to decide between them. It isn't easy, believe me."

Willows said, "You think you know somebody, and then you find out she's an *addict*."

"Well," Parker said, "for someone who feels right at home wasting a gorgeous summer afternoon on three or four hours of tape-delayed baseball, it seems to me you're pretty quick to pass judgement."

"Guilty as charged," said Willows, and tapped on the glass with his badge.

Betty Chan's hand flew to her breast. The *TV Guide* fluttered to the carpet.

Willows smiled reassuringly, held his shield up high where she could easily see it. He tried the door. It was locked. Mrs Chan stared at the detectives for a long moment and then stood up and went slowly over to the television and turned it off.

"Lost the remote," said Willows.

"And her daughter."

"Yeah, that too."

Mrs Chan turned towards them, crossed the room and unlocked the door and slid it open.

Willows and Parker entered the apartment. Parker made the introductions as Willows pushed shut the door. Builders and architects with an eye on the bottom line love sliders because they are cheap, easily installed, maintenance-free, and require less floor space than a normal door. Cops, on the other hand, hate them because they're a thief's dream; usually you can simply lift the door straight up an inch or two and ease it off its track. The locks that come as standard equipment are invariably at the leading edge of flimsy.

Willows wondered if he should advise Mrs Chan to buy a new lock. He decided against it. Advice was cheap but following up cost money. In his experience, people refused to spend so much as a dime on security until the morning they rolled out of bed and discovered the silver was missing, along with everything else they owned that was worth fencing and small enough to fit in the trunk of a car.

There was a clock on the wall – a black cartoon cat wearing white gloves, the fingers pointing towards the hours and minutes. Mrs Chan checked the clock against the watch on her wrist. "I'm sorry, I didn't realize it was so late."

Willows said, "We're a little early. Traffic wasn't as bad as we thought it would be."

"We appreciate you taking the time to talk with us," said Parker. "I know it can't be easy."

The room was furnished with a couch and matching chair upholstered in deep-blue velour. A carved rocking chair stood alone in a corner. "Would you like to sit down?"

Parker and Mrs Chan made themselves comfortable at opposite ends of the couch. Willows moved towards the chair but didn't sit down. A family portrait in a silver frame hung crookedly on the wall behind the chair. Emily Chan was flanked by her parents. They had dressed for the occasion. Mrs Chan was smiling. Her husband looked very serious.

Behind Willows, Mrs Chan said, "Emily was a wonderful little girl."

Parker said, "Yes, I'm sure she was."

"I told her not to get mixed up with that boy. He wouldn't get a job, refused to work."

"Cherry Ngo?"

Mrs Chan nodded. "He always had lots of money. A roll of bills. He liked to take it out and count it out loud. Show off. I asked him once where all that money came from. He laughed at me, as if it was a stupid question and I was a stupid woman to ask him."

"Did Cherry and Emily come to visit with you very often?"

"Many times. Once a week, sometimes twice. They never stayed very long. Ten or fifteen minutes."

"Did Cherry ever bring any of his friends with him when he came here?"

"His brother, once. No one else."

"Joey Ngo."

"Yes, Joey. He seemed like a nice boy. Polite, and respectful. Different from his brother. I think he was very fond of Emily."

"How did Cherry and your husband get along?"

Mrs Chan glanced at Willows. "My husband was afraid of Cherry Ngo. He believed Cherry Ngo was a gangster."

Willows' beeper sounded. He said, "Do you mind if I use your telephone?"

"Just down the stairs. It's in the kitchen, I'll show you."

"Don't get up, I'll find it."

The apartment was narrow, no more than fourteen feet wide. It had been constructed so there was room for an access hallway or stairs plus a room on each floor. The kitchen was about three feet below ground level. A large window provided a view of a light-well. The back door was glass, and wouldn't be visible from the street. A red telephone hung on the wall next to the fridge. Willows called home.

Willy Talbot had left a message confirming that two blood types had been obtained from the Pale Green Shoots washroom. One of the blood types was a match for the specimen that had been collected from Cherry Ngo's heart. The second had come from an unknown donor.

Willows hung up. A long hallway with several doors led to the far end of the apartment. A soft churning sound came from beind the first door. The laundry. He tried the next door and found himself in the bathroom, hit the lightswitch, shut and locked the door. Dozens of small plastic vials crowded the glass shelves of the medicine cabinet. Almost all the prescriptions were made out to Mrs Chan.

Willows wrote her doctor's name and telephone number in his notebook, along with the names of several drugs that were present in quantity.

He crouched and opened the cabinet doors beneath the sink and counter. Towels. Spare soap and toothpaste, a container of cleansing agent. A crumpled brown paper bag containing a box of sanitary napkins.

On impulse, Willows checked the toilet's water tank.

Nothing.

He opened the bathroom door, flushed the toilet and switched off the light.

Mrs Chan was in the kitchen, making tea. Willows asked her if she minded if he and Parker took a quick look in Emily's room.

Mrs Chan hesitated. "No, I suppose not. Are you looking for anything in particular?"

Willows said no, he just wanted to take a look.

Emily's bedroom was on the top floor, separated from her parent's room by an ensuite bathroom. It was a girl's room, a child's room. The walls were decorated with a Laura Ashley print. The wall-to-wall carpet was soft and white and the bedspread was pink with a lacy white fringe. The bedside lamp was in the shape of a polar bear. A tattered copy of *Sixteen* magazine lay on the night table. Parker checked the date – the magazine was almost two years old.

Parker said, "When did Emily leave home, Mrs Chan?"

"A year and a half ago. It was in late December, during the Christmas holidays."

Willows went over to the window, looked out. There was a view of a play area, slides and swings and a tire on a chain, a sandbox. There was covered parking for the co-op residents. An orange City of Vancouver dumpster had been shoved up against a wall overgrown with ivy on the far side of the access road.

Were the Chans planning to continue living in the apartment, or did they intend to move? Willows wondered how heavily the unit was subsidized. It must be tough, walking past that bedroom door.

He said, "Mrs Chan, I'd like to talk to my partner for a moment. Would you mind . . ."

"I'll be downstairs."

"Fine, thank you."

Louvered doors opened on a walk-in closet that ran the width of the room.

Willows said, "Looks like she didn't bother to pack."

"What do you think you're doing?"

"Rousting the joint. Don't just stand there, give me a hand. Look at all this, she couldn't have left with much more than the clothes on her back."

Parker began to work her way through the rack of blouses and skirts. The wire hangers chimed musically. She said, "What are we looking for, Jack, any idea?"

"Mrs Chan said she and Cherry didn't get along. But he visited her regularly, sometimes twice a week."

"But only for ten or fifteen minutes."

"Right."

"You think he stashed his drugs here."

"No," said Willows, "it isn't that at all."

Parker looked at him. "Then what is it?" she said sweetly.

Willows cleared his throat. "You said you watched the soaps. A confession, and I could see it did you a lot of good to clear the air. Well, you've got your dirty secrets and I've got mine." Willows held a blue and white gingham dress up against his chest. "What d'you think, is it me?"

"You're a crossdresser, is that it?"

"Admit it, you knew it all along."

"You're a sick person, Jack."

Willows lifted the mattress. Nothing.

Parker said, "God, sometimes I feel so sleazy."

Willows went over to the bureau. It was painted white, with pink trim. The top drawer was full of underwear. He said, "Claire, you mind?"

"If you're sure you don't want to do it."

"Give me a break. There's stuff in there decorated with giraffes."

"Take it easy, Jack. Don't panic." Parker held up a pair of panties. "Here, pull this over your head and take a couple of slow, deep breaths."

Parker found the baggie of white powder and the pale blue envelope taped to the underside of the drawer. The envelope held a card featuring a fluffy white cartoon kitten whose pink, heart-shaped footprints spelled the words "Happy Birthday". There was a picture, too, a Polaroid.

Parker showed the card and photograph to Willows.

"What d'you think, Jack. Is that who I think it is?"

"Sure looks like it to me."

"Got a nice body, hasn't he?"

Willows said, "Kind of skinny."

"But muscular."

"Especially between the ears, I bet."

Parker said, "Think he killed his brother for her?"

"It's possible. But then, who shot her?"

"Maybe we should go ask him."

"If we can find him."

"I wonder if he's been in touch with the Chans since Emily was shot."

"Let's go downstairs and find out."

Mrs Chan had turned the television back on. Her eyes were rimmed with red, and her cheeks were puffy. Parker found herself wondering what had made her cry – the death of her daughter, or some tragedy that had occurred in the latest episode of *General Hospital*.

Willows sat down on the couch next to Mrs Chan. He said, "Do you know what this is?" and showed her the bag of white powder.

"Cocaine. Or maybe heroin."

"How do you know?"

"From watching television."

"Did you know this was in your daughter's room?"

"Emily never took drugs."

Willows had read the autopsy report. Emily had been three months pregnant, and she was definitely into the coke. He let it ride. "Mrs Chan, I'm not suggesting she used drugs. Not for a moment. I'm only asking if you were aware that this was in her room?"

"No."

"You're sure?"

"Yes, of course. If I found drugs, I would flush them down the toilet!"

"Did you ever do that – find drugs and throw them away?"

"No. But I told Emily that if she ever brought drugs into my house, I would destroy them. And I warned her I would inform the police, as well."

You, maybe, but not me, thought Willows. He'd seen what a couple of months out at Willingdon could do to a kid.

Willows said, "Emily wasn't working, was she?"

"Not for the past few months, no."

"In the days before she died, did she seem different in any way? Worried or concerned, tense?"

Mrs Chan turned to look at Willows. She said, "No more than usual. She was a very unhappy girl."

"She didn't mention anything . . ."

"It made her very angry if I asked her about her personal life. The simplest little question . . . When she came to visit, I didn't want to argue with her."

"What sort of things did you talk about?"

"Television. We talked about what we'd seen on television."

Parker said, "If Joey calls, or drops by, we'd appreciate it if you didn't mention our interest in him."

"Joey wouldn't hurt my child. Is that what you think, that Joey did it?"

Parker said, "Emily had been beaten. Repeatedly. Do you know anything about that, Mrs Chan?"

"No, nothing."

"We want to talk to Joey, that's all, and we don't want to risk scaring him away."

"He won't call. Now that Emily's gone, there is nothing here that he cares about."

"Except this," said Willows, hefting the plastic bag full of white powder.

Parker said, "If he does come, and he asks about the drugs, then you can tell him we searched Emily's room. Otherwise, please don't mention it."

"Yes, all right. What time is it, please?"

Parker checked her watch. "Just past four."

"I missed *Geraldo*," said Betty Chan. "Do you ever watch his show? He's so much fun. That time the identical twins were on, and he asked that man if he ever wanted to go to bed with his wife *and* her sister . . ."

Outside there were several small children digging energetically but to no obvious purpose in the sandbox, while an older child in tattered coveralls made high-pitched engine noises as he steered a remote-controlled car in a complex circuit around the playground.

Parker glanced around. The area was hemmed in by the co-op buildings on all four sides. It was probably one of the safest places to play in the entire city. But the sandbox and swings and brightly-colored plastic slide and other equipment was in shadow even though it was only mid-afternoon. Because of the surrounding buildings, the sun would reach the area for only a few hours each day, even during the summer. The playground was secure, but the lack of sunlight seemed a high price to pay.

Parker's thoughts were interrupted when Willows suddenly shouted a warning, and clutched at her arm. A split-second later the remote-controlled car struck her from behind, smashed into her ankle and rebounded and raced away.

Willows looked for the boy, but he had ducked out of sight, was hiding somewhere, keeping a low profile.

"Damn it," said Parker under her breath. There was a scrape on her skin and her nylon was torn.

"Hit and run," said Willows. "He must've been doing about a hundred and fifty scale-miles per hour. You're lucky you weren't killed."

"Very funny."

"We check all the toy stores in town, maybe we can come up with a lead. No, wait a minute – did you get his number?"

Parker said, "No, but I've got yours, Jack. Knock it off, or I'll buy myself a wind-up Ferrari and chase you all over the squadroom."

They were walking down the narrow road leading to the guest parking lot when the bright red model car suddenly reappeared, racing towards them from behind a hedge of dwarf junipers.

Parker's instinct was to draw her service revolver and shoot the thing to death, but a deep-seated concern for ricochets and paper-work stayed her hand.

She waited until the last second, and then kicked out. The little car veered sharply away, miniature tires scrabbling for a grip on the pavement. It raced thirty feet up the road and then skidded around on its own axis, so it was facing them.

Willows waited. The car shot towards them. He picked up a rock, cocked his arm. The little car veered away and hit the curb and rolled, came to rest belly-up in the middle of the road.

There was a howl of rage from behind the hedge.

Willows walked over to the car. Its wheels were spinning

furiously. He picked the car up and flipped open the battery compartment. Duracells, eight of them.

Across the street, the hedge trembled and then the boy pushed through.

Willows dropped a battery on the road, kicked it with just the right weight and watched it vanish down a storm drain. He fastened the cover on the battery compartment and put the car upside down on the road.

The kid hovered in the shade of the hedge. His face was pinched and angry. He wanted his car back, but not quite badly enough to risk a cuff on the ear.

Willows and Parker walked towards their unmarked car. Willows unlocked his door and climbed in, reached across to unlock the passenger side door. When Willows started the engine, the kid dashed across the road, scooped up his toy and ran back and vanished through an unseen gap in the hedge.

Willows backed the car out of the parking slot.

"Step on it," said Parker, rubbing her ankle. "Let's scram before the little creep gets *our* number."

16

Burnaby. Frank had been there once or twice before, years ago. He couldn't remember why. As he saw it, the municipality was a kind of low-rent bedroom community for the city. Guys who drove trucks lived there, people like that. Lulu had to use a certain amount of friendly persuasion to convince Frank a day trip would be a good idea. Her destination was a sprawling shopping complex called Metrotown.

Frank wasn't keen on the idea. The summer days were slipping by. He'd slept in again this morning, snored away his chance at Claire Parker. The missed opportunity had left him sour-faced and grumpy. What kind of killer was he? The way things were going, he'd be surprised if Newt didn't give him his walking papers, send someone else out to do the job.

It suddenly occurred to Frank – and why hadn't he thought of this earlier – that Newt might slip Rikki's leash. Now there was a scary thought. Frank remembered watching Rikki slice a Thanksgiving roast turkey in a Beverly Hills restaurant. Despite the oily, muttered objections of the joint's maître d', Rikki insisted on using his own knife; a switchblade with a ten-inch blade and weighted handle he'd bought by mail from a specialty shop in Tokyo.

Frank had never seen meat cut so thin – the Mexican was an artist with a blade. But what he'd never forget was the demented glint in Rikki's eye, the bubbling froth of saliva that had appeared in the corner of his sagging mouth, the hiss and moan of his breath and the way the tendons had stood out in his wrists and the backs of his hands as he'd gone to work on that glazed and juicy bird. The look on his face, every last pore contributing to the effect, was – sure I'm having fun, but gimme a *live* bird if you really want to see me enjoying myself.

But no, Newt wouldn't risk sending Rikki across the border to

Vancouver. There was too much fruit in Rikki's cake. You had to watch him every minute, his every move. Frank had heard the story about the guy in the washroom, how Rikki had surgically removed his ear with a stroke so deft it probably had Maneleto rolling over in his grave.

You could get away with that kind of behavior in Los Angeles, maybe. But it was front-page news in Vancouver. Frank told himself that Rikki wasn't a problem. Newt was crazy, but he wasn't insane.

Frank's armpits were damp. He was breathing heavily. Maybe Lulu was right – it would do him some good to get out of the city, grab a breath of suburban air. The reason she wanted to visit Metrotown was to try a shot at another robbery. Frank had been teaching her theory and she wanted to go out in the field and see how well she'd learned her lessons.

Flatly, without being bitchy about it, just stating a simple fact, she pointed out that it seemed only fair he do a little something for her, since she'd spent the last few days waiting on him hand and foot. Besides, she casually added, she'd spent an awful lot of money on her disguise.

"What disguise is that, honey?"

Lulu made Frank turn around and cover his eyes while she changed into her cute little outfit, the dark-green jacket and matching pleated skirt, white blouse and knee socks, round-toed patent leather flats with a shiny black strap. The crowning touch was a Heidi-type wig, blonde and braided.

Frank said, "Holy cow, you look about ten years old. What is that, some kind of uniform?"

Lulu nodded, smiling. The uniform was from a local Catholic girls' school. She'd paid fifty dollars for it from an ice-cream-cone-gobbling hundred and ten pound thirteen-year-old with lots of freckles and no brains.

"Nice," said Frank.

"What d'you think of the wig – is it too much?"

"No, it's great."

Lulu curled up in the tub chair by the hotel window. The pleated skirt rode high up on her thigh as she sat down. Her pale skin gleamed in the light. She said, "So, the overall look, would you say it was kind of sexy, or what?"

"Sexy, yeah. But at the same time, I got to admit I'm not all that comfortable with it. I'm pushing forty, Lulu. You look young enough to be my daughter."

"But you don't have any children, do you, Frank?"

"Nope."

"And I'm twenty-two years old, aren't I?"

Frank nodded.

Lulu held out her arms. "C'mere, baby, and gimme a great big kiss."

Frank wanted to drive to Burnaby but Lulu said she couldn't stand looking at all that urban blight, so they caught the Sky Train – the elevated light transit system that moved commuters in and out of the city – at the subterranean Hudson's Bay Station.

Frank said, "How come they call it the Sky Train? We must be twenty feet underground."

"Don't worry about it," said Lulu, making herself comfortable on his lap. She nibbled his ear. "Just sit back and enjoy the ride." She wiggled her hips. "I'm going to."

There was a crowd at the Metrotown station. Frank's size and the set of his jaw got them through.

They wandered through the mall for the better part of an hour. Roger had a birthday coming up and Lulu had her heart set on a gold wrist chain – a really heavy one, something that would cost in the neighborhood of ten or fifteen thousand dollars, if you bought it.

Frank said, "That's one of the nice things about being a thief – when the clerk asks you what price range you're interested in, you can tell him the sky's the limit, and mean it."

By two in the afternoon, they still hadn't decided who to give their business to.

Frank said, "Let's hit a restaurant."

"What?"

"I'm gonna die if I don't get a cheeseburger in the next ten minutes."

There was a fast-food joint on the lower level with a table available that had a good view of a jewelry store called Silver Threads Among The Gold.

The waitress brought the menus and asked Frank would he like a drink. Frank said no. Lulu ordered a martini the way James Bond liked it, but with an extra olive.

The waitress asked for some ID.

Lulu said, "Watch me drink it – you'll know I've done it before."

The waitress hesitated. Frank caught her eye. He smiled in a neutral kind of way. Indicating the Catholic school jacket, the waitress said, "You teach there, is that it?"

"Advanced Sex Techniques," said Lulu, flashing her milk-white teeth.

"Guess I'll have a beer," said Frank, "to wash down my cheeseburger, double bacon."

Lulu ordered a side salad, no dressing.

Eventually, the drinks arrived. Lulu ate an olive, held her glass up to the light. "I'm going to have to make this last, aren't I?"

"Drinking and stealing don't mix too well."

"But one won't hurt."

"Probably not."

Lulu parted her lips and bit gently down on an olive, pulled it slowly from the toothpick. The olive vanished into her mouth. She licked her lips, chewed slowly, and swallowed. She smiled. "You never lie to me, do you, Frank?"

"Nope."

"Not even when it'd make things a lot easier."

Frank said, "I can't think when that would be." He sipped at his beer. "Is something bothering you?"

"I think I'm in love with you. I mean really in love."

The food arrived. Frank cut his burger in half. The knife blade was serrated but he had a little trouble with the bacon. An image of Rikki flashed across his plate. He pressed down more heavily and the knife cut through. He said, "Maybe we should forget about Roger's present, go shopping some other day."

"Because of one little martini?"

"No, I didn't mean that at all. It's just you've got my mind going in a different direction, and that ain't healthy. If we're gonna do some robbing, it's important to concentrate on the business at hand."

Lulu's eyes darkened, but she held her peace.

Frank said, "How's the salad?"

"Limp."

Frank poured some ketchup on his french fries. "How late's this place stay open?"

"What day is it?"

"Friday."

"Until nine."

Frank had left his Rolex back at the hotel. He said, "What time is it now, about two-thirty?"

Lulu checked her watch. "Twenty-past."

"Is there a hotel or motel around here?"

Lulu said, "We're on Kingsway, Frank. Everywhere you look, there's a motel."

"Why don't we finish lunch, grab a taxi and find someplace close where we can grab a little nap. Later on, if we feel like it, we can come back here and take care of Roger."

Lulu said, "A nap isn't exactly what I'm in need of, at the moment."

"Well whatever."

The motel the taxi driver took them to turned out to be just right – not exactly seedy, but definitely a little run down. Frank opened the window as wide as it would go. He turned on the TV – here they were in late July and it was snowing on every channel. He turned the TV off and went to join Lulu in the shower.

They were back at Metrotown a little after eight. The clerk at Silver Threads Among The Gold was polishing the glass display case. He had a roll of paper towels under his arm and was pulling the trigger on a spray bottle of Windex as if it was a high-powered pistol.

The crowds were thicker than ever. The mall was air-conditioned. Frank smiled. There were at least two good reasons to be there, then. To cool off or pull a heist. He said, "Okay, let's go over it one more time."

Lulu said, "Don't show him the piece unless I mean to use it."

"Right." Frank had loaned Lulu a .32-calibre automatic. The weapon weighed almost as much as she did, even though the magazine was empty. He wasn't proud of the fact that he'd given her a useless gun. But at the same time, he knew from experience that otherwise normal people sometimes went absolutely nuts when they got their hands on a gun. Frank had his eye on a gold chain, not a headline that screamed, BLOODBATH IN BURNABY!

Lulu said, "Speak in a normal voice, and don't talk too fast."

"Good."

"Be careful not to touch anything."

Frank said, "Especially now, since he's just finished cleaning the counter. The cops find any prints that aren't his, they're gonna know right away who they belong to."

Lulu said, "But what difference does it make, if they can't identify us. I mean, since they don't have a record of my fingerprints, how can they make a match?"

"They can't," said Frank. "At least, not until they get their hands on your fingers." Lulu giggled. He frowned and said, "It might seem funny now, but it won't be all that hilarious when they put you away. This's a risky business, and don't you forget it."

"I won't."

Frank glanced around. "After he hands you the gold chain, then what?"

"I tell him to lie down on the floor and stay put for five minutes. That if he doesn't do what I tell him to, I'll kill him."

"Good, good."

"If he stands there like a dummy, I show him the gun."

"*Part* of the gun."

"And if he still doesn't do what he's told, I point the gun at him and repeat my instructions."

"But you don't shoot him."

"I know, I know. Don't be such a *worry-wart*. I'm not going to do anything wrong."

"Okay, fine."

Frank glanced around the mall, failed to spot any stray cops or security personnel. He leaned over and kissed Lulu on the cheek. "Go get 'em, kid."

Lulu walked into the jewelry store. The clerk looked up, saw her coming. He put the paper towels and Windex down on the counter, and smiled warmly. From thirty feet away, Frank saw Lulu yank the .32 out of her purse and thrust the barrel into the clerk's startled face. She said something, Frank couldn't hear what. The clerk nodded, pulled a burgundy-colored tray from beneath the counter. The tray was draped with heavy gold chains. The clerk dumped the chains into Lulu's open purse.

Lulu cocked the .32. What a sound it made. Like the last tick of the world's last clock. The barrel skidded across the clerk's sweaty forehead. Lulu said, "So long, sucker," and squeezed the trigger.

17

The Corvette was still frozen in mid-crash, the shiny nose of the car protruding through the cinderblock wall. But even so, something wasn't quite right. The wild-eyed girl sitting in the driver's lap was a redhead. Willows was pretty sure that she'd been wearing a blonde wig, the first time around.

Some things never seemed to change, though. Bob was still wearing the same blue coveralls unbuttoned half-way down his sagging, furry chest, and the swampy remains of a cheap cigar continued to jut pugnaciously from his mouth.

Bob pointed the cigar at Willows and said, "The cop, right? Where's the pretty lady?"

Willows smiled to take the bite out of his words. "Where she can't hear your dumb-ass chauvinist remarks, Bob. Lucky for you."

Bob's upper lip twitched. His teeth looked rusty. He made a sound like a toilet being flushed, turned his head and spat a shred of tobacco at the floor. "Lookin' for Joey?"

"Is he here?"

"Nope."

"Do you know where he is?"

"Your guess is as good as mine, Detective. Probably better, in fact, since you got the advantage of all that training."

The toilet flushed again. Bob's face was the color and texture of weathered brick. Willows realized he was laughing.

The counterman scratched his chest. His oily fingers played with a silver Saint Christopher's medal. He said, "Joey didn't come to work this morning. Didn't phone in sick, neither. Way I see it, he's gone and joined the swelling ranks of the unemployed." He waved the cigar at Willows. "Gotta match?"

"No."

"I cared about him enough to track him down, first place I'd try is his bedroom. Kid never seemed to get enough sleep, was always nodding off during lunch. Sneak up on him real quiet, you'll probably catch him in the sack, makin' love to his dreams."

Parker started the unmarked car as Willows walked out of the building. He climbed into the car and slammed the door.

Parker said, "What happened, Joey didn't want to talk to you?"

"He wasn't there, pretty lady."

"Pretty lady?"

"That's what Bob called you. The pretty lady."

Parker revved the engine. "Where's Joey?"

Willows shrugged. "He didn't show up for work this morning, or bother to call in sick."

"He's on the lam."

Willows grinned. "Maybe."

"The house?"

"Might as well give it a try."

Parker put the car in gear. "Reminds me of an old joke. Know what they call a guy with no arms or legs who falls in the ocean?"

"Bob," said Willows, slouching low in the seat.

"You heard it?"

"It's an old joke. You said so yourself."

"Another lesson learned," said Parker.

"What's that?"

"Never tell an old guy an old joke." Parker pulled away from the curb. It was mid-afternoon, the temperature in the high seventies. The car wasn't air-conditioned. Willows took off his jacket and rolled down his window. His holster dug into his groin. He unclipped it from his belt and laid it on the car seat. Parker glanced at him but didn't say anything.

Willows said, "You check the air-quality index in this morning's paper?"

"I never read that trash."

"What, air-quality indexes?"

"No, the morning paper. In fact, they've stopped calling it a paper. It's a tabloid now."

"Doesn't matter. They don't have a foldout. Without a foldout, it isn't a tabloid."

"Without a what?"

"Cheesecake." Willows grinned. "Racy snapshot of a pretty woman."

"Knock it off, Jack." Parker was tailgating. She changed lanes and accelerated.

Willows stuck his hand out the window, trying with mixed success to deflect the flow of humid, sticky air towards his face. After a moment, he said, "Speaking of cheesecake, you want to stop somewhere, grab a bite to eat?"

Parker smiled. "No," she said, "I don't."

There was a glossy black Jaguar parked in front of Joey Ngo's house. At first glance, the man on the front porch seemed to be knocking at the door. But as they drew nearer, Willows saw that the man was energetically patching the bullet holes in the stucco.

Parker said, "It isn't often you see a tradesman working in a black three-piece suit, especially in this kind of weather."

"And especially not in this neighborhood, either," said Willows. "In Shaughnessy, I've heard even the plumbers wear a tux."

"But is it a clean tux?"

The man paused to glance at the unmarked police car, and then went back to work. The sound of the triangular metal spatula sliding across the rough surface of the stucco made Parker grit her teeth.

A blob of spackle hit the man's polished black shoe. He knelt and wiped the shoe clean with a scrap of cloth.

By now, Willows and Parker were in the yard, closing fast. The man tossed the spatula in a plastic bucket and used the cloth to wipe his hands.

Willows pulled out his wallet as he climbed the front steps.

The man smiled. "Cops? You don't have to show me any identification, I believe it." He smiled at Parker. "Looking for Joey?"

Willows said, "Who're you?"

"Alan Carroll. The landlord."

Parker said, "Could you show us some identification, Mr Carroll?"

"You want to make sure I'm not the *Star Trek* guy, am I right?" Carroll's black leather billfold was embossed with the Jaguar logo. He showed Parker his driver's licence. "Pretty uncanny, huh? Am I his identical twin, or what?"

"A striking resemblance," said Parker. "Absolutely incredible. Jack, take a look."

"Amazing."

Parker returned the licence, and Carroll slipped it back in his billfold. "Those films seem to come out about every six months," he said. "Every time a new one hits the screen, all of a sudden I can't go *anywhere* without being hounded for my autograph."

Parker said, "I would have thought it'd be kind of nice, being mistaken for a movie star."

"The women falling all over me?"

"No," said Parker, "that isn't what I meant at all."

"Because that part of it's there for me anyway. And as far as the film-star stuff goes, the adulation thing, you can forget about the women. It's the little kids who go crazy. Ten year olds, and like that. Know what the worst part of it is?"

Willows said, "I bet they want to pull your ears, to see if they're real."

Carroll's smile faltered. Willows indicated the house. "You own the building, is that right?"

"What? Oh, yeah. Lock, stock and mortgage."

"Is Joey home?"

"Not unless he's hiding in a duct pipe."

Parker said, "Have you been inside?"

"Yeah, I told him I was going to come around and fix the bullet holes, he was expecting me. When I got here, there was still blood on the porch, and the chalk drawing of that poor girl's body. I was shocked, let me tell you. How Joey could leave it like that beats me." The door was partly open. Willows moved a step closer, peered inside.

Carroll said, "You want to take a look around, go right ahead. Help yourself."

Willows pushed the door open a little wider. He had Carroll's permission to enter the house, but the landlord wasn't living in the house. And Willows didn't have a warrant.

If Joey had killed his brother, the evidence required to put him away could be in the house. Willows thought about it for a moment and then reluctantly decided that the possible benefits of gaining immediate access to the house wasn't worth the risk. He might find the murder weapon under Joey's pillow, but if the court ruled he lacked sufficient grounds to enter the house in the first place, the evidence would be ruled inadmissable.

And Bradley would give him a cute little hand-held stop sign and he'd spend the rest of his career policing a school crosswalk.

Probably he should've arranged for a warrant before he drove to Joey's house. Better late than never. He said, "Excuse us a minute, will you?" and walked Parker down the steps and half-way across the front yard.

Parker said, "A warrant, right?"

"The kid didn't show up for work or phone in. I think we've got reasonable grounds to be concerned for his safety. For all we know, Carroll's right – Joey could be down in the basement, stuffed in a furnace vent. See what you can do, okay?"

Parker, fishing in her purse for the keys, started towards the car.

Willows made his way back to the porch. "Mr Carroll, how long has Joey been living here?"

"He signed a year lease about eight months ago. Him and his brother. When I found out that Joey's chick was living here too, I just about hit the roof."

"Wait a minute. Do you mean Emily Chan?"

"Right, who else?"

"Emily was *Cherry's* girlfriend."

"Maybe he thought so."

Willows said, "What d'you mean by that?"

"I got a phone call last month. Two or three days after I found out I was carrying an extra tenant. The call came about eight o'clock at night, maybe a little later. It was Emily on the line, telling me the sink won't drain, could I come over and fix it or should she call a plumber."

Willows waited patiently while Carroll lit a filter cigarette. The lighter, black anodized aluminum, was also embossed with the Jaguar logo.

"So anyway, it's been a long day, I'm bushed, and I tell her maybe I can make it but probably not. But in the end, I climb in the Jag and zip on over here."

"Why?"

"Excuse me?"

"It had been a long day. You were tired. The sink could wait. Where do you live?"

"Kits Point."

"So why drive all the way across town?"

Carroll shrugged. "Well, mostly to avoid the cost of a plumber. I mean, a plugged sink, it can wait until the morning, but even so, you're looking at maybe a hundred bucks. But there was something else. She sounded . . ."

"Like she was coming on to you?"

"You got it."

"But when you showed up, your plumber's helper at port arms, all she wanted to show you was the sink."

"Hey, it was a lot worse than that. I knock on the door. No answer. So I knock louder. Still nothing. It's at least an hour's drive, there and back. So I try the door."

"You walked in," said Willows.

"I told her I was on my way over. It shouldn't have been such a big surprise."

"She was with Joey?"

"In the living room, on the sofa." Carroll waved at the open door. "You step in, you're right there. Joey's got his back to me, but *she's* looking right at me. Real calm. Winks and puts her finger to her lips, warning me to keep my mouth shut. I start to back out of there. I mean, I can be a wild and crazy guy, but there are limits to how far I'm willing to go."

Across the street, a woman in bright-pink shorts and a matching tank top was pushing a power lawnmower out of her garage, down the driveway towards the parched front lawn. Her hair was in curlers. She had a nose like Bob Hope. She leaned into the machine and then away, yanking at the starter cord. Willows saw Parker roll up the unmarked car's window, to keep out the noise.

Carroll said, "She motions to me, telling me to come on in. When she sees I'm not interested, know what she does?"

The lighter flicked on and off, blue tongues of flame leaping and dying, leaping and dying.

Willows waited.

Carroll said, "Waves her legs in the air and purses her lips and blows me a kiss goodbye."

Willows said, "What about the sink?"

"The sink? Oh, yeah. Cherry phoned the next day, left a message on my machine. Said it was fixed. Tea leaves. I should forget about it."

Parker got out of the car. She locked the door and started up the sidewalk towards them.

Willows said, "You're sure it was Cherry who called, not Joey?"

"Absolutely positive."

"What do you do for a living, Mr Carroll?"

Carroll lit another cigarette, giving himself time for Parker to come within earshot. "I'm in real estate. Got my own company."

"No kidding."

Carroll winked at Parker. "Surprised, huh. What, you had me in corporate law?"

Parker said, "How did you know?"

"Happens all the time. The suit, Jag, thirty-dollar haircut. It all adds up, makes an impression."

To Willows, Parker said, "I talked to Bradley, he's going to get right on it." She glanced across the street at the woman in the pink shorts. "Half an hour. Think she can keep mowing the lawn that long?"

"I hope so," said Willows.

Carroll said, "I've seen stuff on TV, cops with battering rams, sledgehammers. And they always look like they're having such a great time. That house on the east side, that you guys attacked with the bulldozer? In ten minutes there was nothing left but a pile of splinters."

Parker said, "We'll try to avoid using the bulldozer, Mr Carroll."

Carroll fished a pair of sunglasses from his jacket pocket. Mirrored lenses.

Parker and Willows and the woman in the pink shorts watched him climb into his Jaguar and drive majestically away. As the car turned the corner, Parker said, "Is it William Shatner he thinks he looks like?"

"Maybe. I thought his ears were kind of large and pointy, though." Willows checked his watch. "There's a McDonald's a couple of blocks from here. You hungry yet?"

"Not particularly."

"We've got plenty of time until that warrant arrives. I'm going to go grab a burger. Want anything?"

"Not for me."

"Coffee?"

"Okay, a coffee. A small coffee."

"Salad? You sure you don't want a salad?"

"Okay, fine. I'll have a salad."

"What kind of dressing you want?"

"I don't want any dressing."

Willows held out his hand.

Parker slammed the car keys into his palm. "And I don't want cream for my coffee, either."

"Back in fifteen minutes."

"Take your time," said Parker, and meant it.

*

Willows was in the lane behind the house, stuffing a small tree's worth of McDonald's packaging in a battered garbage can when the search warrant finally arrived.

The uniformed constable who'd courier'd the warrant across town was bored, and looking for a little action.

"Need any doors kicked in?"

Willows said, "You *see* any doors that look like they need to be kicked in?"

Playing to Parker, the cop said, "They *all* need it, you ask me."

Parker said, "That attitude cuts no ice with me, sonny."

Walking back to his patrol car, the cop tried to stare down the woman in the pink shorts and hair curlers on the far side of the street, who was pretending to mow her lawn.

No luck there, either.

The house was fairly small. There were about eight hundred square feet on the main floor. The living room, kitchen, bathroom and bedroom all radiated from a central hallway. There was a three-piece bathroom and another bedroom in the basement. Joey Ngo's body wasn't stuffed in any of the furnace ducts, or anywhere else.

In the bedroom, Parker slid open a bureau drawer. It was empty. She tried the other drawers. They were all empty. Parker could hear Willows prowling around upstairs, the rattle of cutlery in a drawer. Was this where Emily and Joey had made love? The room had a single small window. She pulled aside a curtain torn from a scrap of black cloth, letting in a flood of light.

There were four deep indentations on the surface of the scruffy carpet. A piece of furniture had stood there until recently, and been moved. Parker stared at the empty bureau. It was about the right size. She made her way back around the bed, got a grip on the bureau and tilted it away from the wall. The plaster was dented. There was a dark smear of blood.

Parker went to the foot of the stair and called Willows.

There was more blood on the wall, minute high-impact splash patterns that came from several directions and heights and indicated a protracted struggle. Marks on the walls suggested that several larger stains had been washed away.

Parker said, "A fistfight?"

"That's what it looks like. A good, old-fashioned bare-knuckles brawl."

"Between Joey and his brother. Or either one of them and Emily. Maybe that's how she got her bruises."

Willows nodded, although it seemed to him that Emily had been beaten repeatedly, over a considerable period of time. He said, "We better take another look at both autopsy reports."

"And get the techs in here," added Parker.

They'd need to organize a stakeout, too, in case Joey was stupid enough to come back. Willows said, "Busy day, all of a sudden."

Parker nodded. Where was Joey, what was he thinking? Was it worth staking out the Chan apartment? The coffee was already turning to acid in her stomach.

18

The clerk's eyes rolled up in his head. His legs buckled. The glass countertop briefly flattened his nose and then he disappeared behind the display case.

Lulu tried to stuff the utterly useless .32 in her purse. The gun wouldn't fit because of all the gold chains. She walked back to where Frank was waiting, gave him a coldly scornful look and handed him the pistol. Frank dropped the weapon in his jacket pocket. Lulu hurried back towards the jewelry store.

Frank said, "Hey, where you think you're going!"

Lulu rolled the unconscious clerk over on his back. There was a rapidly swelling lump on his forehead. His nose was bleeding, but not much. He wasn't as heavy as he'd looked. His wallet was in the inside breast pocket of his suit, which had a Mens Shop label, price tag still attached. Ninety-nine dollars and ninety-five cents.

The key case was in one of the little pockets in his vest. Lulu unlocked a display case, pulled out a tray and dumped the contents into her purse. She glanced over the counter to see what Frank was up to, then knelt and kissed the clerk daintily on the cheek.

Moments later, Lulu took Frank's arm and they strolled casually towards the excalator that would carry them up to the ground floor.

Lulu said, "That was a pretty sneaky thing to do."

"What's that, honey?"

"Take the bullets out of the gun."

Frank said, "I didn't. It was equipped with a noise suppressor. Nice shot, by the way."

Lulu gave him a quick look, saw he was kidding. She said, "What would have happened if the guy hadn't fainted?"

"Who can say?"

"No, I mean what if he'd grabbed me, or something?"

"Then I'd have wandered over and rescued you, just like we worked it out."

Lulu shuddered, and pressed close against him. "I'm cold, Frank."

"A little scared, is all. You'll get over it."

"Armed robbery. It's a lot harder than it sounds. I felt so all alone. And when I walked up to the counter, got close to him, he seemed so . . . *big*. I was afraid he'd remember me, every little thing, and that he'd tell the police." Lulu squeezed Frank's arm, his rock of a biceps. "Suddenly I was worried that he'd hit me and take away the gun and shoot you. Shoot my lover." She peered up at him with adoring eyes. "I decided I couldn't let that happen, Frank."

"So you figured you'd take charge of the situation, bump him off while you had the chance."

"I wasn't thinking very clearly, was I?"

Frank shrugged. "Everything worked out okay. Rog is gonna be happy as a clam when he sees what you got for him. His only problem is he'll have to pump iron for a few months to build up enough strength to wear all that heavy metal." Frank smiled. "He better be careful, with all those muscles and all that gold, that he don't get mistaken for Mr T."

Lulu said, "I'll do better next time."

Frank had his doubts about that, because as far as he was concerned, there wasn't going to *be* a next time. One brush with a first-degree murder rap was more than enough. Lulu was all he'd ever wanted in a woman, the whole ball of wax. But at the same time, certain dark aspects of her personality scared him half to death. That big book of photographs. All those dead fathers. He'd known from the start that she had a problem defining reality. That's why he hadn't been all that surprised when she'd tried to blow away the clerk, why he had taken the bullets from her gun in the first place. She was beautiful, but dangerous. If they hoped to survive, they were going to have to be very careful and awfully lucky.

Lulu, studying Frank's monolithic profile, knew exactly what he was thinking. They were so *close*. As if they were twins, or something. It was like, anytime she wanted, she could peek inside his brain and see all the stuff that was going on.

And he was absolutely right; she was dangerous, both to him and to herself. And there was nothing she could do about it, he was right about that, as well. It was up to him to watch over her. Left to her own devices, she didn't have a chance.

But he was wrong about her not doing a better job next time.

There *was* going to be a next time, and soon. And her gun would have *bullets* in it!

No more of this stupid fainting stuff. The next time somebody messed with her, he was going to *die*.

Frank remembered a guy he'd known in the joint, a slouchy little black fag lifer worked in the library, who'd told him that the eyes were the windows of the soul. Frank had reacted by slugging the dude in the mouth. Afterwards, lying in his cell thinking about it, he realized he'd tossed the punch because of the guy's faggy tone of voice rather than what he'd actually said, since Frank hadn't understood what the words meant.

That had been years and years ago. Only now, right this minute, as the escalator crawled upward and he and Lulu and a couple of pounds of eighteen-carat gold made their slo-mo getaway, did Frank finally pick up on what the fag had meant.

What he saw in the glacial windows of his sweetie's soul was lust – a lust for violence, for wealth, and for power. The big three.

Scary.

Frank wanted to take the Sky Train back into the city. He'd found that he liked being up high, sitting in the bright blue seat and looking down at the gnarled traffic and houses and apartments, through brightly-lit picture windows and into people's lives. It was a strange kind of fun, getting that quick peek as the train blew by. He hadn't said anything to Lulu, because it had all happened so fast and he didn't quite believe his eyes but, during the trip out, there had been a man and a woman making love in front of a mirror, in the living room of a track-level apartment. Maybe they were still there.

Not that Frank was a voyeur. It was just weird, that's all, and he'd thought Lulu might be interested or curious. But no, she wasn't. His violent baby wanted to take a cab back to the hotel. Anything less would be anticlimactic.

Frank waved at the traffic. "It's gotta be at least a forty-five minute ride. We're looking at twenty bucks plus tip, maybe more."

"We could steal a car."

"Forget it."

Lulu pouted, but stopped short of stamping her pretty foot. "I want you to show me how to steal a car, Frank."

"Well, I'm not gonna."

"Why not?"

"You'd only get yourself in trouble, is why."

"Oh, I get it. You can steal all the cars you want, anytime you feel like it, because you're a man. But I'm a woman, and women are supposed to stay home and vacuum, right? Stay home in the vacuum and vacuum."

They were standing on the sidewalk, waiting for the light to change and the illuminated sign to change from an orange palm to a white pedestrian, so they could cross in safety. Six crowded lanes of traffic streamed past at about twenty miles an hour. Thousands of shiny bright cars, polished metal, glass. Radios blasting, engines throbbing. From the presumed safety of their vehicles, women stared at Frank. A kid pointed at him, and laughed soundlessly. Men, busy driving, chose to ignore him. A van squealed its tires. There was a TV inside, Frank could see the screen, and then it was gone. He believed he heard a faint electrical crackling drifting across the air from Metrotown. Kingsway wasn't a healthy place to be. The air stank of burnt rubber and exhaust fumes and endless frustration. Frank could feel his lungs trying to take it all in, deal with it.

There'd be cops all over the place by now. How much would the clerk remember?

A taxi cruised towards them. It was in the far lane, but its roof light was on, signalling that it was vacant. Frank whistled shrilly, waved his arm. The driver's head came up. He spun the wheel and shot across two lanes of traffic. A hubcap scraped the curb. Frank yanked open the rear door and they climbed in. The driver's hair was combed straight back and was too thin to hide his rash. His eyes were a flat green, dull and lifeless. His gaunt, sunken cheeks were a network of hundreds of tiny broken scarlet lines of the sort that signal "road under construction' on maps.

Lulu said, "Granville and Georgia," and they lurched into the flow of traffic.

Lulu put her hand on Frank's thigh. "Isn't this fun?"

Frank said, "Fasten your seatbelt. It's the law."

Click.

"And I wouldn't mind if you got rid of the rug, now that you don't need it any more."

Lulu tilted her head and removed the hairpiece, tossed it out her open window.

"Better?"

Frank nodded. He watched as Lulu brushed her hair that was the genuine article but looked like a cloud, all soft and shimmery. She said, "I don't know how Sinatra stands it."

Frank said, "Stands what?"

"Wearing a wig. They're so hot, and they itch."

"Cheap ones. I bet he spends a couple thousand each, easy." Frank mulled it over. "The quality he'd be used to, we're talking all natural fibers. So that would take care of the itching problem. And his wigs aren't nearly as thick and luxurious as yours, so there wouldn't be as much heat build-up. Plus, the guy's a star of the first magnitude. So wherever he goes, it's air-conditioned like crazy."

"Star of the first magnitude, where'd you read that?"

Frank said, "At the barber's probably."

Lulu put on her sunglasses, the Vuarnets with the shiny black plastic frames and oversized lenses so dark it was impossible to see her eyes, whether they were open or shut, angry or bored, full of laughter or tears. She said, "You think I look silly in this outfit, don't you?"

"No, it's great. Really."

"If I'd shot that poor clerk, we'd both be in a lot of trouble, wouldn't we?"

"Not as much trouble as him," said Frank, smiling. "But yeah, you're right. Cops don't forget about murder. Five minutes or fifty years, somebody'd be thinking about that clerk from time to time. Looking to find out who we were, and bring us down."

Lulu said, "You did the right thing, giving me an empty gun."

Frank grinned. "Oh, I don't know. You wouldn't have missed him, that's for sure."

By the time they hit Granville and Georgia the meter read twenty-three dollars and forty cents. Frank folded a fifty in half, slapped it down on the dashboard. As they got out of the car, Lulu said, "If I'd known armed robbery was so darned expensive, I might've suggested we try something else."

Frank smiled. God, thought Lulu, what a hunk. Being in love was even more amazing than she'd dared dream it might be – why, they'd been together almost a whole week already, and she still couldn't get enough of him. She grabbed him by the arm, pulled him towards the hotel.

Frank glanced down at her, surprised, and she gave him a look that made him think of steam boiling off a damp roof on a day suddenly gone hot and sunny. He was pushing forty. Although he had lived parts of his life at warp speed, he'd somehow managed to avoid dying young. In his time, he had flirted with death more than once. But no matter how perilous his situation, a crucial part of him had somehow always managed to keep a certain distance, maintain the cool; up until the afternoon Lulu knocked on his door, and the need for her had ripped through him, blinded him and brought him to his knees. And also, come to think of it, robbed him of his limited ambition to do Parker and head back to sunny Calif.

So when Lulu clutched his arm and he looked down at her and saw what was in her eyes, he knew exactly what she needed, wanted, demanded.

Because – and wasn't it simple – he needed it too.

19

Inspector Homer Bradley rolled the dead cigar stub in his fingers, studied it so intently it might have held the key to the universe.

Willows leaned against the wall next to the door, his hands in his pockets, a picture of studied indifference. It wasn't just Willows' posture that gave the game away – if he'd requested the meeting, had something he wanted to tell Bradley or needed from him, Willows always walked right up to the Inspector's cherrywood desk, got as close to his boss as courtesy allowed and then spoke his piece. But when the situation was reversed, when it was Bradley who wanted something from Willows, the detective always hovered by the door, poised for a quick exit.

The two men, Parker thought, were a generation apart but so much alike. The way they preferred to approach a problem was exactly the same – peripherally, from an acute angle, rather than head on.

Then, when they were sure of their adversary, both cops liked to attack with everything they had, kick down doors, smash whatever happened to be in their way.

Bradley, using his index finger and thumb, squeezed his cigar so hard it made a tiny squeaking sound, like a panicked mouse. A few nutbrown flakes of tobacco drifted down on the cover of a file folder. Bradley picked up the folder and tilted it towards the wastebasket, shook it gently. "So at this point you've narrowed your list of suspects down to the max – you're pretty sure Joey's been a real bad boy, right?"

Willows nodded.

Bradley turned to Parker. "You concur?"

"I can't think of anybody I'd rather arrest. Where was Joey when Emily was shot? Cherry assumed he was down in the basement of the house, and so did we. But the way we see it now, he had the black Honda or whatever he was driving that night parked nearby. All he had to do was slip out the basement door, jump in the car, drive around to the front of the house and pull the trigger, lose the car and sneak back into the basement. He could've made the round trip in five minutes or less, depending where he had the car parked."

"The car was never found, is that correct?"

Parker nodded.

Willows said, "The night of the shooting, Cherry was completely out of it. Joey didn't have much to say, either, and who can blame him. He'd tried to bump off his brother and shot his sweetheart instead."

"You think. Could be that when Joey found out she was pregnant he decided to knock her off before she got around to telling Cherry."

Willows said, "No, I don't think so. It was dark, the range was about fifty yards. He was pissed at Cherry for beating on Emily. He wanted to terrify him, punish him by making him feel what Emily had felt – fear, and plenty of it."

"Does Mrs Chan know Emily was pregnant?"

"Not yet."

"It'll come out at the inquest." Bradley turned to Parker. "You'll have to tell her before then."

"Why me?" said Parker belligerently. "Why not Jack? Is it just because I'm a woman?"

"You misunderstand me, Claire. I meant you and Jack, not you personally." Willows started to say something but Bradley cut him off. "What's the word on Joey. Got any leads?"

"Our best bet's to stake out the house. He's just a kid. He'll come home sooner or later, if only because he's got nowhere else to go." Willows grinned. "We're closing in on the end of the month. Alan Carroll isn't the kind of guy who's going to wait around for his rent money. With the vacancy rate we've got in this city, I can't see Joey risking an eviction."

Bradley said, "Faulty logic, Jack. Joey's got a cell reserved in his name for the next twenty-five years, and he knows it."

Parker said, "It's possible he's been calling me. There've been messages on my machine."

"What kind of messages?" said Bradley.

"Heavy breathing."

"First Cherry phoned you – or at least you think he did. Now it's his brother. But neither one of them has anything to say."

Willows said, "If Cherry had her number, Joey could have got it off him."

"You better change your number," said Bradley. "If Joey really wants to get in touch, he can phone you here at work."

From her desk, Parker phoned Emily Chan's parents. Mrs Chan picked up, and Parker told her that there was an outstanding warrant on Joey Ngo, and that Joey was to be considered armed and dangerous.

"What shall I do if he comes here?" Mrs Chan sounded on the verge of panic. Parker had intended to warn, not terrify her.

"Don't open the door, or try to talk to him. Go to the phone and dial nine-one-one. Can you remember that?"

"Yes, yes."

Parker said, "We're going to try to keep a patrol car in the neighborhood at all times. But really, Mrs Chan, I just called to keep you informed. I don't think you need to worry about Joey. You have no reason to fear him and we don't expect he'll come anywhere near you."

"But what if he does?"

"Then use the telephone, and a policeman will be there in minutes. Do you understand?"

"Yes."

"Fine," said Parker. "If anything develops, we'll be sure to let you know. In the meantime, promise me you won't worry, all right?"

"Promise," said Mrs Chan faintly.

Parker added a few more words of reassurance, and hung up.

Willows checked his watch. Orwell and Spears had taken the first shift in the round-the-clock stakeout of Joey's house. Oikawa and Kearns were up next and he and Parker had the dawn patrol. The smart thing to do would be to drive home, throw something in the microwave, wash it down with a beer and hit the sack. He said, "Been a long time since we paid Freddy a visit."

"Think he's managed to stay in business without us?"

"We'll never know unless we take the time to go and find out."

"I'll meet you there," said Parker. "I don't want to have to come all the way back for my car. And I'm only staying for one drink, okay?"

"Yeah, sure."

"One drink," said Parker, "and one drink only. I mean it, Jack."

Willows said, "Look, if that's the way you feel about it – that you're being pushed – why don't we just forget the whole thing?"

Freddy sidled up to the booth wearing a pair of Nikes with bright orange laces and a fluorescent orange swoosh, baggy pink cotton pants patterned with baby-blue arrows, and a short-sleeved neon green silk shirt garnished with hula girls whose voluptuous and apparently naked bodies were strategically located behind clumps of lurid yellow and mauve flowers. Just in case there was any doubt, the word "Hawaii" was scripted across the shirt's pocket in fiery red letters.

"Nice *ensemble*," said Willows, shading his eyes with his hand.

Freddy said "It's the kind of outfit appeals to the ladies, Jack. Twenty years in a blue suit – what would you know about high fashion?" Smiling broadly, he turned to Parker. "Clothes make the man, right. So go ahead and admit it; I turn your crank, don't I?"

Parker made a production of edging across the seat to the far side of the booth, putting as much distance between herself and Freddy as possible.

The bartender sadly shook his head. "This is such a goddamn conservative town. Every minute's another punch in the face."

Parker said, "I'll tell you one thing, Freddy. If you're walking across the street and somebody hits you with a truck, at least you'll know why they did it."

"Hey, if you think I look good now, you shoulda seen me when I got off the plane. It's the tan that brings out the colors, makes 'em glow."

"What plane?" said Willows.

"The plane from Hawaii."

"You were in Hawaii?"

"How'd you guess? No, don't tell me. From the way you're dressed, you gotta be a highly trained detective."

"And you're a highly trained bartender, Freddy, if memory serves."

"Cutty Sark, right, on the rocks for the gentleman and the lady's straight up, water on the side. Doubles?"

Willows nodded. Simultaneously, Parker shook her head, no.

"Gotcha," said Freddy, and gave Parker an exaggerated wink.

Willows said, "Bring us a menu when you come back, Freddy."

"One menu," said Parker firmly.

"You don't like the food, izzat what you're telling me?"

Parker smiled. "The food is wonderful, it's the preparation that turns my stomach."

"Comical cops." Freddy sighed heavily, and started towards the bar. "I gotta tell you, there's nobody I'd rather pass time with, except my therapist."

There was a big color television suspended over the bar, an identical set half-way down the row of booths and a third facing the cluster of tables down by the rear of the building. All three sets were on the same channel; TSN, The Sports Network.

Parker said, "You ever bowl?"

"A few times. Once or twice."

"Ten pin?"

"Yeah, I think so." The last time had been several years ago, during Annie's birthday party – at Annie's request he and his wife, Sheila, had taken their daughter and several of her friends to a local alley. Willows had bowled a few frames, knocked over a few pins. It wasn't nearly as much fun as fishing for trout.

But then, at the time, he'd had no way of knowing that he, Annie and Sheila only had a few birthdays left together, that his wife would soon leave him, and take Annie and Sean with her.

Willows could feel himself slipping into a morbid frame of mind.

Freddy thumped his tray down on the table, eased into the booth beside Parker. "It's been a long time. Mind if I join you for a minute?"

"Tick, tick," said Parker.

Willows said, "Your round."

"Naturally, Jack." Freddy distributed the drinks, sipped at his Coke.

Willows said, "So what's the problem?"

"'Scuse me?"

Parker and Willows exchanged a look. Parker said, "Let's put it this way, Freddy – what's the problem?"

"No problem." Freddy snagged a chunk of ice, bit down hard. "Well, okay, I got a flea in my ear. But nothing worth bothering a couple of hot-shot homicide cops about, believe me."

Willows picked up his glass, held it to the light of a Budweiser sign. The glass looked clean, and the color of the Scotch was just about right. "Hit the punch line, Freddy."

Freddy demolished another ice cube. "Extortion, it's still a crime, right?"

Parker said, "What's the bite?"

"Three-fifty a week, but it just got bumped to five hundred."

"Anybody we know?"

"The guys I'm talking about, they're real nasty, and real serious. But experienced, they ain't. So I doubt it."

"How long've they been hitting on you?"

"This is the third week."

Willows said, "When's the next payment due?"

Freddy leaned across the table, peered at Willows' watch.

"It's twenty-past six, Freddy."

"They're due any time now. When you two waltzed in, I thought for sure that Sally'd dropped a dime. I mean, you ain't been around in months and then, bingo, there you are." Freddy's smile was so forced it looked as if he'd got all dressed up in someone else's teeth.

Parker said, "How many are there?"

"There's two of them, but somehow it always seems like a whole lot more. The top honcho's a little Italian guy. Tony. His muscle's a black dude. Calls himself Crow. I got no idea what his real name is either, except it ain't Bill Cosby. They come in here, help themselves to the booze, muss my hair and eat the pickled eggs . . ."

Willows said, "Can you describe them – aside from the fact that they're heavy eaters?"

Freddy savaged another ice cube. "Black guy's got a chrome-plated revolver long as my arm. Last week, after I paid his boss the three-fifty, know what he did?"

"What, Freddy?"

"Told me to open my mouth and close my eyes, and put a bullet in my mouth. The guy stuck a bullet in my mouth, Jack. Made me swallow it down. Is that a sick personality, or what?"

"They threaten you?"

"Yeah, you bet. Said if I messed with them, black dude'd stick his gun against my head and pull the trigger until there was nothin' left to shoot at."

"That's a threat, all right," said Parker.

Willows toyed with his Scotch. He glanced past Freddy towards the bar and then said, "Stay calm and follow my lead."

"Jack, I don't think I'm up for this."

Parker glanced up as the two hoods moved in. The Italian guy who called himself Dino looked a little like Al Pacino, but without Pacino's brains and good looks. There was another major difference, of course. Pacino was an extremely talented actor, and Dino was extremely bad.

The black, Crow, was about six-four, wide in the shoulders and narrow in the hip. No neck to speak of. He was wearing a black shirt and black jeans tucked into knee-high black leather boots reinforced with shiny metal shin plates and pointed toe-caps. His hair was cut short and a jagged picket fence of razor-cut lightning bolts marched around his bony skull just above ear level. His black silk shirt was loose-fitting and wasn't tucked into the jeans. Willows, studying his posture and the way he held his hands, decided the gun was hidden in the waistband of his pants.

Dino had a complexion like a bruised banana, smokey-green eyes. He wore a hi-style lightweight cotton suit and the kind of pointy black shoes favored by ballerinas. His long black hair was combed straight back and looked as if it had been trained with a frying pan. When he spoke, he sounded as if he started each day by gargling with a cup of warm olive oil.

"Tell your pals to beat it, Freddy."

Freddy said, "Scram, Jack."

Willows said, "Take a hike, sweetheart."

"Huh?" said Parker.

"*Now*, sugar!"

Parker cast her eyes demurely down and slid out of the booth. Until that moment, Freddy hadn't even noticed she was chewing gum.

Crow pointed at Willows. "You too, whitebread."

Willows leaned back in the booth. "My deal with Freddy is I gotta stick around until I've sweet-talked you two dummies into refunding his money."

Crow said, "Say whaaaat?"

Dino put both hands flat on the table and leaned over Freddy. "Five hundred bucks, that's how much you owe me. Pay up, or your customers are gonna wish they was wearing asbestos suits."

Willow said, "How fast are you, Crow?" He slipped his hand under his jacket and drew his .38. "Faster than a speeding bullet?"

Crow said, "Don't shoot, man. Nothing's happening. *Relax*."

Several hours later, Parker sighed, and massaged her aching hand. When she'd first thought of joining the force she had imagined all sorts of dangers, but writer's cramp hadn't been one of them. She glanced up from her desk, caught Willows' eye. "It's always the same, isn't it – the bust takes ten seconds and the paperwork lasts forever."

Willows nodded distractedly, went back to the task of chewing on his pen.

Dino Nathaniel McGuire and the black called Crow had been booked, fingerprinted, escorted across the alley to the remand center and tucked snug in their beds for the night. Except for Willows and Parker and Eddy Orwell, who'd wandered in half an hour or more ago, the squadroom was deserted.

Orwell had been working quietly at his desk, but now he suddenly said, "Got any paperclips, Jack?"

"Yeah, and I'm going to keep 'em."

"I'm all out, I just used my last one." Orwell held up the daisy chain he'd been making, turned it so the thin metal links caught the light. Willows had wondered what he'd been up to, to hold his attention for such a lengthy stretch of time. The links reached from Orwell's hand all the way to the carpeted floor. Dolefully, he said, "A chain to bind me, and tie me down."

Willows and Parker exchanged a quick glance. Parker said, "Have you been drinking, Eddy?"

"Had a few beers. I'm not *drunk*, I'm just, I don't know . . ." Orwell cast his eyes up to the ceiling and made a sort of pushing motion with his hands, as if he feared the building was about to collapse. "*Despondent* best describes the way I feel, I guess."

Willows smiled, and had to turn away.

"Isn't funny, Jack."

"You're right, Eddy. Nobody's arguing with you."

Parker said, "What's the problem?"

"Judith hates me."

"Don't be ridiculous."

"And she's gonna leave me."

"No, she isn't."

"If she hasn't already gone and done it."

Parker said, "How can you say that? I've seen some of the stuff she packs in your lunch. She's obviously crazy about you."

"Used to be, maybe. Once upon a time, a long, long time ago." Orwell wrapped the paperclip chain around and around his wrist. "She's pregnant. I told her I didn't want to be a daddy. Wasn't ready for it. And she, well, she took a swing at me and told me to get out and not come back."

Parker said, "Judith's *what*? Did you say pregnant?"

"The bunny seemed to think so."

Parker sank a little deeper in her chair. She said, "Maybe when you've both had time to think it over . . ."

Orwell's fist thumped down on his desk. "I've *been* thinking it over!" he shouted. "I've been doing nothing *but* think it over!"

Willows said, "Take it easy, Eddy. You'll wake up the janitor."

"She's so darn stubborn. Won't answer the phone. I've been calling all day. The machine's turned off. It rings and rings, and I hang up and I can still hear it ringing . . . I'm afraid something terrible has happened to her." Orwell studied the floor. "This feeling has been growing inside of me all day long. Tragedy. Something bad has happened to my wife, or is going to, and there's nothing I can do about it. It's like a premonition." He spread his arms wide. "I'm afraid to go home."

Willows said, "You still living in Port Moody?"

"Yeah."

To Parker, Willows said. "Can you clear the last of this for me?"

"No problem."

Willows snatched his jacket from the back of the chair. "Eddy. Let's hit the road."

"Jack, I can't ask you to drive me home. It'd take you at least an hour and a half, to get there and back."

"We'll take my car. You'll have to figure out a way to make it in to work in the morning."

"Dan Simpson lives about six blocks away. Danny'll give me a ride."

"C'mon, Eddy. Let's go."

"Maybe Judith and me'll work things out. A kid . . . I can handle it." He turned and waved goodbye to Parker, slapped Willows on the shoulder. "Funny how things work out, sometimes, isn't it?"

Hilarious, thought Willows. But maybe it wouldn't be quite so funny when Eddy found out that *he* was paying for the gas.

20

Newt liked his suite, which was no great surprise considering how much it was costing him – three hundred eighty smackers a day plus various provincial and federal taxes. He unpacked, hung up his clothes and yanked open oak-veneer drawers until he found the Gideon Bible, which he stuck in his suitcase, so he wouldn't forget it.

Rikki said, "What you want another of them things for?"

Newt smiled. "Bored, Rikki?"

"You betcha. What's happening man? Nothin'."

Newt said, "Watch a little TV, why doncha. Relax, you'll live longer." He picked up the phone, dialled a local number. Rikki picked up the TV guide, studied it, then grabbed the television's remote control and stabbed viciously at the buttons with the index fingers of his left and right hand. It looked to Newt as if Rikki was hitting the buttons simultaneously. His face was grim, upper teeth biting down hard on lower lip, eyes bulging just a little. Newt had to ask.

"What're you up to, Rikki?"

"Tryin' to tune in two stations at once. Cosby on five, Clint Eastwood on twelve. Really be something, check 'em both out at once."

"Right, right."

Newt listened to the phone. It was still ringing, and every ring sounded exactly the same. He was going to let it ring no more than dozen times before hanging up, but thanks to Rikki's bugbrained electronic tinkering, he had lost count. One of these days someone would invent a phone that kept track for you. It'd ring at the other end, but all the caller would hear were numbers. One, two, three . . . Newt wondered how many numbers the phone company would program into their equipment. He pictured kids going for a world record, getting into a million rings or more . . . Nah, they'd have to put a limit on it. A hundred rings, maybe. That oughtta be enough. Jeez, what in hell was he thinking about – he was loonier than Rikki, and with less excuse.

"Yeah, what?"

Startled, Newt jerked the phone away from his ear. He cleared his throat, identified himself. It had been a few years. The guy on the other end of the line, Slick was his name, on account he used so much Brylcreem on his hair, had to think about it for a long time before he recognized Newt's voice. And then he called Newt by his old name, 'Junior', which he'd stopped using the day daddy bought the farm. Slick was full of questions – where had Junior been the past couple of years, had he done some time, or what? Newt told him about the name change and got down to business. How much for an Uzi or Mac-10 or M16, basically any reliable automatic weapon that was available for immediate delivery, plus extra magazines and, say, five hundred rounds of ammunition.

A figure was named. Newt squeaked. The line went dead. Newt threw the phone at the wall and made a dent in the plaster. So much for old pals. He dialled the number again and said, "Yeah, okay. You deliver?" He listened quietly for what seemed to Rikki to be a very long time, then gently cradled the phone. He printed an address in large block letters on an embossed sheet of hotel stationery, gave the address and eleven hundred and eighty dollars to Rikki.

"What's this?"

"It's an address, what's it look like?"

"I don't know my way around this fokin' town. How'm I gonna get anywhere?"

"Remember the lobby, Rikki? No? Okay, remember the train, remember how much you liked the model choo-choo? That was the lobby, where you saw the train. Now, listen real careful. First you get in the elevator and push the button that's pointing at your feet. When you get to the lobby, go to the desk and ask for a road map of the city. Tell the guy where you want to go. Get him to point the address out on the map, draw some lines. Ask if one of 'em will go with you."

"Go with me to pick up some guns?"

"Canadians are real friendly, you'd be surprised how much they'll go outta their way for a stranger." Newt wound up like a major league pitcher about to deliver a 100-mph fireball, tossed Rikki the keys to the rental. "Just get the hell out of here." He made a brisk flapping motion with his arms. "*Vamanos.*"

"I know what you're saying to me, I unnerstand English real good."

Newt waited with rapidly growing impatience as Rikki crouched in front of the mirror, combed his hair, moved in close to check his teeth, made sure his zipper was up. Newt watched him drag his shoes sideways on the carpet to give them a better shine. It was the slammer that did it to you, took away any sense of urgency, time passing faster than it should, and leaving you behind.

When Rikki'd finally gone, Newt dialled room service and ordered a cheeseburger deluxe, glass of icewater. He hung up, left the room and prowled the halls until he found an ice machine. He'd forgotten to bring along the little plastic bucket, and was forced to carry the ice back to his room in his cupped hands. His suitcase held a fifth of Wild Turkey Kentucky bourbon. Newt poured himself a fat one and thought about how good it was going to feel to get the job done, head back to LA.

It was weird, how the caper had started. A couple of years ago he'd read about Frank in one of the Vancouver papers, given him a call and, more out of idle curiosity than anything else, offered him a job. Frank had turned out to be a real gem. He didn't over-indulge in drugs, kept his big hands off Newt's bimbos and out of Newt's cookie jar. What more could he ask, especially at the wages he paid?

Then, a few months ago, Newt had been unceremoniously ditched at the tailend of a long and frustrating night by a woman with big brown eyes and black hair – a rarity in LA where, at times, it seemed as if everyone had sky-blue eyes and tangled blonde hair and had been hatched out of the same vat. The woman had reminded Newt of Parker; set him off. He'd rambled on for hours about the Vancouver homicide dick and homicide jane who'd had such a negative impact on his life.

Settled comfortably into his bourbon and deck chair beneath the late-night stars, Newt reminisced about the evening, about five years ago, that he'd exchanged gunfire with Willows and Parker and caught a .38 special in the chest, had most of his hair burned off and got his Trans Am impounded. And how his daddy – bless his soul – had put up a quarter-million cash bail so Newt could skip if he needed to, and how a lawyer who cost a lot more and was therefore a lot smarter than the Crown Attorney had eventually got him off due to what the judge termed an unconstitutional delay in proceedings.

Towards the happy end of his tale, Newt decided more or less on the spur of the moment that it'd be nice to bump off Parker. Why he hadn't told Frank to knock off Willows while he was at it, he couldn't say. Probably because although both cops had been shooting at him, it was Parker's round that had put him down, caused him such agony and pain. In any case, the idea of hitting both cops at once simply hadn't entered his mind . . .

Until now. Nah, forget it. It'd be impossible to whack both of them and make it look like an accident. Even the cops weren't that dumb.

The burger arrived. Newt ate it at the table by the window, washing each bite down with a measured mouthful of bourbon and water. Robson Square, the open space down at the far end of the Law Courts, was lit up by zillions of tiny white lights that hung from the trees like the sparkly bloated corpses of so many dead fireflies. Newt chewed on his burger and drank his liquor, watched the cars roll slowly by, the funereal drift of people on the sidewalks. Vancouver was a weird town. Laid back, but very tense, with the highest crime rate of any major city in the country. Newt smiled at a parking meter. Maybe that was why he felt so much at home, because of all the robbery and murder.

He found himself thinking about Felix, his poor old dad, and the sprawling house he'd owned in West Van, on the far side of the harbour, high up the mountain in the British Properties. The house had a terrific view. You could see the whole city if you climbed up on the roof and stood on the chimney.

Newt scooped up some bits and pieces of fried onion that had fallen out of the burger. He licked his greasy fingers, leaned over and wiped them dry on the bedspread. His favorite thing about the house in the Properties was the heart-shaped swimming pool in the back yard, with its walls and bottom painted hot pink, the underwater lights. Because of a couple of moonlit skinny-dipping episodes he'd indulged in, and the inevitable complications that followed, Newt found himself remembering Misha, his dad's sly youngstuff sweetheart who'd done him wrong.

What was that sleek beauty up to now? Badness, no doubt. Offenses to the Criminal Code.

Newt overreached himself trying for the telephone, fell out of his chair. Sitting on the floor, he dialled room service and, slurring his words somewhat, asked if they could fix him a banana split. No problem. Was the whipping cream the real thing, or out of a pressurized can? His choice. Newt ordered the latter, and then, as an afterthought, tossed in a request for a double order of onion rings.

He'd sunk the split and the onion rings and the top half of the bottle by the time Rikki made it back home. His main Mex had a brand-new mouse under his left eye, fresh blood on his knuckles.

Rikki reached down deep into his pants pocket and gave Newt his money back.

Newt counted it slowly, but even so, kept losing track of the amount. He tossed the roll on the bed. "He did something stupid, didn't he?"

Rikki nodded, his slicked-back hair flashing like chrome under the lights.

"What happened, he tried to stiff you for a couple extra bucks?"

"Yeah, yeah. Like you say."

"But you're a macho guy, proud, and you refused to go along with it, so the dummy lost his temper and popped you one."

Rikki nodded, grinning.

"Took you by surprise, otherwise he'd never of laid a finger on you."

"Almos' broke my nose. I seen flashing stars, all colors."

"Blue, red, green . . ."

"And yellow," said Rikki, smiling. "There was lots of yellow."

"So then what happened?"

"What's the guy's name?"

"Slick."

"Yeah, Slick. Slick don't have no guns. The house I meet him at? He don't live there. Know what he tried to do? Mug me, steal the money. Whadda creep."

"So what happened?"

"I cut his friend up quite a bit. Slick scrambles away but not too far. I cut him up too, pretty good."

Newt said, "So we still need some guns."

"Don't worry about it. I'm thirsty, let's go down to the bar and get a drink."

Newt said, "Cheaper to buy a bottle at a liquor store, drink in the room."

Rikki, already heading for the door, totally ignored him, which came as a shock. Newt reached out to grab the stupid little greencard bastard by the scruff of the neck so he could pound some sense into him, then thought better of it. Frank and his bimbo wouldn't be drinking in *their* room, no, they'd be yukking it up at the piano bar, enjoying the good life at Newt's expense.

They took the elevator down to the bar, and there they were, those two lovebirds, sitting right where Newt knew they'd be. It was as if he had some strange power over them, that made them materialize exactly where he imagined them to be.

Newt stared at the back of Frank's head as he strode briskly across the ornately patterned carpet towards the bar, concentrating on sending out such venomous vibes that Frank couldn't help but pick up on them. With each step he took, Newt anticipated Frank turning towards him, his eyes wide with shock, whimpering pitifully as he realized what deep shit he was in.

But Frank was having too much fun; or Newt's psychic powers weren't up to scratch. And when Frank finally did notice Newt and Rikki standing beside him, his reaction was to beam hugely up at them, happy as a clam.

"Newt, what a pleasure! I was just telling Lulu all about you."

"Yeah?" Newt stuck his hands in his pants pockets, tried to lean against the piano but grossly miscalculated the distance. Losing his balance, he staggered against the piano player, who cursed into the microphone, fended him off with one hand and improvised with the other. The sharp edge of the baby grand caught him in the ribs and knocked the wind out of him. Anguished, he sank to his knees.

Lulu said, "Nice to meet you, Newt." The mini-guy with Newt was so darkly tanned he made Richard Prior look anaemic. He was wearing a mustard-colored suit and the biggest belt buckle she had ever seen, a huge carved slab of silver. "You must be Rikki, right?"

"You heard about me?"

"Saw your picture."

Rikki frowned. Was amazing, how many people thought because you from Los Angeles, you was in the biz.

"At the post office," Lulu explained.

Rikki glared at Frank. Frank said, "It's a joke."

"Yeah?" Rikki helped Newt to his feet, stared at Lulu as he whispered something in Newt's ear. He tried to sneak a look down Lulu's neckline. She gave him a friendly smile.

Frank made a show of examining his watch. A gold Rolex, Newt couldn't help but notice. Jeez, if Frank'd used his charge card to buy it, he'd kill him. Frank, still studying the watch, said, "You're out pretty late, for a couple of guys from California. Stayed out of trouble, I hope."

Newt eased on to the stool next to Lulu. He'd never seen such pale skin. He said, "We been cruising around, admiring the town, how clean the streets are."

Lulu said, "How'd you get the cut, Rikki – staring too hard into a mirror?"

The bartender arrived with a fresh B-52 for Lulu and another double Glenfiddich straight up for Frank.

Newt saw that Frank and the bimbo were running up a tab. Was the bimbo gonna pay? Newt didn't think so. The bartender waited. Newt ordered a glass of icewater, Rikki a beer. The bartender went away. Newt rested a clammy hand casually on Lulu's naked shoulder, leaned across her to speak to Frank. The cash register needed a new ribbon, but from where he was sitting, it looked as if the bill was $111.48. Newt felt a high-pressure ridge bearing swiftly down on his cortex. His water arrived, and he rolled the cold glass across his burning forehead.

It had to be *his* money that was being guzzled down – Frank didn't have that much of his own.

Frank said, "So, when'd you get in, Newt?"

"Earlier."

"Have a good flight?"

"What's to enjoy? Know what an airplane is, Frank? An elevator with wings." Newt gave Lulu's creamy white shoulder a squeeze. "So who was your last date; Bela Lugosi?"

"Excuse me?"

"You're so pale," said Newt. "Or didn't you notice?"

"I'm an albino."

Rikki stared at her.

Newt said, "Know how to make a blonde's eyes gleam? Shine a flashlight in her ear."

Frank started to turn towards him.

Lulu said, "Look, I'd really appreciate it if you took your hand off my shoulder."

"And put it exactly where, honey-pie?"

Lulu said, "So far up your ass you have to open your mouth to wave goodbye, sport."

Rikki made a cheerful gurgling sound, wiped beer from his chin.

Newt suddenly took an interest in the piano. After a few minutes of snapping his fingers out of time with the music, he said, "Tough chick, Frank. But can she cook?"

But it was much too little and far too late, and he knew it, and so did they all. Newt sipped moodily at his glass of water.

Frank became aware of someone testing the limits of his peripheral vision. He looked up. Roger. He waved, and Roger went away.

A few minutes later, Phil Estrada showed up, gliding so smoothly across the carpet towards them that Frank glanced quickly at Estrada's feet to make sure he wasn't wearing roller skates.

Rikki gave the security man a quick, fierce look that ran from Estrada's shiny black shoes all the way to the soft flesh beneath his chin. The way Rikki took in Estrada reminded Frank of the way he'd seen a guy on the Santa Monica pier gut a fish, very fast and all at once. Phil didn't seem to mind. He smiled at Lulu with every tooth in this mouth, then turned to Frank and said, "Going to introduce me to your new pals?"

Before Frank had time to react, Rikki said, "Time to call it a night, huh?"

Newt nodded his agreement. He finished his icewater, pointed at Frank and said, "My suite, tomorrow morning at ten sharp. Be there or be square."

Frank nodded.

Phil Estrada smiled at Newt. His teeth looked as if they'd just been bleached and sharpened. He said, "You gentlemen staying at the hotel?"

Rikki drank the last of his beer and put the empty glass down on the baby grand's keyboard. The piano player glanced up at him. Rikki said, "Know something, man? You play like my dog sings."

"He need an agent?" said the musician, not missing a beat. Phil Estrada chuckled softly and patted him on the shoulder and wandered off.

Lulu waited until she was sure Newt and Rikki and Phil were absolutely and positively beyond earshot, then turned to Frank and said, "Why didn't you *do* something?"

"Like what?"

"Oh, I don't know. How does 'kill them both' sound for starters?"

"Take a look around. What d'you see? A bartender, piano player, that guy over there with the beard, Phil, those two lovebirds holding hands in the corner table . . ."

"Fiftieth anniversary," said Lulu, "aren't they sweet."

"Rog probably hiding behind one of the potted plants. *Witnesses*. I blew away Newt and Rikki, even though they clearly deserved it, any one of those people could point me out in court, testify, and drop me in the slammer for the next quarter-century. That movie, *Alien.* You ever see it? By the time I got out, it'd be like *Stagecoach.*"

Lulu smiled. "That's who you remind me of, John Wayne."

"Forget it. He was a good guy. I'm a bad guy."

"Not from my point of view. And besides, people change, Frank."

"That's right. They get older, and less optimistic." Frank knocked back the rest of his Scotch, signalled for another. "Slower, too. I wouldn't stand a chance against those guys, not the two of them."

"Aren't you forgetting something?"

"What?"

Lulu pointed at herself. "Me."

Frank's eyes were dark, full of sorrow.

Lulu took his hand in hers, kissed the knuckles one by one. "What're we going to do?"

"Survive," said Frank. "I think probably that's the main thing we oughtta work on right now – surviving."

"You're saying we should make a run for it?"

Frank said, "I don't like this. I don't like any of it. Rikki – nobody'd miss him. And Newt, he ain't never gonna be in line for the Nobel Prize. But at the same time, I worked for the guy a couple, almost three years. His checks never bounced. Christmas, he'd pay for a trip to Palm Springs, we'd eat turkey and play golf all weekend, it never cost me a dime."

"Sure, and what'd you do for him?"

"That's just it – almost nothing. Laughed at his dumb jokes. Chased away the door-to-door aluminum siding guys. Drove him wherever he wanted to go. Broke a few arms."

"You ever kill anybody?"

"No of course not."

Lulu turned to the piano player, who seemed twice as big as he'd been a couple of minutes ago. "We're trying to have a private conversation, just the two of us. Go slide down to the other end of the bench, if you don't mind – and play a little louder." To Frank she said, "Is this how it worked – you did the light stuff and Rikki was the heavy?"

"More or less."

"So why'd Newt send you to Vancouver to kill a cop?"

Frank said, "Like I tried to explain already, Parker shot him a few years back, and he had this crazy idea of getting even, taking her down. And he figured I wouldn't mind doing the job, because I'd been shot too, and knew what it felt like."

"Painful."
"Yeah."
"But Parker didn't shoot you, did she?"
"No, but she'd rousted me, had been on my case."
"Doing her job, that's all."
"I know, I know."
"What's her first name?"
Frank hesitated, then said, "Claire."
"How could you shoot somebody with such a pretty name, Frank?"
Frank hung his head in shame. "I dunno."
"When Newt asked you, did you act like you wanted to do it?"
"Not really. In fact I said I'd just as soon take a pass."
"Then why didn't Newt send Rikki? He *likes* killing people, from what I saw."
"You got that right."
"Well then?"
Frank mulled it over. He really hadn't thought about it. "Maybe Rikki pushed him into it, sending me. Me and Rikki don't get along too good."
"Why's that?"
"I couldn't say. Rikki's pretty crazy about himself, if you know what I mean. The guy shaves three or four times a day, is always cleaning his fingernails, combing his hair. He carries a toothbrush with him everywhere he goes, I've even seen him use it at the table, between courses."
"He's a vain person, is what you're saying."
"In spades. But here comes the funny part. Suppose we're out at a nightclub or restaurant, or maybe some dopester's birthday party . . ." Frank trailed off, not sure how to put it. He tossed Newt's credit card – the card had Frank's name printed on it but because Newt was the principal cardholder he was responsible for all the bills – down on the bar.
Lulu said, "I know what you're going to say – that the girls trample Rikki on their way to good old Frank." She smiled into his eyes, ran her fingers through his hair. "You know why that is, don't you? It's because women can tell that you're all man, and Rikki's nothing but a lowlife bantam-weight slimeball creepoid slug."
"You kind of like me, is that it?"
Lulu trailed her fingers lightly over his thigh. "Is this a room key in your pocket, or are you glad to see me?"
The bartender scooped up Frank's card, drifted away and idled

back moments later. Frank tipped a fat twenty per cent and signed with a flourish.

Lulu tugged at his arm. He followed her across the lobby, into a waiting elevator, up to their room. He was tipsy, but not drunk, and believed there was no immediate need to worry about Rikki or Newt. They'd leave him alone until Parker had been killed.

He slipped the key into the lock and pushed open the door. The room was dark, quiet. Lulu pulled him on to the bed, switched on the bedside lamp with it's ten-watt bulb and sexy pink shade and there was Rikki, inches away from them, smirking like a fiend.

21

At five o'clock in the morning the street was quiet except for the despondent gargling of a solitary unseen crow, and the muted drone of detective Dan Oikawa's electric razor.

Oikawa spotted Willows in the rear-view mirror as the unmarked Ford pulled in behind his beige chevy. He raised his hand in greeting.

Willows turned off the engine, and he and Parker got out of the car. Oikawa switched off his razor and put it in his jacket pocket, gratefully accepted the coffee and greasy bag of donuts Parker handed him.

"Breakfast, great." He pried the lid off the coffee. "Got any cream?"

"In the bag."

"Perfect, perfect."

Willows leaned against the car. There was a rumpled sleeping bag in the back seat, a battery-powered travel alarm clock on the ledge beneath the rear window. He said, "Where's Ralph?"

Oikawa dumped a plastic container of cream into his coffee, put the lid back on and shook the cup, removed the lid and tossed it on the floor of the car. "He ran off in a huff when I refused to share my toothbrush." Oikawa blew on the coffee, sipped gingerly. "Nah, the truth is, he had to take a leak."

Willows nodded. "Any action, so far?"

"Not until the donuts showed up. Morning paperboy's about due. I suppose that's something to look forward to." Oikawa probed the bag. "Get any cinnamon?"

Parker said, "There's two each of cinnamon, plain, and chocolate. You owe me three-fifty."

"That include the coffee?"

Parker nodded.

Oikawa said, "Catch you later, payday's on Wednesday, right?"

The crow started up again. Parker scanned the area, located it in a mature apple tree in the back yard of the property adjacent to Joey Ngo's rented house.

Oikawa fished a cinnamon donut out of the bag, bit into it, chewed and swallowed, drank some coffee. "It started up about half an hour ago, crack of dawn." He took another bite out of the donut, a bigger one this time. "I was sitting in the car, trying to keep my eyes open. The sky started to lighten, fade to blue. Then I saw this streak of pink, very thin, appear just above the horizon. Like someone had opened a door just wide enough to peek outside. There it was – *the crack of dawn.* I never realized what the expression meant; always thought it was supposed to be noisy – sort of like a gunshot."

Oikawa ate another donut and wiped his fingers on a paper napkin. "I took a hike down the alley, to try to find out what the damn crow was yelling at. You wouldn't believe the size of the lady's underwear hanging on the line in the back yard. Maybe that's what the damn bird's so excited about."

Willows looked up as the front door of the rancher across the street from Joey Ngo's house swung open. A plump redhead in a pink nightgown glanced quickly up and down the street. An early riser, thought Willows, eager for her morning paper.

Then Ralph Kearns stepped on to the porch, finished tucking in his shirt, gave her a quick kiss and trotted diagonally across the sun-bleached slope of the lawn towards the sidewalk.

Willows said, "How long has he been in there, Dan?"

"Beats me, Jack. Timing him ain't part of my job description."

Kearns grin faded as he noticed Willows and Parker watching him. His stride faltered, and he glanced back over his shoulder, as if hoping to survey the scene on the porch from Willows' perspective.

Oikawa dipped in the bag for a third donut, and then remembered there'd only been two cinnamon and that he'd already eaten them both. Chocolate or plain? He mulled it over, but only for a moment.

Kearns spotted the bag of donuts. Was he smiling cheerfully, or smirking lasciviously? Parker couldn't make up her mind.

Kearns lit a cigarette. "You guys are here a little early, aren't you?"

"Looks that way," said Willows.

Kearns suddenly became very serious. "Now hold on, Jack. I know what you're thinking, and you're wrong."

"What am I thinking, Ralph?"

"That Barbara – Mrs Hinton – looked like pretty hot stuff, wearing that nightgown, showing all that leg."

"No, that wasn't what I was thinking at all."

Kearns glanced at Parker, back to Willows. "Lemme tell you what really happened."

All that sugar was giving Oikawa a powerful thirst. He popped the lid off the second cup of coffee. It was still hot. He added cream and went through his ritual of putting the lid back on and shaking the cup. There were three donuts left; two plain and a chocolate. He stole a quick, furtive look at Kearns. The guy had been up all night, probably he was exhausted, and a blast of sugar was exactly what he needed. But Kearns seemed a lot more interested in explaining the situation to Willows and Parker than grabbing breakfast.

Oikawa snatched the last chocolate donut out of the bag.

Kearns said, "There's one of those plastic milk jugs on the floor in the back of the car, full to the brim with four litres of cop piss. A little while ago, just before you showed up, I had to go again, couldn't hold it another minute. Stakeout or not, my bladder was killing me, know what I mean?"

Willows said, "Yeah, I think I get the picture." He glanced at Parker. "Claire, are you managing to follow along?"

Parker nodded, continued to watch the street.

Kearns said, "So I take a hike up the alley, and I'm waddling like a duck. Another minute and I'm gonna wet my pants. And guess what – there's no place private to take a leak! All the garages are locked, there's no bushes to hide behind . . . Then I see Mrs Hinton, she's in the back yard, filling her bird feeder. And naturally she's a little worried about this strange guy prowling around at five o'clock in the morning . . . So I flash my badge, explain the situation. And because she's a good citizen, ready and willing to do her civic duty, she lets me use the can."

Willows said, "Don't you think you should've tucked in your shirt before you left the house?"

"Jack, I see your point, but I was in a hurry to get back to the stakeout. Danny was all alone in the car. I was *worried* about him. This kid we're after, Joey Ngo, he's killed a couple of people, right? So naturally the only thing on my mind is my partner's safety. Come *on*, Jack. Everybody has to use the toilet, it's a natural human function. I've heard of guys who've *died* because they tried to hold it too long . . ."

On the far side of the street, high up in the apple tree, the crow guffawed loudly.

Parker, her back to Ralph Kearns, smiled widely.

Oikawa finished his second cup of coffee. He caught Parker's smile and misinterpreted it. Wiping a few last granules of sugar from his mouth, he said, "A four-donut breakfast. Maybe I'm pushing forty, but I still got a few good moves."

Parker said, "I never doubted it."

Oikawa adjusted his belt, letting it out a notch.

The sun was low on the horizon, smearing the flawless blue sky with streaks of yellow and orange. The door to the blue rancher opened and the red-haired woman came out. She was wearing lime-green shorts and a matching tank top. She made her way to the far side of the house, turned on a tap and filled a green plastic can with water. Oikawa fumbled in his shirt pocket for his glasses.

Willows walked around to the far side of Oikawa's unmarked car, reached through the open window and tapped the detective on the shoulder. Oikawa jerked upright, clutched at the steering wheel, gave Willows a sheepish look.

Willows said, "All that coffee, your bladder must be pretty full too, by now."

"Well . . ."

Willows said, "Why don't you take a stroll over there and ask the nice lady if you can use her facilities?"

"C'mon, Jack. Be reasonable. I ask to use the can, she's gonna slap my face. Or worse."

"How long was he in there?"

Oikawa shrugged, stared out the windshield. "You're gonna have to squeeze that out of him. But why bother? Nothing happened, nobody got hurt."

Willows said, "If we're right about Joey Ngo, he's already killed two people. You better straighten Kearns out or get yourself a new partner. Nobody's luck lasts forever. When he goes down, chances are good he'll take you with him."

"Yeah, well . . ."

The car rocked as Kearns opened the far side door and settled himself in the passenger seat. He fastened his safety belt. "Let's roll, partner."

Oikawa started the car. Willows stepped back. It was just past six and the sun was still low in the sky, but the city was starting to come alive, the dull throb of traffic drifting down to them from 41st Avenue, the closest main artery.

Oikawa put the Chevy in gear. He took his foot off the brake and the car began to creep forward.

Willows said, "Think about it, Dan."

Oikawa punched it. The Chevy bolted down the street.

The redhead went back into her house and shut the door.

Willows and Parker climbed back into their unmarked Ford. Willows backed the car fifty feet up the street, into the shade of a chestnut tree. The sightlines were still pretty good. He turned off the engine, reached behind him and rolled down the rear side window. It was starting to get hot – by the end of the day the temperature would hit the mid-eighties.

Parker said, "He'd been drinking, hadn't he?"

"He might've had one or two."

"Dan won't turn him in?"

"Would you?"

Parker said, "No, I guess not. But I'd get rid of him, find myself a new partner, and do it fast."

Willows adjusted the rear-view mirror so he had a better view of the street behind them. The crow had been silent but now it started up again.

Parker said, "I got another one of those phone calls last night. The heavy breather."

"Get your number changed."

"There's a new system – call alert – it's about twelve bucks a month. Every time you get a call, the number's displayed on a small screen. No more anonymity."

"But lots of crowded phone booths," said Willows. He heard the sound of tires on pavement, twisted in his seat.

Oikawa's beige Chevy pulled up alongside the unmarked Ford. Kearns, grinning, jerked his thumb over his shoulder. A skinny Chinese kid about fifteen years old was slumped in the back seat. Kearns said, "We caught him in the alley, coming out of a garage." He flicked the stub of his cigarette out the window, across the hood of Willows' car. "It's all over, Jack. Except for the congratulations."

"Congratulations, Ralph." Willows raised his voice a little. "Hey, Dan."

Oikawa leaned forward so he could see past Kearns. "What?"

"On your way downtown, do yourself a favor and stop off at a lumberyard."

"Why?"

"So you can buy a stick to hit yourself over the head with."

Oikawa's face tightened. He slammed his foot down on the gas and the car shot down the street.

Parker said, "Who the hell was that?"

"Beats me."

"Kearns thinks he's nabbed Joey Ngo, doesn't he?"

Willows smiled.

Parker said, "Think Dan got the message?"

"We'll hear about it soon enough, if he didn't."

A trio of crows warily circled the apple tree. The birds drifted slowly down, their wings flaring as they sideslipped into the topmost branches and settled cautiously into the foliage like so many elderly, overweight, black-clad Victorian dowagers easing into a particularly uncomfortable chair.

"Breakfast time," said Parker.

"Maybe." He'd caught a crow once, when he was a teenager, with a simple trap made of a baited box with one end resting on the ground and the other held up with a stick tied to a length of twine. Captured, the bird made a horrible squalling sound that tricked him into thinking he'd mortally wounded it. He would never forget the swarm of crows that had descended upon the scene from every point of the compass, and screamed at him until he freed their comrade. It was like the Hitchcock film, *The Birds*, but much more terrifying.

The crows in the tree were making a similar sound now, an urgent, high-pitched squawking. Another larger flight of crows flew in from the east, out of the rising sun, and vanished into the tree. The air, suddenly, was heavy with the rustle of wings as a flock passed directly overhead.

Willows grabbed his walkie-talkie.

Parker said, "You going to take a look?"

"It was a lot darker when Dan was over there. He couldn't have seen much, even with a flashlight."

Parker checked the battery light on her walkie. "Stay in touch, Jack."

Willows got out of the car and walked across the road, disappeared in the narrow gap between Joey Ngo's house and his next-door neighbors'. Parker checked her watch. She'd learned long ago that in situations like this minutes often stretched into hours and, that under certain circumstances, a few seconds could last forever.

As he crossed the street, Willows clipped his shield to his jacket pocket. The grass between the houses was still heavy with dew, the moisture darkening the leather of his brogues. He saw that the houses were separated at the back by a low, sagging, picket fence. Climbing over the fence was impossible; the boards looked rotten and he was sure they'd collapse under his weight. He pulled at one of the pickets. Wood crumbled under his fingers. The picket came away in his hands. He yanked two more pickets from the fence, crouched low and crawled through the gap.

Now he was in the back yard of the home next to Joey Ngo's house, the yard with the apple tree. A narrow sidewalk ran down the middle of the yard, from the lane to the house. There was an open carport on the right. A sagging clothesline led from the house's enclosed back porch to a tall wooden pole. Oikawa hadn't exaggerated when he'd described the size of the undergarments hanging from the line. You could, Willows thought, sail a boat.

The apple tree was near the back of the yard, its wide, heavily leaved branches overhanging the roof of the carport and spreading out over the lane. The tree was more than thirty feet high. Its gnarled trunk was thick and rough, drifted with amber sap. Willows could hear the crows muttering, the scrabble of their claws as they shifted restlessly in the topmost branches.

He had expected that they would abandon the tree by now. But it was the tallest tree on the block. Maybe it was an habitual gathering place and that was why the birds were so reluctant to leave. Or perhaps there was another reason. Most of the crop seemed to have been picked. He peered upwards, squinting against the glint of the rising sun into the dark green foliage.

He turned and looked behind him, at the house. He was unobserved. He turned back to the tree. The branch which looked most promising was about five feet up and was thick enough to carry his weight easily. He slipped out of his jacket and hung it on the fence. His brogues hadn't been designed for tree climbing. He would have to go carefully, or risk a nasty fall.

He grasped the branch with both hands, bent his knees to give himself a little more spring, and then pulled himself up, hooked a leg over the branch and desperately clutched at another, higher branch. High above him there was a shriek of alarm. Unseen wings beat at the air and made it tremble. A few leaves and bits of twig drifted down. Willows caught a glimpse of the flock racing away from him, flying due south, and then they were gone, and he was alone in the tree.

Almost alone.

Willows worked his way up the tree until he was about twenty feet above the ground. He could see the glint of his badge – he'd forgotten to remove it from his jacket.

Joey Ngo had climbed a little higher, but not much, before straddling a fork in the main trunk. The rope went around and around his waist and there was a lot of it to spare. It looked as though he'd intended to hang himself, and thought better of it.

Joey was wearing black jeans, a white shirt, Adidas running shoes. No socks, no belt. He'd shot himself in the chest. The wound had bled hardly at all, indicating that he had died very quickly. Judging from the angle of the exit wound, there was a good chance the bullet had passed through his heart.

He'd been a handsome boy, and had wanted to spare his face. The crows, of course, had their own ambitions.

Joey's left hand hung straight down by his side. His right hand was in his lap, and still held the pistol – a .45-calibre Colt semi-auto. The hammer was cocked.

Chunks of dark brown pulp stained the white shirt in the immediate vicinity of the wound. Willows shifted his position, carefully circled the body. He was fairly sure the bullet had passed through Joey's left hand. Chunks of dried pulp clung to the palm of the hand.

Sweet potato.

Willows had seen enough – more than enough. He climbed back down the tree, braced himself, and dropped the last five feet. He retrieved his jacket, put the badge back in his wallet. A spent .45 casing lay among a patch of bluebells hard up against the carport.

Willows retrieved his jacket and made his way back through the gap in the fence. Parker watched him from the car as he strolled across the street.

She said, "He was up in the tree, wasn't he?"

Willows nodded. She reached for the radio to call it in. Evidence technicians, a photographer and medical examiner, uniformed cops and assorted brass as well as the body removal services people would soon be swarming around the apple tree. The neighborhood was peaceful now, but it wouldn't last.

"How did he do it?"

"Shot himself," said Willows. His cop's training warned against taking anything for granted, making even the most insignificant assumption. But cop instinct told him it was all over. Joey Ngo had fallen in love with his brother's girlfriend, Emily, tried to frighten or maybe even kill Cherry because he beat her, and muffed the job in the worst possible way. Then he'd bought a sweet potato to use as a silencer and shot his brother to death. And now he'd killed himself. Fair enough.

Except, if you thought about it for a minute, it didn't work. Cherry stole the sweet potato, not Joey – Mrs Minotti had ID'd him. Probably Cherry had intended to use the potato as a silencer when he found out who'd killed Emily; not that he cared about her – he'd be worried that the shots were meant for him. He showed his gun to Joey, planned to give him a demonstration. Maybe he'd even suspected Joey of Emily's murder, put the question to him. There'd been a struggle . . . Willows gave up. He'd never know what happened. It was as simple as that.

Parker radioed in the call. She climbed out of the car and locked it, went around to the back and unlocked the trunk. The first thing that had to be done was isolate the crime scene.

Willows said, "I'll get that," and reached past her and grabbed a spool of bright yellow plastic "police line – do not cross' ribbon. How long it would last depended on the boldness of the neighborhood's children. Not that you could always blame the kids. Willows had seen adults walk off with the stuff. What they did with it, he had no idea.

Parker slammed shut the trunk.

Willows said, "Would you mind waking whoever lives in the house. I don't want them looking out the kitchen window without knowing what to expect."

"You going to string the ribbon?"

Willows nodded.

Parker said, "Why don't I string the ribbon, and you can have the pleasure of breaking the good news – there's a corpse in your apple tree, but don't *worry*. We'll take it away as soon as we finish trampling your garden."

Willows started across the street, leaving Parker no option but to tag along. Over his shoulder, he said, "My great big feet have already stomped all over the crime scene. Yours haven't."

"Since you put it so nicely." Parker split away, towards the house.

Willows had just finished stringing the ribbon when the back door of the house swung open and Parker stepped outside, steaming cup in hand. Coffee. He could smell it.

Parker lifted the mug in ironic salute. An elderly woman wearing a blue and green floral-pattern blouse and faded denim overalls appeared in the narrow space between Parker and the doorframe. The woman was huge, with a wild mass of white hair and bright blue eyes. She said something to Parker and then waved at Willows. He waved back. Parker started down the stairs, the woman close behind.

"Jack, this is Miss Eloise Simpson."

Willows said hello, switching the roll of tape to his left hand so he could shake. Eloise Simpson's hand was calloused, her grip firm. She smiled at Willows with the finest teeth that money can buy, and said, "Claire tells me you have a lovely garden but it's being neglected. I think that's terribly sad. Nature can't be trusted. You must keep a watch on her, or she'll go completely out of control, like an unattended child."

Parker said, "Miss Simpson saw Joey climb into the tree."

"Call me Eloise, please."

Willows said, "When did you see him, Eloise?"

"About nine o'clock, just as it was starting to get dark."

"Nine last night?"

"Yes, of course."

"Did you say anything to him?"

"I didn't see the point. Why make a fuss? If the birds don't get them, the children will. That's been my philosophy all along, and I intend to stick with it."

Willows caught Parker's eye. She gave him a look he'd never decipher in a million years, and hid behind her coffee cup.

Willows said, "You thought Joey was climbing into the tree to steal some apples?"

"What other reason could he have had?"

"My partner didn't tell you?"

"I thought I'd leave it up to you, Jack."

Willows felt a flash of anger, resentment. He and Parker had been together a long time now, but every time he thought he was beginning to understand how her mind worked . . . The spasm of anger passed. Yeah, they'd been together a long time. Too long for Parker, maybe. The job had a way of wearing people out; it exhausted them physically and emotionally. Some cops dealt with the problem by growing a shell so thick that nothing could get through it. Willows believed that to some extent it was an inevitable reaction. There was nothing you could do about it. The job gnawed away at your soul, and you grew scar tissue. Every cop knew it, and every cop – or at least every *good* cop – secretly wondered how much the job had changed him, what he'd lost. Up there in the apple tree, with childhood memories of other trees drifting towards him on the sweet morning breeze, Willows had protected himself by focusing on the bits and pieces instead of the whole ball of wax – the human being that had been Joey Ngo. It was a reflex action. He always fought it. But it was tough, sometimes.

The eyes, they said, were the windows of the soul.

Tell it to the crows.

Willows took Eloise Simpson gently by the arm. "Is there any more coffee?"

"Why, yes. Would you like a cup?"

"Please," said Willows, guiding her back inside. She was barely five feet tall, but had excellent posture. He'd never seen such brilliant blue eyes. He held the screen door open for her. She smiled warmly up at him, and despite the circumstances, he was charmed. Eloise Simpson's house was brown stucco with green trim. It should have been made of gingerbread studded with a rainbow of candies, smothered in frosting white as her hair.

22

Lulu couldn't believe the way Frank was acting. Talk about *morose*. Like he'd just found out his new zip code was located in the Valley of the Doomed. Her wonderful guy. Hard as a sidewalk. Tough as nails. And just look at him now.

It was ten o'clock in the morning. They'd been up since seven. During those three hours Frank had hardly spoken a word to her. She was hungry, on the verge of crankiness, but he refused to let her leave the room or even pick up the phone and call room service.

Because Newt might call, summoning them to breakfast, and he didn't want his boss frustrated by a busy signal.

Frank, watching her, knowing exactly what she was thinking and not blaming her one little bit, said, "Why don't you see if there's something on TV?"

"Because there isn't, that's why. There never is, and everybody knows it."

"I thought you kind of liked Merv."

"I hate Merv."

"What about Geraldo?"

"The guy can't even pronounce his own name." She brightened. "I like the way he does his hair, though. And hasn't he got a wonderful sense of humor?"

Frank lit a cigarette. It tasted terrible. He'd never been one of those guys who smoked before breakfast. Plus he'd been trying to cut down, so he'd live longer. Now wasn't *that* a good one?

Lulu wandered around the room, picking things up and putting them down. The air was hot and stuffy. She'd turned the air-conditioner off because something had gone wrong with the fan and the noise bothered her, and now she wanted Frank to open a window but couldn't bring herself to ask. What if he was so petrified of Newt and his scumbug buddy that he couldn't move? What if he tried to open the window and didn't have the strength? Lulu felt utterly betrayed by this new turn of events. Since their late-night meeting with Newt and Rikki, the *ooze* twins, her lover had been a stranger to her, silent, brooding, ineffectual. He'd been the pillar she had finally decided to lean on, and now it seemed he could hardly hold himself up, never mind her.

All that training, and she'd bet on the wrong horse!

She went over to the window and looked down. Under the spotlight glare of the sun, the streets and buildings were black and white, monochromatic. Even the cars and pedestrians struggling for control of the intersections seemed to have had all the color bleached out of them.

She tried to unlock the double-glazed hotel window and chipped a nail. Brother! Just when it seemed that things couldn't get worse . . . Behind her, the bed creaked. Then Frank was standing beside her, kissing her wounded finger with a simple tenderness that made her shiver all over. Effortlessly, he pushed open the window.

Lulu said, "We're going to have to kill them, Frank. Newt and Rikki. Both of them."

"In alphabetical order, or what?"

"If we don't do it to them, they're going to do it to us. Did you see the way the little creep stared at me?"

Frank nodded.

She said, "I'm not just talking about Rikki. I mean *both* of them."

"I know what you mean, honey."

"Then you damn well know what those filthy, perverted little sewer-brains were thinking about, don't you!"

"Like you were something sizzling on a barbecue, that they couldn't wait to slap down on a plate and dig into," said Frank.

Lulu gave Frank an over-the-shoulder look. "So tell me, what're you going to do about it?"

Frank waited until a guy in a black three-piece suit was clear and then flipped his cigarette out the window. Amazing, the way he'd mellowed during the past few days. He said, "That's what I've been trying to figure out; how to handle the situation."

"Rikki terrifies me. He makes Charlie Manson look like Mr Rogers."

Frank smiled.

Lulu put her arms around him, got up on her tippy-toes and kissed him in the hollow of his throat. "That little worm wants me real bad. You better believe he'll do anything to get me, too." She leaned away from Frank and ran her fingers through his hair as she stared deeply into his eyes. "I'm not being manipulative, Frank. You saw the way he looked at me. We both know exactly what it means."

Frank lit another cigarette, pulled the smoke down deep and squeezed it with his lungs.

Lulu said, "I'd kill him myself, but he might be a bit too much for me, my first time out." She grinned mischievously, struck by a sudden thought. "You made a mistake when you wouldn't let me waste that Metrotown jewelry store clerk. I could've used the practice."

Frank said, "I wish you wouldn't talk like that."

"Why not? I thought you liked it."

"I do, kind of. It's exciting, because you look like such an angel, all sweetness and light, and then you open your mouth and some of the things you say . . ."

"What?" Lulu was starting to enjoy herself. The nature of Frank's work and her knowledge of the time he'd spent in prison had colored her expectations. The first time she'd said something and he had blushed, she'd been almost speechless with surprise.

"I dunno." Frank shrugged massively, the muscles under his freshly pressed yellow shirt with pink buttons causing the material to swell briefly, in the way the glassy-smooth surface of the ocean bulges when a large mammal is about to breach. Without consciously thinking about it, Frank had come to realize that body language was by far the most effective way of conveying emotion to his new girl. He shrugged again, but in a subtly different way, indicating a kind of freckle-faced, straw-in-the-hair boyish confusion. "To look at, you're such an angel."

"Frank, what a nice thing to say."

"But when you open your mouth, Jeez, sometimes you sound like you're on a day pass from hell."

Lulu giggled, held him a little tighter.

Frank said, "You like to shock people. I could see it in your eyes, the first time you did it to me."

"You could, huh."

"But deep inside, you're not like that at all. And you know something – you can act like a hard-ass all you want, but you're always gonna pay a price."

The telephone warbled, but to Frank it sounded more like a vulture than a canary.

Lulu said, "What price is that?"

Frank picked up. It was Rikki, inviting them up for brunch. Frank still had a few moves left. He let the invitation hang for a moment and then said, "Okay, sure. As long as there's lots of coffee and I ain't expected to eat any fresh fruit."

Rikki said, "Tell the truth, Frank, Mr Newton don't expect you to do much of anything."

Frank waited, not saying anything, giving Rikki lots of time to take another shot at him or hang up. After a moment, the line went dead. Frank disconnected, turned to Lulu and said, "Hungry, honey?"

"Does it matter?"

Frank said, "Not yet, but soon."

They caught an elevator up to Newt's posh tenth-floor suite. The door was ajar. Frank knocked twice.

Lulu said, "Why don't we just walk in, show some initiative. It isn't as if they aren't expecting us."

"It ain't polite. In a situation like this, you gotta show some respect." Frank knocked again, not too loudly. Adopting the stance of a pallbearer, he waited patiently for Newt to shake the wax out of his ears.

But it was Rikki who came to the door, a loaded fork in one hand and a steak knife in the other. Casually, he waved them inside.

The suite was a little larger than Frank's, but not much. There was a lean-out-the-window view of Coal Harbour. Next to the window, a quartet of wing chairs snuggled up to a table laid for four.

Newt was wearing green suede deck shoes, baggy white cotton pants rolled half-way to his knees and held up with a shiny red belt of woven leather, a short-sleeved cotton shirt in pastel splashes of pink and blue and green. He looked as if he was going to finish breakfast and then go audition for a front-row seat at a Beach Boys concert.

Newt waved a champagne flute at Lulu and patted the chair next to him. "Sit, baby. Grab some chow."

Frank took Lulu's hand in his big paw, gave her a quick squeeze. They sat down, Newt scattering scrambled egg across the carpet as he used his fork to direct Frank into the chair on his left, leaving Lulu no choice but to sit between Newt and Rikki – the aftershave twins.

Frank eased a serving cart out of the way. The table was crowded with silver-plated heating dishes of eggs and bacon, white toast, croissants, cute little jars of jam, a silver coffee pot, huge bowl of fruit salad and several bottles of Calona Pastel Peach Champagne.

Newt said, "There, now. Ain't this cosy? Rikki, serve the lady."

With his slick black hair and icy, glittering black eyes, the crisp white shirt, matt black suit and matching tie, black silk socks and mirror-polished size seven black patent-leather shoes with the custom-made elevator heels and needle-sharp stainless steel toe caps, Rikki might have been the headwaiter at a razorwired maximum security institution, or maybe the chief warden at a kennel for the terminally rabid. He said, "Sure 'ting, boss," and slapped a mountain of scrambled eggs on Lulu's plate.

"Bacon?"

Lulu shook her head.

Rikki hoisted a bottle of Pastel Peach. "Thirsty?"

"No, really."

She was fading, had gone about two shades paler than normal. Frank had to do something. He snatched at the coffee pot and filled her cup. She glared at him. He gave her a pleading look. Verbal semaphore. *Please be patient.*

Newt shoved his plate out of the way, wiped his mouth with a napkin the size of a small parachute. "Where's my grapefruit?"

Rikki was staring at Lulu, looking her over as if she was something that was on sale, twenty per cent off but maybe still not quite worth the price. Frank had a very strong urge to snap his neck. Instead, he reached across the table and handed Newt half a juicy plump Indian River grapefruit.

Rikki drained his flute glass, licked his lips and poured himself a refill.

Frank emptied the rest of the bottle into his glass, sipped cautiously. Rikki was watching him. Frank wiped his mouth clean with the back of his hand, put the glass back down on the table and gently pushed it away.

Newt used his fork to stab a slice of grapefruit. He dipped the grapefruit in the sugar bowl and then popped it in his mouth, leaned way back in his chair and chewed thoughtfully, swallowed. He said, "I asked you to do a little something for me, Frank. At the time, it didn't seem like it was gonna be a major problem." Newt leaned across the table and playfully jabbed at Frank with the fork, the tines dimpling Frank's cheek. "But look what's happened – nothing. Absolutely zero."

"Zilch," said Rikki, winking at Lulu.

Grinning maniacally, Newt said, "I trusted you like a son. And you let me down, Frank. You spent thousands of my hard-earned dollars, and dropped me on my ass."

"Ouch!" said Rikki, wriggling in his chair and making his eyebrows dance, flashing his pearly teeth.

Frank poured himself some coffee. The pot had a valve, you had to twist a little handle. The coffee was very hot. If he threw the cup in Rikki's face, blinding him, he could take all the time he wanted to beat Newt to a pulp.

But that wasn't what he wanted, not really. Newt was right; he'd been good to Frank and Frank had let him down.

He added cream, sipped.

Newt said, "What I require, Frank, is an explanation. Take it from the top, and try not to skip over any of the good parts. What I'm saying to you, don't make me ask a lot of questions, I'd hate to lose my temper in front of the lady."

So Frank went over the whole story, more or less. He told Newt about the flat tire and the bad luck and the trip out to Metrotown and the kid trying to sell tickets on the BMW. Newt smiled a couple of times and once he even laughed out loud.

Three cups of coffee later, Frank finally ran out of monologue, and Rikki jumped on him with both feet.

"Yeah, man, but what you done *recently*?"

Frank said, "I guess you missed my point. I've been trying to explain that the job doesn't interest me any more. The Corvette's still in the garage, far as I know. Take it if you want it."

Newt said, "But I don't understand. What d'you mean, you lost interest? What *happened*?"

Frank glanced at Lulu. She was watching him, a smile in her eyes. They locked in on each other. Frank said, "I fell in love."

Rikki said, "Ain't that sweet," and stuck two fingers in his mouth and made a nasty gagging sound.

Lulu said, "You're a really ugly person, Rikki. And I'm not just talking about your face. I mean deep inside you, where it counts." She turned to Newt. "You guys sleep together, is that the attraction?"

Newt giggled, and shook his head, indicating neither denial nor confirmation.

Rikki, staring at Frank, slowly withdrew his fingers from his mouth, wiped them dry on the lapel of his black suit.

Newt said, "I called statement enquiries, Frank. My charge card's been taking a beating. Unless the clerk made a mistake, you've spent almost five thousand bucks in the last few days, and I got nothin' to show for it. No *body*."

Frank reached inside his jacket, came up with a small blue box with a red ribbon around it. He tossed the box to Newt and said, "This ought to take care of what I owe you."

Newt stared suspiciously at the box, then shrugged and ripped it open. Inside was a heavy gold chain, the broad flat links smooth and lustrous, looking solid and rich. He tilted the box so the chain slid into the palm of his hand, gauged the weight of it, smiled and turned to Lulu. "Gimme a hand with this, willya?"

Lulu was careful not to touch him as she draped the links across his wrist, fastened the clasp.

"Nice, Frank. But it ain't five grand's worth of nice, not by a long shot."

Frank reached into his sagging pockets and dumped the rest of the jewelry store loot on to the table. The pile of tangled gold chains and rings was about four inches high and eight inches across. A chip diamond sparkled in the light.

Newt said, "What'd you do, rob a jewelry store?"

"There's close to five pounds of gold there, most of it eighteen carat."

"Yeah, okay . . ." Newt studied the ceiling. After a few moments he said, "What the hell. I can't make you do what you don't wanna do. Rikki can play bumper cars, I guess, as good as you."

Newt gobbled the rest of his grapefruit while Frank told Rikki where he'd parked the Corvette, and explained his reasons for using such a noisy car. Rikki listened politely, sipped at the Pastel Peach champagne, his eyes steady on the small mountain of gold.

Newt said, "You two lovebirds stick around until we finish our business here, understood?"

Frank nodded.

"Don't leave town, in other words." Newt grinned. A fragment of pink Indian River pulp was lodged between his two front teeth.

In the elevator, as they glided silently back down to their room, Lulu said, "We've got to kill them both, Frank."

"No we don't. Everything's taken care of, and no hard feelings."

"If we don't do it to them, they're going to do it to us. You saw the look on Rikki's face, in his eyes. He's a killer, pure and simple."

"Simple, maybe, but not pure."

The elevator doors slid open. They walked slowly along the thickly carpeted corridor. The doors to the suites were mahogany, with brass numbers. Frank patted himself down, looking for his key. They came to their room. Frank slipped the key into the lock, pushed open the door. The maid had come and gone. A vase stuffed with baby's tears and long-stemmed white roses stood on the bureau.

Lulu read the card, snatched the roses out of the vase and threw them on the floor.

Frank said, "Rikki?"

Lulu stomped the roses into the carpet, didn't stop until there was nothing left but an unrecognizable pulp.

Frank said, "Since I met you, I've changed, I feel different about things. Like maybe it wouldn't be so bad, being a normal human being, leading a normal kind of life. I ain't saying I want to go somewhere and grow *wheat*, but maybe . . ."

"Wait a minute, back up." A thorn had done its work. Lulu licked a drop of blood from her wounded thumb. She said, "The reason I fell for you in the first place was because you were such a wild and crazy guy. And now you want to settle down – lead a normal kind of life? Y'know what that sounds like to me, Frank? *Death!*"

The phone rang. Frank picked up. Rikki asked him if Lulu liked her flowers.

"She's right here, you wanna say hello?"

What Rikki wanted was to check and make sure he had Parker's correct address. Be a shame, he said, to hit the wrong woman and have to go back and do it all over again.

"Good point," said Frank. He gave Rikki Parker's street and apartment number, waited the five minutes or so it took Rikki to write it all down, and then hung up and searched the phone book for the list of government-controlled liquor stores. There was a number for general enquiries. Frank dialled the number and asked the clerk at the other end if he could please give him the price of a bottle of Calona Pastel Peach Champagne. The guy put him on hold, came back on the line a minute with the good news. Frank thanked him, and hung up.

Lulu said, "What's so funny?"

"Nothing."

"Then what're you smiling at?"

Frank said, "I guessed four ninety-five. I was only out a nickel."

23

Popeye Rowland removed the pince-nez from his left eye, puffed up his cheeks and clouded the surface of the glass, then polished it against the creamy white sleeve of his shirt and screwed it back in place. He smiled dolefully. "I always wanted to make it to the top of the ladder, Jack, but this isn't exactly what I had in mind."

"Life's full of surprises."

"If you're lucky." The ME reached out and plucked an apple from a nearby branch. Birds had been at it, and worms. He tossed the apple at a garbage can in the alley, missed. "See where the bullet hit the tree?"

Willows nodded. The bullet that had ended Joey Ngo's life had exited between his shoulder blades and lodged in the tree trunk. He remembered a suicide's bullet that passed through the victim's throat and then a neighbor's kitchen window, killing a man named Barclay as he'd sat at the table reading the paper and eating his cereal.

Popeye said, "Everything looks just right, Jack. Textbook perfect. The positioning of the kid's prints on the weapon, the position of the weapon itself, location of the ejected cartridge." Popeye glanced towards the house and covertly helped himself to another apple. It too, was riddled with worm holes. "We won't know for sure until the autopsy, but the angle of the entrance and exit wounds looks exactly right for a suicide." Popeye studied the apple, turning it in his hands. "I hear you like to fish for trout. Ever wet a line out of season?"

"Can't say I have."

"You ought to give it a try. Take my word for it, trout always taste better when you catch 'em illegally. Being up here in this tree reminded me of that fact. I haven't raided a fruit tree for over thirty years, ever since I was a kid. That's why there'll always be cops,

Jack. Because some people never forget how much fun it was to jump the neighbor's fence and steal what doesn't belong to them."

"That's your theory, is it?" Willows kept turning Eddy Orwell's blood-stained VPD card in his hand. The card had Parker's home phone number written on the back, and Willows had found it in Joey Ngo's shirt pocket. Somehow, Cherry had lifted Parker's number off the Rolodex on Orwell's desk when he'd made the phone call after the interview. Then he'd passed the number on to his brother – or maybe Joey had found it on Cherry after he'd shot him. Either way, Willows had a hunch Parker wasn't going to receive any more anonymous phone calls.

"Yeah," said Popeye, "that's my theory."

Joey had unbuttoned his shirt and exposed his chest – another strong indication of suicide. Popeye squinted as he examined the wound in Joey's left hand. The muzzle of the pistol had been pressed firmly against his body when the trigger was pulled. Trapped gases from the explosion had burst his flesh, producing a typical star-shaped wound.

Popeye's nail-bitten finger hovered an inch above the bullet hole. The summer breeze moved the leaves of the apple tree just so, and for a moment, a stray shaft of sunlight brightly illuminated the wound, so that it seemed magnified, grossly enlarged. In the blackened area immediately surrounding the wound, a considerable amount of unburned powder residue was clearly present on Joey's skin.

The gun had been photographed and then pried from Joey's grasp. There were abrasion marks on his thumb and the soft web of tissue between the thumb and index finger of his right hand. These marks were consistent with the working of the weapon's slide as the gun automatically pumped another round into the chamber. Fragments of flesh and splashes of blood across the lower wrist and knuckles of his right hand were intermingled with ruined pulp from the sweet potato. There was no blood on the inside of Joey's hand or corresponding area of the gun's grips.

The lab would search for lead particles, metallic residue from the percussion cap, copper from the spent cartridge, traces of gun oil from the weapon's barrel. A series of comparative shots using the gun and identical ammunition would be fired in the police lab at 312 Main Street. Infra-red photography would serve to intensify the zone of powder residue depositing; just one of many factors that together would indicate suicide or murder. Chemical examination of the gunshot wound would reveal barium, lead and antimony, forcefully expelled when the primer detonated.

Popeye said, "I remember one guy, this was a few years ago, before your time maybe, during the autopsy they found two bullets in his head. But there was no doubt at all he'd shot himself. Know what happened?"

"He used two guns."

"Nope, just the one. The ammunition was about fifty years old, had lost its zip. First time the guy pulled the trigger, the bullet lodged in the barrel. So the poor sap took another shot at it, so to speak. The gun should've blown up in his face, but it didn't. Lucky, I guess. Had that coroner scratching his head, though." Popeye stared blankly at the laundry blooming on the clothesline. "There was a logger I heard about, bit down on a blasting cap. This was first thing in the morning, way out in the bush, at the breakfast table. Guy's head snaps back. He drops his fork. Fifty or sixty guys digging into their ham and eggs, yelling logger bullshit at each other, most of them didn't even realize anything had happened. And I heard you couldn't tell there was anything wrong by looking at him, he showed no external signs of damage at all, except his eyes were a little bulgy." Popeye nodded thoughtfully. "The main thing is to get the job done, I guess. Whatever works, works. Want me to sum up?"

"Help yourself."

"Okay, see his eyes – the corneas are still clear. Rigor mortis is present, but by no means complete. The way he was holding the gun, so tightly, was due to what we professionals call 'cadaveric spasm'. Run across it before?"

Willows shook his head, no.

"It isn't all that uncommon. Takes place immediately at the time of death, especially with suicides. Guns or knives. It's often confused with rigor mortis. The important thing is, you can't fake it. Somebody blew Joey away, there's no way he'd have held on to the weapon so tightly."

Joey's left arm hung straight down. Blood had pooled in his hand, darkening the flesh. Popeye pressed a finger firmly against the discolored skin, held it there for a moment. The skin did not blanch, indicating that at least four hours had passed since the time of death.

Popeye said, "In my professional and highly esteemed opinion, it is certainly possible that the deceased could have produced the injury that caused his death – a bullet through the heart. My learned estimate is that the fatal moment occurred seven to nine hours ago. He's dead as a doornail, in other words, and likely to stay that way for all of eternity, poor soul."

Popeye backed carefully down the ladder. "I trust that when you go after the bullet, you'll be careful not to inflict too much damage on this lovely tree, Jack."

In the hours immediately following the discovery of Joey Ngo's body, the crowd that gathered behind the police lines of flimsy yellow plastic tape grew fat and prospered on the novelty of scurrying television crews, the arrival of the aggressively anonymous mud-brown Body Removal Services wagon, the aimless wanderings of lantern-jawed cops and unbelievably relaxed homicide detectives, the chatter of on-the-spot reporters with their blow-dried hair and airbrushed complexions. Mel Dutton, watching a particularly glamorous blonde reporter seduce her network's minicam, turned to Willows and said, "Know how to make a blonde's eyes sparkle?"

Claire Parker, as she and Willows strode briskly across the street towards the crowd and their unmarked car, was positively ID'd as the Channel Eleven late-night news anchor. Willows, it was assumed, was her producer, or lover, or both.

A woman thrust a scrap of paper and pen at Parker, and yelled the anchor's name and asked her for an autograph.

Parker signed with a flourish as Willows started the car. She allowed the woman to engage her in small talk, returned the paper as she climbed into the car, but kept the pen.

Willows leaned on the horn, and the crowd scattered. The pen was a ballpoint, bright green with a thick line of black running from top to bottom.

Willows said, "You kept her pen?"

"It's a souvenir, from Bermuda." Parker held the pen sideways at eye level, so Willows could easily read the bold block letters, admire the sailboats and sun. She said, "Whenever I use it, people will ask me when I was there, and I'll tell them I never was, and give them an odd look, like they're weird, or something."

"Brilliant."

"It's a fair trade. She's got a story too – how the overpaid TV bitch stole her favorite pen." Parker gave Willows a quick smile. "Besides, Popeye just walked off with mine, so I needed one."

"He's a sneaky guy. I've heard he's got a drawerful of disposable lighters." Willows checked his watch. Ten-past one. "Want to go somewhere, get something to eat, maybe a beer?"

"We've got a mountain of paperwork ahead of us, Jack. Why don't we order take-out from the office?"

"Because I want something fresh and hot."

"And a beer."

"And a *couple* of beers, to wash the smell of Joey Ngo out of my throat."

There was a Pizza House half a block up, on the left. Parker spotted it a split second after Willows. "Forget it, Jack."

"Mushrooms, green pepper . . ."

"And anchovies and draft beer."

"I haven't had anything to eat since five o'clock this morning. I get cranky when I'm hungry. You ought to know that by now."

"You'll never know how much it hurts to have to turn you down, Jack."

"Fine. But if I start growling, try not to take it personally."

Two blocks later, Willows made a sudden left turn across two lanes of traffic, parked in front of a bright red, freshly painted fire hydrant.

"Need to take a leak?" said Parker, grinning at her own dumb joke.

Willows flipped down the sun visor, displaying his "Police Vehicle" sticker. "There's a restaurant right around the corner. Tommy's. I had lunch there a couple of months ago, it was terrific."

"What's that supposed to mean, there's three tables and a fifty-foot bar?"

Willows slammed shut his door, checked to make sure it was locked. He glared at Parker across the hot metal surface of the roof. "If Joey's gun matches up with the bullets that killed Emily and Cherry – and I bet you a tossed green salad with caloriewise dressing it will – we've cleared two murders and a suicide. Not a bad day's work, Claire. Reason enough to hoist a cold one."

A dozen arguments sprang to mind. Parker filed them away for future reference, and matched Willows stride for stride as he marched up the sidewalk and around the corner towards the restaurant.

A fat, almost-larger-than-life papier-mâché Holstein hung suspended over the restaurant's double glass doors. The cow was impaled on a sturdy iron rod, but the intent was apparently to fix the poor beast in space rather than viciously slaughter it. To Parker, the bulky corpse hinted darkly of relatives that had met a similar fate, and now waited patiently inside, disguised as hamburger patties and steaks.

Willows pushed open the door, held it for her. The restaurant was more empty than not, and they were given a table by the window.

Parker ordered a spinach salad, glass of icewater.

Willows said, "I'll have a pint of whatever you've got on tap, and a hamburger with swiss cheese, bacon and mushrooms. But could you hold the green pepper and substitute lettuce for the beans sprouts?"

"That's a number fifteen, the blimpburger."

"It is?"

The waitress smiled. Her lipstick was a dark, glossy red – the color of an overripe apple. Willows glanced away, and Parker knew exactly what he was thinking. The worst thing about the job was how the foulness of it sometimes caught you by surprise, filled your mouth to overflowing. Parker reached across the table, gently squeezed Willows' hand.

It was a moment of unexpected intimacy, unsettling and powerful. Parker smiled at Willows, and he smiled back. They might have been lovers, and perhaps they were.

The waitress went away. There was a moment of absolute silence, and then Parker said, "So, how goes the battle?"

"What battle is that?"

"For custody."

Willows shrugged. "Her lawyer calls my lawyer. My lawyer calls her lawyer. They whisper to each other, the long distance charges pile up, but who knows what they say?"

Parker's water arrived, and Willows' beer. He drank half the glass and sighed.

Parker said, "You aren't contesting the divorce, are you?"

"I want a chance to be a father to my children, that's all." Willows drank some more beer. "Why did you bring this up?"

"Because you've been telling me you've got them for the month of August, but you don't seem to have made any plans. What d'you expect them to do for entertainment? You should get yourself organized, make sure that when they're with you they really enjoy themselves."

The food arrived. Parker waited until the waitress was out of earshot and said, "Your wife phoned me this morning, at the office.

Farley took the call. She left a message, said she wanted to talk to me."

"I told you she was going to call. She's worried about me, remember? Not *that* worried – just enough to want to be reassured that I'm doing okay, getting by."

The food arrived. Parker used her fork to stab at her salad. She said, "So what the hell am I supposed to tell her, Jack? That it's a wonderful life, or you miss her like crazy and would do anything to get her back?"

Willows had lost his appetite and regretted the beer. He should have ordered something stronger – a quarter gram of arsenic on the rocks, or maybe a couple of pints of 86-proof ethanol, with a twist of lemon.

Parker pushed her spinach salad aside. "I can't take any more of this, I feel like a damn bunny rabbit." She indicated Willows' congealing hamburger. "You want that, or not?"

"Every last pound." Willows cut his burger in two, held the plate out to Parker. "Help yourself."

"Cowburgers. What a concept." Parker took a bite, made a face. She chewed and swallowed and said, "Joey fell in love with Emily, didn't like the way Cherry treated her. He decided to kill Cherry, but, his first time out, made a rookie's mistake and shot Emily. Then died of remorse, so to speak. Tell me something, Jack."

Willows cocked an eyebrow.

Parker said, "Is that how it happened, did I *miss* anything?"

"Cherry might've figured out that Joey shot Emily, and decided to kill him. I doubt that's what happened, though."

"Why is that?"

"Partly because they were brothers, but mostly because Cherry didn't seem to care what happened to Emily."

Parker nodded, remembering the interrogation room, Cherry's attitude.

Willows pointed to the cowburger. "You finished with that?"

"Definitely."

Willows flipped open his wallet, dropped some money on the table.

Out on the sidewalk, Willows found that he and Parker were standing very close to each other and that she was looking right at him, directly into his eyes. She said, "Tell me something – how can things be so complicated and so simple, all at once?"

Willows realized, with a sudden vertiginous lurch of the heart, that Parker wasn't talking about Joey and Emily. He stared down at her. The heavy summer air was adrift with chunks of grit, stained pale blue with exhaust fumes and gridlock malice. Parker's huge dark eyes were vulnerable as any first offender's. Willows stared at her for a long moment, then turned without a word and strode briskly towards the waiting unmarked car.

24

While they were waiting for the limo to show up for the ride out to LAX, Newt and Rikki had passed the time arguing about the wisdom of taking a gun into Canada. Newt agreed with Rikki that there was no real difference between the two countries except taxes were criminally high in Canada. But he pointed out that even so, LAX-VCR was an international flight. Consequently, they were likely to encounter pesky customs officers with dogs that liked to snort luggage.

Rikki'd said, "What about the Glock? Can I at least take the Glock?"

He was talking about an Israeli-designed and produced semi-automatic handgun that was built mostly of hi-tech plastics. Rikki believed that if you disassembled the weapon and were reasonably creative about how you stowed the pieces, it was virtually impossible to pick up on an X-ray machine.

At the time, Newt hadn't seen any point in taking what he considered an unnecessary risk; he could always arrange to get hold of a gun in Canada. But now that he was in Vancouver, the situation was different. Frank had a gun. At least, Newt presumed he did. Rikki, on the other hand, didn't, thanks to Slick's double-cross. It wasn't a situation Newt felt comfortable with. Weird, the way Frank had turned out. Newt didn't believe any of that stuff about falling in love. There was something else going on. Maybe, after all the rounds he'd absorbed, Frank had become gun-shy.

Newt had been shot only once, and that was years ago, but he remembered it as clearly as if it was happening to him right this minute. Remembered being knocked flat on his ass by Parker's .38 wadcutter, a lucky shot that struck him in the chest, punctured a lung and deflected across his ribcage, the collapsing flesh and shattering bones playing a wheezy bagpipe dirge that brought tears to his eyes and almost killed him, it sounded so painful.

And he remembered the surgeon, Epstein, paying him a visit a few days after he hit the emergency ward, the guy all piercing blue eyes and aftershave and hairy forearms, wearing a thousand-dollar silk suit. The doc seemed to picture himself as some kind of hero. Laying each word of eternal wisdom down firm and heavy as a paving stone, he informed Newt that he'd come *that close* to being in a situation where the only date left in his appointment book was the autopsy.

Newt had licked his cracked dry lips and said, "What pissed me off, I couldn't swear to it in a court of law, but I'm pretty sure she was aiming at my popsicle."

Epstein folded his hairy arms across his chest and gave Newt a cool look.

Newt grinned and said, "Be a major tragedy, wouldn't it, getting your popsicle shot off."

The Hippocratic Oath had lost most if not all of its impact since the invention of the BMW. And Epstein was as much a human being as anybody else. The look he gave his patient was equal parts malice and disgust. As far as he was concerned, the little creep could go into post-operative shock and roll over and die.

Newt saw the look in the surgeon's eyes and knew what it meant. The pain was starting to get to him, but as Epstein headed for the door, Newt yelled, "Man, you're such a tight-ass, I bet every time you fart you break a wine glass."

Finally, the toilet flushed and Rikki wandered out of the bathroom. Newt told him what was on his mind, that he wanted him to take another shot at getting some guns.

Rikki said, "Where I gonna go?"

"Frank."

"Offa Frank?"

Newt chewed on a cuticle. "No, Rikki, what I mean is maybe Frank could help you get a gun. He's a local guy, knows his way around."

Rikki thought about it for a moment. Newt watched the wheels turning, flakes of rust falling out of Rikki's ears. Rikki said, "Why don't I just take Frank's gun offa him? Save some money."

Newt swallowed the tiny fragment of raw flesh he had chewed from his own body. He said, "You take Frank's gun away from him, you're gonna have to shoot him with it or he's gonna take it back.

No offense, but this ain't the kind of fleabag hotsheet back-alley bordertown motel you usually hang out at. You blow somebody away, even Frank, people are likely to call the cops."

"Screw da *policia*," said Rikki. "I kill 'em all!" But he was smiling as he spoke, in a jovial mood despite Newt's excessively cautious nature. He loved spending his boss's hard-earned cash, and there was nothing he'd rather buy than a *pistola*. But it was even better if you could get the piece for free, or at least keep the cost to an absolute minimum. And despite his kidding around, he knew how to find a gun – all he needed was a phone book and a taxi.

In the hardware department of a nearby store, Rikki peeled a couple of twenties off the thousand-dollar roll Newt had given him, and bought the biggest pair of boltcutters they had in stock.

The closest sporting goods store was ten minutes and a twelve-dollar taxi ride away. Rikki paid the driver with another of Newt's sweaty twenties. The boltcutters were wrapped in heavy brown paper. A bell suspended above the store's door tinkled cheerfully as he stepped inside. The guy down at the far end of the store by the cash register glanced up, smiled. There was a long rack of shotguns and rifles behind him, and a safe as big as three refrigerators that looked to be about a hundred years old that had to be where the handguns were kept. Rikki ambled the length of the store, the boltcutters, still wrapped in brown paper, dangling loosely at his side. The guy behind the counter was in his mid-forties, slim, with short black hair and a trim moustache. He was staring at Rikki's package, frowning. Probably figured there was a rifle or shotgun in there that needed to be repaired. Rikki swung the boltcutters around as if to place them on the counter and then accelerated and widened the arc, caught the man high on the temple and wiped the sudden look of surprise right off his face, brained him.

He jumped the counter, stripped the brown paper off the boltcutters and used them to cut through the heavy chain securing the rifles and shotguns. After a moment's hesitation he chose a 12-gauge Remington pump. There were boxes of shells under the counter. Rikki smashed the glass, loaded the weapon with three rounds of double-ought, cranked one and laid the shotgun on the counter. The man on the floor groaned wearily and rolled over on his side. Rikki whacked him on the ear with the cutters, knelt down and frisked him. The guy's name was Barry Chapman. He had thirty-four dollars in his wallet, and an American Express card. His key ring was in his back pocket.

Rikki started in on the safe, trying the biggest keys first, working his way around the ring.

The telephone screamed at him. He dropped the keys, scooped them up. Now he'd lost his place and would have to start over again.

The telephone rang fifteen times, each ring sounding to Rikki like somebody yanking a big zipper on his heart. The silence, when the ringing finally stopped, was even more terrifying.

The safe had two doors. Each door had it's own lock, one at the top and the other at the bottom. It took him what seemed like a very long time to figure out that the doors opened simultaneously or not at all. Inside, there were three brand-new and totally illegal fully-automatic Kalashnikov assault rifles, ammunition, and about sixty handguns of various calibres, most of them tucked away in factory cardboard boxes.

Rikki, squinting at the labels on the boxes, yelped with delight as he spotted the pair of .40-calibre Smith & Wesson stainless steel semi-autos. He ripped open the boxes, snatched at a 40-round box of 180 grain copper-jacketed Winchester hollow points, ejected the pistol's magazines. Each gun held eleven cartridges plus one in the chamber. Loaded, the weight was close to four pounds. The Smith was the official handgun of the FBI; emphasis had been placed on accuracy and reliability, muzzle velocity and penetration and expansion. The hollow points did a fine job of blowing away blocks of gelatin; the FBI's "tissue-simulation medium". A clean hit'd put a bad guy on his ass, all right. But the really nice thing about the pistol – from Rikki's point of view – was that it'd kill the good guys just as dead as the bad.

He stared down at Barry Chapman. What if the guy woke up, grabbed the phone? Rikki stepped over his body, ripped the telephone's cord from the wall. Okay, fine. What if he woke up and went outside and started yelling and screaming – or grabbed a Kalashnikov? Rikki racked the slide. The safety was a two-way button mounted at the rear of the trigger guard. He used his index finger to push the safety off, moved a little bit further away from Chapman and aimed carefully, then remembered to take a quick look out of the window. The street was empty. He shot Chapman in the knee, the impact of the hit making the body twitch.

Rikki said, "There now, that didn't hurt a bit, did it?" He eased the Smith's hammer down and made sure the safety was on and then stuck the pistol in the waistband of his pants. The other gun and six boxes of ammunition went into a brown paper bag. He grabbed the shotgun and then decided to hell with it, the weapon was too big to fit into the paper bag, someone was sure to notice it.

Chapman wasn't bleeding very much. Rikki wondered about that, but only for a moment. He had other things on his mind. Making his getaway. The hit and run. How to deal with Frank, sweet talk the albino, with her skin so soft and white it looked like she bathed in moonbeams.

Busy, busy, busy.

The taxi ride back to Granville and Georgia cost him another thirteen bucks, plus a dollar tip. He sat down on a bench near the hotel and worked it out. His total costs for the caper were sixty-three dollars plus change. Subtract the thirty-four he'd lifted from Barry Chapman's wallet and his net profit was one thousand dollars less twenty-nine. Except there was no way Newt would let him off that easy. Or maybe he would. Rikki sat there on the bench, the sun on his face and the paper bag heavy on his lap, the Smith's stainless steel four-inch barrel digging into his crotch. What could he tell Newt he paid for the guns, what was the most he could hope to get away with?

Rikki watched the girls go by. Were they as pretty as California girls? He couldn't make up his mind. He had a thing about blondes. In LA, just about everybody was a blonde. Otherwise, what was the point? He found himself once again thinking about Lulu. He stood up, adjusted his pants and strode briskly towards the hotel.

Newt pulled back the slide and saw that there was a shiny fat round in the chamber. He carefully eased the slide back, took a bead on himself in the mirror and then gave Rikki a quick sidelong glance and asked him how bad was the damage.

Rikki said, "Seven-fifty for the pair. Plus I buy 'em in a bar, had to pay for a couple rounds of *cervesa*."

Newt smiled and held out his left hand, the one that wasn't holding a gun.

Rikki added, "Plus two hundred for the bullets – less than a buck apiece." Smiling, he dipped into his pocket and dragged out a pair of twenties and a ten.

Newt snatched the money out of his hand. Rikki was stealing from him, no doubt about it. He'd have to do something about that, back in Laguna Beach.

Rikki said, "So, we're all set. We got the shiny guns, fancy car, good looks."

"I want it done tonight," said Newt. "Or tomorrow morning, when she goes to work."

Rikki amused himself juggling three of the big .40-calibre hollow points, tossing them up and snatching them out of the air. His hands hardly moved. He was pretty good, Newt had to admit.

Newt said, "I got tickets on a Delta flight leaves in the morning, we gotta be at the airport by ten o'clock."

"All of us?" said Rikki.

"Just you and me, kid."

Rikki grinned broadly. The way Newt had said it, the words sounded like they were a line out of a movie. "What about Frank, and the albino chick?"

"I thought you were gonna take care of that for me."

Rikki nodded slowly. "Yeah, sure. No problem."

Newt said, "That's why you bought all those bullets, remember?"

"Seen 'em around?"

Newt said, "They'll show up, don't worry."

Rikki tossed the bullets on the bed. He said, "Watch this," and tried his fast draw. He was pretty slow, but this was due mostly to his concern that the Smith's front sight might rip his pants. He said, "I wish there was some place I could try this baby out, make sure it works."

"You'll get your chance soon enough."

As had so often happened in his life, Newt was right for the wrong reasons. Usually the bottom line was more or less where he expected it to be, so his flaws of logic didn't matter.

This time, unfortunately, it was going to matter a great deal.

25

Rick Conroy nodded hello to Farley Spears, pushed Orwell's chair across the grey carpet until it bumped up against Willows' desk. He spun the chair around and sat down, resting his forearms on the padded back. His hands dangled loosely.

"Notice how I'm sitting?"

Willows said, "Yup."

Conroy grinned. "That's right, you got it. Cowboy style. Gary Cooper got his first big break by turning his chair around and sitting on it like this during his interview for *The Winning of Barbara Worth*, made way back in nineteen-twenty-six. Of course, Gary actually was a cowboy, before he became a film star. In one of his early roles, he played the white knight in *Alice In Wonderland*." On the other side of the squadroom, Farley Spears snorted disdainfully. Conroy looked at Spears and said, "That was way back in nineteen-thirty-three. You'd have been too old to want to go and see it, I guess."

Willows said, "What can I do for you, Rick?"

"Cooper was tall, dark and handsome. He had a slow and deliberate way of talking that made people want to hear what he had to say. *I*, on the other hand, am short, pale and sweaty. Also balding. And when I get nervous I talk too fast and sound like Pee-Wee Herman on amphetamines. Plus I bite my nails. So why did the brass pick *me* to do the stand-up comedy?"

"Because you're so obviously unqualified for the job," offered Spears.

Conroy said, "Be quiet, old man. Go back to your crossword puzzle and stop interrupting." To Willows, he said, "I'm probably the ugliest guy on the force. Don't laugh – it's true. I look like Michael J. Pollard gone to seed."

Willows didn't quite catch that one. He let it show.

"Remember *Bonnie and Clyde*? Pollard was pumping gas at some run-down station out in the weeds. They robbed the joint and he helped steal the money, went along for the ride. Big mistake."

A shadow moved across the square of pebbled glass in the door of Inspector Bradley's office.

Conroy said, "He in there?"

Willows nodded.

Behind the door, someone shouted incomprehensibly. A fist was slammed down on a desk – they'd all heard *that* sound often enough to recognize it.

"What's going on?"

"Beats me," said Willows. Bradley's door had been shut when he'd arrived at the squadroom. No one had gone in or out.

Conroy shrugged. "So, Pollard. Remember him now?"

Willows nodded. "Yeah, sure. Face like a caved-in pumpkin. I don't see the resemblance, Rick."

"No?"

"You're twice as ugly. No contest."

Conroy smiled. Until recently, he'd been an ace vice cop. Now, thanks to the department's policy of rotation, he was suddenly the community relations officer. Gone forever were those happy days of screaming with rage and fear, kicking in doors. The primary skill his new job required was an ability to knock softly and wait forever. So far, it hadn't been an easy transition.

Willows said, "So what can I do for you, other than put you out of your misery?"

"The Joey Ngo case. Everybody wants the gory, lurid details. Was it murder or suicide? Did the kid bump Emily and his brother? Can we wrap all three deaths, or what? Gimme the straight goods, Jack. The public's got a right to know."

Willows smiled. "Parker's at the autopsy. She's due back with the preliminary report any time now. But we won't have anything official until the coroner's report comes in. That could easily be a month or more away. So I have no idea when we'll wrap up the other murders. We know Emily and Cherry were both shot with the same gun. If it turns out to be the weapon we found on Joey – and it will – I'll recommend we close all three files."

Conroy said, "Yeah, but you haven't got a match on the gun yet, and it probably won't happen until tomorrow at the earliest. I talked to Goldstein about ten minutes ago. He's got that triple went down in the Japantown warehouse this morning, plus the poor sap was beaten to death in the gunshop. You hear about that?"

Willows shook his head, no.

"Guy named Chapman, Barry Chapman. Was kneecapped with a handgun and then had his head beat in with a pair of boltcutters." Rick mimed biting a chunk out of the back of Orwell's chair. "Know what Goldstein told me when I asked him how he was coming along on *your* case?"

"What?"

"Wanted to know why I was in such a rush – pointed out that everybody involved is dead as a doornail, and likely to stay that way."

There was another burst of yelling, sharp and ironic, from Bradley's office.

Willows shrugged. "You know how it goes, Rick. The investigation is ongoing. New information when and as it becomes available."

"You're a natural, Jack. How's this for a bright idea – why don't *you* take my job?"

"I'd quit first." Willows wasn't kidding, and he let that show, too. He'd been a policeman almost twenty years, a homicide detective for as long as he cared to remember. He'd always been better at being a cop than playing the role of father or husband. He believed his devotion to the job had cost him his wife and family. There were times when the grief of his loss brought him to his knees. But there was nothing he could do. The job had him by the throat. He was incapable of change, and he knew it and accepted it.

But there were limits. He spent too much of his time behind a desk as it was. Being a cop meant hunting bad guys, tracking them down and putting them away. The day Bradley told him he was out of homicide was the day he handed in his badge.

Conroy was staring at him. "You all right, Jack?"

"Yeah, sure." The varnished door at the far end of the squadroom swung open. Orwell, and then Parker.

Conroy said, "I heard Eddy's marriage is going down the tubes."

"Judith's a slow learner," Spears said from his desk. "But she's making progress."

Orwell closing fast, pointed a stiff finger at Conroy and said, "What're you doing in my chair?"

Conroy said, "Probably nobody told you, but there's gonna be a major press conference in about ten minutes. The Japantown shootings. We're expecting fifty or sixty people. Television, the papers, radio. The Chief told me to round up as many chairs as possible."

"Bullshit."

Conroy turned to Parker. "Got anything for the press?"

"Never," said Parker firmly.

Conroy stood, pushed Orwell's chair across the carpet towards the squadroom door. A castor squeaked. He said, "I'll get it back to you in a couple of hours, promise."

"Yeah, sure. But what'm I supposed to sit on in the meantime?"

Conroy unlocked the squadroom door, shoved the chair through it and towards the elevator.

Orwell said, "Hey, wait a minute!" His glare carried the length of the squadroom. Conroy turned and waved as the elevator doors slid open. He pushed the chair inside and turned and yelled, "Gotcha, Eddy!"

Orwell bolted after him.

The elevator doors slid shut.

Willows said, "So how'd it go?"

Parker tossed the file on her desk, sat down. "I never want to see another autopsy as long as I live."

"That sounds about the maximum time frame."

Parker grinned. "The coroner's convinced Joey died of a self-inflicted wound. He told me that even if Joey came back to life and grabbed him by the lapels and told him who did it, he'd still call it a suicide."

Farley Spears said, "I remember a case where a guy with an inoperable brain tumor left a handwritten three-page note, went into a locked room and blew his brains out with a twenty-gauge shotgun. Five years later, his back-yard neighbor confessed that she'd killed him because he kept stealing her roses. The detective who'd handled the case – his name was Ted Nolan – didn't believe a word she said. In fact, nobody believed her except the crown prosecutor and the judge. She got mandatory life. Nolan was so humiliated, he resigned and ran off to Saltspring Island to raise sheep. This happened about thirty years ago. My rookie season." Spears smiled at Parker with yellow teeth and watery blue eyes. "Never take anything for granted. That's the lesson that case taught me and I hope never to forget."

"*Sheep?*" said Willows.

Spears scowled into his crossword. He printed a word and then reversed his pencil and laboriously rubbed it out. The door at the far end of the squadroom banged open and Orwell, his face red as a brand-new wagon, bulled in dragging his chair behind him. He slammed the chair against his desk, chipping the paint. Spears glanced up at him.

"What the hell do *you* want?" snapped Orwell.

"Seven letters. Preferred vessel of acrobats."

Orwell said, "The chief was in the elevator. He took a look at my chair and told me if my ass was *that* tired, I oughta book off sick and go home."

Willows laughed. Orwell sat down at his desk. He yanked open a drawer and pulled out a tennis ball. He squeezed the ball in his fist. The tendons and muscles of his wrist and arm bulged ominously.

Parker and Farley Spears exchanged a look. Nobody said anything.

Orwell wheezed and grunted. A seam tore and the ball collapsed. He stared at it for a moment and then tossed it on his desk.

Farley said, "Gosh, this is more fun than a day at the beach."

"What's that supposed to mean?"

"Don't shoot, Eddy. It was a compliment. You're supposed to be flattered."

Orwell said, "I'll flatten you, wiseguy," and shut his eyes and began to massage his temples.

Parker said, "Tumbler."

Spears nodded, bent over his crossword.

Mel Dutton, his jacket slung over his shoulder and the armpits and chest of his pale-blue shirt dark with sweat, sauntered into the squadroom. He walked over to Orwell's desk, tapped him on the shoulder. "You given any thought to what we talked about, Eddy?"

"What's that?" said Orwell.

"Memories, and how they fade. The baby."

"Judith and me talked it over," said Orwell. "We decided we're gonna get a camcorder. Motion pictures, Mel – it's the latest thing. And like Judith said, why would we want somebody like you taking pictures of our baby – so he'd look nice and dead?"

Dutton glanced at the crushed remains of the tennis ball lying on Orwell's desk. "When the great day finally arrives, try to remember not to squeeze the little guy too hard, okay?"

Orwell said, "Thanks for the advice, you're a pal," and went back to massaging his temples.

The door to Inspector Bradley's office swung open. Ralph Kearns was first out. His face was pale, shoulders slumped. Oikawa was right behind him. Both detectives looked exhausted, as if they'd just finished a marathon. Oikawa softly closed the door.

Dutton said, "Never mess with a paperboy. Those kids are *nasty*."

Kearns gave him a sour look.

Dutton said, "So you guys still cops, or what?"

Kearns said, "You tell 'em about it." He gave Oikawa a quick look of warning. "I gotta have a cigarette, or I'm gonna die."

Oikawa said, "It turns out the mother is a lawyer. The way she tells it, the kid's in terrible shape, crazy with guilt. Shock. Loss of self-esteem. He may never recover. Why, he even had to quit his paper route."

"Think of the loss of income," said Dutton. "Could be as much as twenty, thirty bucks a month."

Oikawa grinned despite himself.

Spears said, "So what happened? What was Bradley yelling about?"

Oikawa picked up Orwell's tennis ball. "Man, what a life." He tossed the ball in the air and neatly caught it. "It ain't as if we didn't have a *reason* for picking the kid up – he was crouched down between a couple of houses at the far end of the block, peeking in somebody's basement window. Ran like hell when he saw us. And he fit Joey's description, more or less."

"Mostly less," said Willows.

"I admit it, we jumped too soon. Ralph was feeling a little touchy about slacking off during the stakeout. He wanted to make the bust. Is he going to do it again? Believe me, I hope not." Oikawa pried the two halves of the tennis ball apart and looked inside. Empty. "What happened is, the inspector made a couple of calls, found out the kid – he's fifteen years old – has a record even longer than my . . ."

"What?" said Parker.

"Arm," said Oikawa, blushing. "The kid's a born thief. If it ain't nailed down, he'll steal it. And if it is nailed down, he'll go steal a hammer. Daddy can hardly wait until his son graduates to adult court where some hard-ass judge puts him away for a couple of years."

Spears said, "So what *was* Bradley yelling about?"

"Well, I guess he felt obliged to point out that we didn't know the kid was a thief when we busted him."

"Cop instinct," said Spears. "That's why you nailed the punk. Cop instinct."

Oikawa smiled. "That's what Ralph said just before the inspector blew his top."

"Anyway," said Spears, "what's important is that the kid's mommy backed water."

Oikawa nodded. "There was some movement on both sides. We had to go over to the house, promise the kid we wouldn't bother him anymore."

"Cease and desist your harassment of the child," said Spears. "Fair enough."

Oikawa lowered his voice to a conspiratorial whisper. "Ralph was terrified. The kid's mother scared the hell out of him. We drive over there to tug the forelocks and he's wriggling around in his seat, can't stay still for a minute. I ask him what's the problem and he tells me he can't get comfortable – it's the cork."

"*The cork?*" said Spears, grinning broadly.

"Yeah, sure. Enjoy yourself. In all the years Ralph and I've been partners, I've never heard him tell a joke or even laugh at one. He wasn't trying to be funny – the only thing holding him together was his suit."

The laughter abruptly died as the door to Inspector Bradley's office swung open. Bradley crooked a finger at Willows and Parker.

Spears said, "It's the Japantown triple. They got Sandy Wilkinson and Bob Kaplan on it, and now they want you."

Willows, pushing away from his desk, had a hunch that Spears was right.

26

The town was full of Jeep Cherokees, boxy little four-wheel-drive vehicles that maybe weren't as quick as a Corvette, but were inconspicuous simply because there were so many of them. Rikki took a taxi across the Lions Gate Bridge and stole a charcoal-grey model from a dealer's overflow lot off Marine Drive. As he broke into the vehicle, strings of blue and red and white plastic flags that marked the perimeter of the car lot snapped in the breeze, applauding his efforts.

Rikki had never bought a new car, or even a used one, come to think of it. He'd stolen plenty, but probably it was a different kind of thrill. *The pride of temporary ownership* – whoever heard of that?

The Cherokee's engine turned over, caught. Rikki gingerly pumped the gas pedal. Six cylinders. He tried the lights and turn signals, radio. Everything worked. He put the Cherokee in first gear and floored it out of the lot, turned West on Marine, towards the bridge. A few years ago, a distillery had spent several hundred thousand dollars stringing lights along the top of the bridge. The lights followed the shape of a slightly flattened-out "M", and looked like a limp advertisement for McDonalds. The illuminated bridge was beautiful at night, but from Rikki's point of view its attraction was also a bit tainted, in the sense that it had the same kind of tawdry superficial appeal as the car lot's gaudy plastic flags. But then, there were miles of car lots on Marine Drive – so maybe the bridge was an appropriate gateway.

Rikki cruised past a Dennys restaurant, a motel, and then another restaurant – this one with a flock of giant fiberglass parrots perched on the roof. He swung on to the approach to the bridge, was swallowed by the flow of Mercedes and BMWs from West Vancouver. Far below him and to his right were rows of permanently immobilized mobile homes, the floodgate-controlled waters of the

Capilano River, lights of a major shopping center. Most of this was reservation land, though you could look for days and never see an Indian.

The bridge was three lanes wide. Above each lane were twin rows of green and red lights which controlled the flow of traffic. Cars and trucks and buses in the middle lane zipped past Rikki at a combined speed of one hundred miles an hour and more, and the blur of onrushing steel at times seemed only inches away. The drivers were paying more attention to the bridge's spectacular view of the ocean and park than the road. Rikki gripped the Cherokee's steering wheel so hard he had a feeling he'd never be able to wipe his fingerprints away. He reached the apex of the bridge. A seagull raced screaming past the windshield. On the horizon, a massive island seemed to rise up out of the sea, and almost directly below him, a huge freighter churned the dark-green water creamy white.

There was almost too much to look at. Rikki had a nice view of the Stanley Park seawall, people strolling along singly and in groups, riding bikes, jogging. He caught a glimpse of Siwash Rock – a pillar of dark stone local legend said had once been a man. The shrill whine of the Cherokee's all-terrain tires changed pitch as he reached the south end of the bridge, roared past the thirteen-ton pair of concrete lions and hit the cement surface of the causeway. The blare of traffic doubled in volume as the Cherokee shot beneath an underpass. He tried to imagine what the causeway must be like when it was raining or snowing. A nightmare – far worse than anything LA had to offer.

The road climbed slightly. There was a solid wall of green on both sides, then a turnoff into the park. He was tempted to dip into the greenery, take it easy, start breathing again. He'd like to catch one of them fatass Canada Geese, watch the light go out of its beady little black eyes as he wrung its neck. Light a driftwood fire on the beach, cook that bird and tear it apart with his fingers, lick the grease and watch the sun go down. But he had a really heavy date with the cute lady detective, and it was important he didn't stand her up.

Newt had inherited most of his wealth but spent every penny as if *he'd* been the one who'd died to earn it. The hotel mini-fridge wanted eighty-five dollars and fifty cents for a bottle of Charles Heidsieck. He was thirsty, but he wasn't crazy. At a government liquor store – and there was one on Alberni, hardly more than a block away, the champagne would be half that price or less.

"Frank."

"Yeah, what?"

"We need something to lubricate our celebration. Why don't you go get a breath of fresh air and a couple bottles Dom."

Frank glanced at Lulu, who was busy following along with an exercise program on television.

Newt said, "She can stay here, keep me company."

"Won't be cold."

Newt frowned. He said, "I wouldn't expect her to be."

Frank said, "I'm talking about the champagne, not Lulu. You order from room service, it'll be ice cold. I buy it off the shelf, it'll be room temperature. You like warm champagne, Newt?"

"I'll order some ice. Ice is cheap. By the time Rikki gets back, it'll be cold enough. Now get outta here, Frank." Newt smiled, but there was nothing in it. "Stop arguin' with me, will ya?"

Frank glanced at Lulu, hoping she'd have something to say, help him out. She was lying on her side on the carpet, wearing orange day-glo lycra so tight you could see the little dimples on either side of the base of her spine. She caught his eye and scissored her leg, pointing her polished red toenails at the ceiling. A wisp of platinum hair drifted into her glacial eye. The sound the lycra made when she brought her legs together was whispery and wet. Frank headed for the door. Lulu's leg came up again. She pursed her lips and airmailed him a kiss goodbye.

Newt sprawled out on the bed. The elevation provided by two pillows allowed him to watch Lulu's reflection in the mirror. She had a better body than any of the TV sports chicks, for sure.

The screen flickered. Commercial time. Newt said, "You and Frank getting along okay? I mean, I noticed you don't seem to do a lot of talking."

Lulu rolled over on her stomach. Newt's heart went bumpety-bump. She said, "Frank's no black belt at idle chatter, if that's what you mean."

Newt wasn't sure what he meant, exactly. Or what she meant, either. He probed again.

"A woman your age – Frank's old enough to be your father."

"Yeah, that's one of the things I liked about him when I first met him, his maturity."

Newt mulled that one over, focusing on the fact that she'd used the past tense. Was the bloom already off the rose?

The string of commercials ended. Lulu rolled over on her stomach, on to her hands and knees. She gave Newt a smile that lingered just a fraction of a second longer than he expected, then turned her attention back to the television. Newt stared greedily at her as she extended her right leg straight out behind her, held the pose for the count of five. Now the left leg. Lycra, the miracle fabric. Newt's lungs ached. He suddenly realized he'd been holding his breath.

Lulu turned so her back was to him. She rocked on her haunches. There was a thin sheen of sweat on the back of her neck, her shoulders. She said, "Is my back straight?" Newt nodded stupidly, and then said yes. His voice was dry, cracked. She glanced over her shoulder at him, smiled. Newt licked his lips.

On the television, the top chick and her team of synchronized identical triplets were slowing up, cooling off. Lulu came gracefully to her feet, uncoiled smoothly and effortlessly as an astronaut – as if gravity had nothing to do with her. She turned off the TV and, much to Newt's amazement, was suddenly lying beside him on the bed.

She stared at him for a moment, from a distance of no more than six inches, and then sighed, and closed her eyes. Newt tried not to look at too many places at once. Despite the ferocity of her workout, she smelled fresh and clean, the healthy fragrances of her toothpaste and shampoo and soap mingling with the subtle carnality of her thousand-bucks-an-ounce perfume.

Newt slipped an arm around her tiny waist. The lycra whispered as she moved a little closer towards him. Her eyelashes fluttered – Newt was wound so tight he actually *heard* them.

Lulu grabbed a pillow and bunched it up, making herself comfy. The Smith lay there on the sheets, shiny and big as the front bumper off a pre-war Cadillac.

"Big gun," said Lulu softly.

"Rikki picked up a pair of 'em," said Newt, "one for him and one for me."

"There was something on television, a man was shot and then hit over the head . . ."

Newt made his face go slack with dismay. He said, "Rikki's such a jerk. I don't know if I'll *ever* be able to teach him to pull his punches. There oughtta be some kind of obedience school for guys like him, know what I mean? 'Cause if you can't train 'em, sooner or later, you gotta put 'em down."

Lulu shut her eyes and concentrated on her breathing, keeping it under control. A man had been murdered, a guy with a wife and three kids. God help her, she couldn't remember his name.

Newt said, "Wanna hold it for a minute?"

The phone rang. Lulu's eyes popped open. She looked frightened, terrified.

Newt had to lean over her to get at the phone. His lips brushed the nape of her neck. He tasted salt – or maybe it was just a trick of his feverish imagination. He picked up.

Frank said, "I'm at the liquor store. They got a pretty good selection of champagnes, but they all sound the same and I can't remember which kind to get."

Newt told him.

Frank said, "Hold on a minute, lemme borrow a pen from the clerk and write it down."

Newt waited.

Frank said, "Okay, but go slow."

Newt rolled his eyes at Lulu. He wondered why he'd ever been afraid of Frank, the Killer Snail.

Lulu was sitting on the edge of the bed, a dazed look in her eyes.

Newt gave Frank the information he needed. Frank asked if it was okay if he went somewhere and had a bite to eat. No problem, said Newt, take as much time as you want. Frank said he wasn't *positive* he wouldn't come straight back from the liquor store. Maybe he'd grab a bite and maybe he wouldn't. He just wanted to clear it first, was all.

Newt hung up and said, "That was Frank." He studied his watch. "He'll be back any minute, I guess."

"Are you afraid of him?"

"No way," said Newt quickly, before he had time to think about it.

"I am."

"Yeah?"

"He yells at me. Sometimes he hits me."

Newt's eyes crawled across her body with the random determination of a thousand ants.

Lulu said, "Here and here . . ."

"Where it doesn't show?"

She nodded. Her pale hands twisted in her lap.

Newt said, "You want me to get Rikki to take care of him?"

"Then he'd think I belonged to him, wouldn't he?"

"Yeah, yeah." Newt hadn't bitten his nails in years, but he was biting them now.

"Couldn't you just send him away somewhere. On a job. Do you have any friends in Colombia, for example?"

"Nobody I'd trust. Besides, would he leave without you?"

"If there was enough money in it."

Newt said, "Buying people never works. Want to know why?"

"Tell me," said Lulu. She glanced up at him and then quickly lowered her eyes. Her voice was sweet as honey and soft as a feather pillow. She sat there on the edge of the bed, waiting to be instructed.

"Because the money always runs out, and then they want more, and in the end there's never enough. So you gotta find a more permanent way to take care of them – what you shoulda done in the first place."

"People are greedy."

"Right, exactly. And you can count on 'em to always take the easy way out. Know why LA is so violent?"

Lulu, her eyes wide, shook her head.

"It ain't." Newt smiled. "It just seems that way, 'cause people are always finding bodies. The reason for that is, most major cities in America are on a river. You wanna get rid of a guy, all you gotta do is buy him a pair of cement overshoes and take him swimming. You look at a map of LA, you'll see a river. But like everything else in the city, it ain't real. Ever been to LA?"

"Not that I remember."

"The river's lined with concrete, walls and bottom. Most of the time there ain't enough water in it to drown a midget."

Lulu's eyes widened with amazement.

Newt said, "You didn't know that, huh?"

"There's a lot of things I don't know," said Lulu softly, giving him a quick shy look and then casting her eyes demurely down.

Newt said, "I could teach you, if you wanted . . ."

Frank found the wine in a little alcove at the back of the store. Thirty-nine dollars and seventy-five cents a bottle. He paid with a hundred. The clerk was in her low twenties. She had long red hair and was wearing a baggy green sweater and jeans so tight it hurt Frank just to look at them. He counted the freckles on her cute little nose while she counted out his change, remembered as he was turning away to ask her for a dollar's worth of quarters.

There was a phone booth across the street. Frank dropped a quarter and dialled information, asked for the number of the police department's major crimes section. He waited a moment and then a computer with a voice like the Tin Man all grown up gave him the number. He wrote it down on the brown paper liquor store bag. The Tin Man gave him the number again. Frank said thank you, and hung up. His quarter dropped into the change slot. He used it to dial major crimes. A woman answered. Frank asked for Parker. *Detective* Parker was out. Did he want to leave a message? Could he please speak to *Detective* Jack Willows? Willows, too, was out. When was he due back? The woman patiently asked him again if he wanted to leave a message.

Frank hung up, waited for a break in the traffic and then trotted across the street. There was a burger joint on the top floor of the building on the corner. He went inside and climbed the stairs, got a table by the window. He ordered a cheeseburger and onion rings, a bottle of Budweiser. The service was quick but he made himself eat slowly, biting off little chunks of time and grinding it to a pulp with his jaws.

By the time he got back to the phone booth, almost an hour had passed. He wondered how Lulu was doing. They were in a tight situation, and he knew she could go either way but that no matter what she did, she'd overreact.

He dropped a quarter, carefully dialled the major crimes number.

Detectives Willows and Parker were still unavailable. Frank tried to decide what to do, and failed.

Lulu rested her hand gently on Newt's knee. She said, "What are you going to do about Frank?"

"Forget him. Wanna come back to California with me?" Newt struggled to think of the advantages. Disneyland. The tar pits. Hollywood.

"It sounds wonderful, but . . ."

"But what?"

"My skin can't take the sun."

"Don't worry about it. You and me, we ain't *daytime* people, we're . . ." Newt struggled to find the words. He smiled like an octopus – his teeth, all jumbled together at the front of his mouth, seemed to swallow his face.

"Creatures of the night?"

Newt's mouth opened wide to let the laughter spill out, and in the same moment, the door opened wide and a man with a brown paper bag for a head walked into the room.

Lulu relinquished her grasp on Newt's trembling knee.

Frank put the bag down on the table by the window. He said, "The ice didn't get here yet?"

"Any minute now." Newt reached for the phone. "I'll give 'em another call, and then I thought maybe the three of us could go somewhere nice for dinner."

Frank patted his stomach. "I'm ready."

Newt turned to Lulu. "You know this town better'n me or Frank. There a decent steak and lobster joint in the neighborhood?"

"Coal Harbour, it's down by the entrance to the park. There's a place not far from there, right on the water. We could drive, be there in ten minutes."

"On the water?"

Lulu nodded, smiling.

"Perfect." Newt turned to Frank. "Sound good to you?"

"Yeah, sure."

Newt said, "Then it's all settled, ain't it."

The phone rang again. Frank picked up, listened for a moment and then handed the receiver to Newt.

Rikki said, "I'm at a phone booth. I got the wheels and everything's all set. How're things at your end?"

"Fine," said Newt.

Rikki held the phone towards the street as a huge diesel truck roared past, then hung up and climbed back in the Cherokee and drove the two blocks to Parker's apartment. He wished he had some tapes so he could try the tape deck. He ran the dial across the radio, fooled with the presets, turned the radio off and pawed through the Cherokee's glove compartment and studied the manual. It was printed in English and another launguage that Rikki, after a considerable amount of heavy thought, figured must be French. He listlessly fiddled with the power windows and seat adjustment controls, sniffed the rich, brand-new smell of the Jeep's leather upholstery.

Where in hell was she?

Man, but he was bored.

An old woman wearing a grey sweatshirt and matching pants came out of the apartment with a marmalade cat in her arms. She walked out to the boulevard and lowered the cat to the grass. The cat was on a gold leash that terminated in a rhinestone-studded collar. Or maybe they were real diamonds, who could say? Rikki powered down his window and turned and watched the old lady follow her cat slowly down towards the far end of the block.

By nine o'clock, the light was starting to fade, and so was Rikki. He was hungry, had to take a leak, was out of cigarettes. He turned on the radio again. He found the CBC French-language station, and then, at the far end of the dial, Hindustani and Italian and Chinese-language stations. But no Spanish broadcast. Probably he was the only Mexican in three thousand miles. He grew homesick, bad-tempered. At twenty-past nine a clown in a battered yellow Volkswagen Rabbit pulled up alongside the Cherokee and asked was he leaving. Rikki snarled, and spat on his windshield. The clown drove away.

At nine-thirty, a light came on in Parker's kitchen. Rikki peered up at the window. He couldn't see Parker or anybody else in there. No sign of movement. Was she home, or did the light have an automatic timer? Rikki checked his watch. He was pretty sure the light had gone on at exactly nine-thirty. He got out of the Cherokee, urinated into the gutter, zipped up. The old lady with the cat had never come back – or if she did, Rikki hadn't seen her.

It suddenly occurred to him that the apartment block had to have a back entrance, maybe even an underground parking lot. What was the *matter* with him? He stuck the Smith in the waistband of his shiny black pants and shut the Jeep's door and trotted across the street.

Parker's apartment was on the third floor, front. He hit the elevator button and the doors slid open and he stepped inside and punched *tres*.

The door to the lady cop's apartment was sheet steel painted beige. There was a spy hole set into the metal on a level with the top of Rikki's head. He got up on his toes and peeked inside, was rewarded with a fish-eye view of what was probably the living room. The apartment was quiet, still. Rikki knocked again, three times, hard enough to bruise his knuckles.

Nada.

Rikki pressed his ear to the door. Silence. He glanced up and down the empty hallway and then checked the locks. There was no way he could get in without busting something, leaving visible signs.

But it was getting tiresome waiting in the car. He knocked on the door again, and then stepped back and drew the Smith and pointed it at the spy hole.

Nobody home.

He took the elevator back down to the ground floor and looked up the building's supervisor in the tenant directory.

The super's name was Bruno Grebinsky. He answered the door with a paper napkin stuffed into the open neck of his dark-brown shirt and an empty fork in his hand.

Rikki said, "Mr Grebinsky?"

The man nodded, chewed and swallowed. He was in his sixties, probably. Thin on top and thick in the middle. Gold wire-frame glasses. Rikki shoved the barrel of the Smith into his belly, backed him up until there was room to kick shut the door.

At the far end of the living room, there was a dining alcove. A woman sitting bolt upright at the table with her back to them said, "What is it, Bruno?"

Rikki said, "I need the key to apartment three-one-seven."

Probably because she didn't recognize his voice, the woman turned in her chair. Rikki pointed the gun at her, and then swung back to her husband. The woman said, "I told you it was a mistake, renting to the police." Bruno handed Rikki the master key. He said, "I hope you know what you're doing, young man."

Rikki turned two of the dining room chairs back to back. He tore the electrical cords from the toaster and a blender, tied Bruno to one of the chairs, and used the telephone wire to tie up his yackety wife. Bruno had eleven dollars in his wallet. He looked like the kind of guy who kept his life savings under the mattress. Rikki went into the bedroom and checked the bed. Bad guess. He went through the bureau. He'd done a lot of B & Es when he was a kid. It'd always given him a kick, poking around in other people's lives, fingering through their tiny stupid secrets.

He found a thick wad of fifty dollar bills hidden in a mismatched pair of socks in the bottom drawer of Bruno Grebinsky's bureau. He stuffed the money in his pants pocket. There was some costume jewelry that he doubted even the marmalade cat would want. He went back into the living room. Grebinsky's face darkened as he saw the socks dangling from Rikki's hands.

Rikki said, "Open wide." He stuffed one sock into Bruno's mouth, the other into his wife's.

Tears ran down the super's face. His wife had told him not to rent to cops. And she had spent hours yelling at him about putting their life savings in a bank, where it was safe. God, he'd never hear the end of this.

Grebinsky spat out the sock Rikki had shoved into his mouth. He cursed Rikki and strained against the wire that held him.

Rikki said, "Watch yo" mouth!" His thumb snatched at the hammer as he tried a fast draw on the Smith. He had practiced the move for hours in front of a mirror, never had any problem. But this time it was different. This time, the Smith's blade front sight snagged on his fancy silver belt buckle.

The muzzle blast singed Rikki's pubic hair. He felt something tug at his stomach muscles, tear through him, rip him up inside. He sat down hard.

Mr Grebinsky stopped shouting.

Rikki had dropped the Smith. He couldn't seem to find it anywhere. He stared hard at Bruno Grebinsky. "What happened, old man?"

"You shot yourself, you fool."

Rikki nodded. Yeah, that was *his* blood, all right. He should've known. He climbed slowly to his feet, wandered over to the sofa, stumbled and collapsed on to the soft pink cushions.

There was blood on the carpet. Blood on the sofa. He was soaked in blood from his waist to his ankles. How much blood had he lost? Lots. Too much. He fumbled with his shirt. The entrance hole was just below and to the left of his belly button. The hole didn't look all that big, but there was a lot of blood, it was pumping out of him in a dark and solid river that overflowed his lap and spilled across the sofa.

Rikki remembered loading the Smith. How heavy and fat the .40-calibre bullets had felt as he'd pushed them into the magazine. And now one of them was inside him, deep inside him. He cleared his throat. He said, "You gotta get me an ambulance."

Bruno Grebinsky said, "You should have thought of that before you pulled the phone out of the wall, young man."

"I been shot . . ."

"You want help, come and untie me."

The wink of brass caught Rikki's cloudy, wandering eye. The spent cartridge lay on the carpet three or four feet from him, in the path of a slow-moving delta of blood.

Rikki covered himself with his hands, attempting to staunch the flow. He tried to press down on the wound but had no strength. Blood trickled from between his fingers. He tried to yell for help. His screams were whispers.

Bruno Grebinsky said, "You were going to murder us, weren't you?"

Rikki shook his head, no.

"Then why weren't you wearing a mask?"

It was an easy question – he simply hadn't bothered to think that far ahead. He'd always been the kind of guy who liked to take things one step at a time. He tried to explain all that to the dumb-ass super, but when he spoke, his lips failed to move, and nobody heard him.

Rikki's head lolled on his shoulder.

Mrs Grebinsky closed her eyes, but Bruno sat there in his chair with his beef stew congealing on the plate and watched Rikki die. He didn't feel the least bit sorry for the man. The colder-than-an-icecube look in Rikki's eyes when he'd shoved the big pistol in his stomach had erased any sympathetic feelings he might have had.

And there was the fact that the gun was right there by the sofa, partly hidden by a cushion but within easy reach, should Rikki happen to spot it.

Rikki watched out of the corner of his eye as the blurry puddle of blood crawled slowly towards the spent cartridge. The gun must've had a hair trigger, or maybe there was something wrong with it and that's why it had been in the gunshop. What terrible damage the bullet must have done, to leave him feeling so numb, lifeless. After a little while, exhausted, he shut his eyes.

When he was sure that Rikki was dead, Bruno Grebinsky worked a hand loose and untied himself and then walked stiff-legged and trembling into the kitchen and dug a steak knife out of the drawer and carefully cut free his wife. Rikki had tied the wires a bit too tightly. Her wrists stung. He held her in his arms, spoke softly and reassuringly to her. The other phone was in the bedroom. When she had managed to get herself under control, he asked her to please go and call the police. As soon as she left the room, he retrieved his five thousand hard-earned dollars from Rikki's pants pocket. A few of the bills were drenched in blood. He went into the tiny kitchen and rinsed his hands and the money under the tap.

From the bedroom his wife yelled that the police were on their way and she had to stay on the line until they arrived.

"Fine with me," said Bruno under his breath.

Before they left the hotel, Newt left messages at the lobby, the bar, and both restaurants, so that if Rikki got back to the hotel in time, he'd know where to join them. While Newt was busy leaving messages, Lulu told Frank about the gun Newt kept under his pillow, and how it had come into his possession. Frank listened carefully to her whispered rush of words. He looked a little disappointed, but not at all surprised.

The Coal Harbour restaurant was right on the water, just as Lulu had promised. It was a big place, post and beam construction, lots of dark wood and seating for two hundred or more. The problem was there weren't too many windows, and none that overlooked the water.

During dinner, Newt paused about every two or three minutes and gave Frank an odd look and said, "Where the hell's Rikki?" or, "Where did that little Mex bastard get to?" or something along those lines. Frank varied his replies to the best of his ability but after awhile he started repeating himself. By the time the main course arrived, he'd begun to feel stupid saying, "Beats me," or, "Wish I knew!" over and over again, and had reduced his response to a hunching of the shoulders, an empty shrug.

Newt eyed Frank suspiciously as he wolfed down his dessert; a monstrous wedge of chocolate cake slathered in ice cream and imported strawberries.

A fresh bottle of wine arrived. Frank didn't remember ordering it, but let it pass. Lulu took full advantage, trying to wash away the tension. Meanwhile Newt continued to slaughter his dessert, showing it no mercy. The ice cream had turned to slush but he didn't seem to mind. Frank noticed that Newt's glass still only had the waiter's fingerprints on it. He asked Newt if there was something wrong with the wine. Newt, blinking rapidly, said he was saving himself for the champagne.

Frank figured Newt had another reason to stay sober. He was deeply saddened. He'd always been a good and faithful servant. Since the move to sunny California, in almost as many years as could be counted on one hand, he had never once let Newt down. Now, suddenly, he'd made three serious mistakes in a row: screwed up the hit and run, bled his borrowed credit card dry and met a woman Newt wanted to take away from him. He suspected the way he'd abused Newt's credit card was by far the worst of the three offenses – not that it made any difference.

The bottom line was that Newt was after his ass. And judging from the agitated way he was beating the last of his strawberries and ice cream to a mushy red pulp, he was in a real hurry to get the job done.

Frank drank some water. That was one of the things he liked about the city – you could drink the water right out of the tap; even though it was mildly chlorinated, it tasted pretty good. The things you took for granted. He realized his mind was wandering. Jesus. Sooner or later, it always came down to those three precious words – *him or me*. He glanced at Lulu, admired her profile; the way she sat in her chair, erect and self-possessed. She was wearing skintight high-gloss lycra in vertical black and white stripes and had dyed her hair to match. Man, if zebras ever watched pornographic movies, she was what they'd pay to see. It had taken him awhile, but Frank had slowly grown used to the attention Lulu never failed to attract. When people first looked at her it was because she was an albino, pure and simple. But then, Frank knew, it was her stunning beauty and reckless nature that stopped them in their tracks, made them turn to sneak another look.

She was a gorgeous woman. He didn't blame Newt for wanting her, or plotting to take her away from him. He almost spoke up, and told Newt as much.

The waiter arrived with the bill. Newt reached for his jacket, pushed away from the table and headed for the washroom. Frank studied the bill, then turned and looked behind him. Newt was at the phone, pushing buttons.

Frank wondered if Rikki would be waiting for him in the parking lot. He decided no, the parking lot'd be too risky. Newt would worry about Lulu, that she might start screaming, making noise.

The hotel, then. Probably in his suite and not until they'd managed to separate him from his woman.

The bill was two hundred and ten dollars and change. Not a bad dent, considering the wine came to almost a hundred, and Newt's cake all by itself was just under eight bucks. Lulu helped Frank work out the tip. Since he'd red-lined his credit card, he had to pay cash. Newt came back to the table, looking impatient. Frank dropped a fat wad of five and ten dollar bills on the table, slipped his arm around Lulu's waist and gave her a quick kiss. He wanted to tell her not to worry, that everything was going to turn out fine, but somehow, he couldn't quite bring himself to speak the words.

Newt said, "I'm gonna take a leak. Wait for me at the car."

Frank didn't like the way Newt was staring at him, as if his bladder problems were all his fault. Or maybe it was Rikki he was mad about. Well, what was Frank supposed to do, wave his napkin in the air and hope Rikki would drop out of it? Hardly believing his luck, he watched Newt stroll stiff-legged across the restaurant and turn off down a narrow hallway.

"Got any quarters?"

Lulu started digging into her purse. Frank resisted the urge to tell her to hurry up, it was a question of life and death.

There was a public phone in a little alcove next to the washrooms. Frank dialled the hotel. No answer. Wherever Rikki was, it was somewhere else. Frank glanced over his shoulder, hung up and quickly dialled major crimes. A guy answered this time, a male with a soft, confident voice. No Parker. No Willows. Frank pitched his voice as high as it would go and said, "You getting this on tape?" There was no answer. He gave the guy the name of the hotel and Newt's room number and told him if the cops were still looking for the guys who shot Barry Chapman, it was a good place to start. Naturally the dispatcher asked him for a name. Frank hesitated for a moment and then figured what the hell, if he was gonna be a snitch he might as well do the job right. He gave the guy Newt's full name and Rikki's and then brief and not entirely objective description of both of them. Then he said, "You get all that?" The dispatcher wanted to know who was calling. Almost as an afterthought, Frank told him about Rikki's plan to bump Claire Parker.

Then he and Lulu went out to the parking lot to see what was there.

CD logged Mrs Grebinksy's call as Frank was hanging up, and dispatched a blue and white to the scene. By then, Parker and Willows had done what they could at the Japantown crime scene and were on their way back to 312 Main to hit the paperwork. Parker's address leapt out at her from the unmarked car's Motorola radio. Willows made an illegal left turn, pulled up next to a payphone and called central dispatch. Dispatch filled him in on the reported threat to Parker's life. Whether Rikki had accidentally shot himself or committed suicide was at that point unclear. In any event, he'd taken himself out of the picture. Newt, however, was still alive and well and presumably at the hotel. Dispatch had already alerted the Emergency Response Team.

Willows informed dispatch that he and Parker would be joining the party.

*

Back at the hotel, there was still no sign of Rikki. Newt excused himself and went into the bathroom, flushed the toilet repeatedly to cover the dismal growl of his retching. He splashed cold water on his face, gargled with mouthwash the color of diluted blood, and retrieved the twin of Rikki's .40-calibre Smith & Wesson semi-auto from its new hidy-hole at the bottom of a stack of fluffy hotel towels. He ejected the magazine to make sure the bullets hadn't mysteriously disappeared. Nope, they were all there. He slammed the magazine home and racked the slide, gingerly lowered the hammer and stuck the gun in his jacket pocket and checked himself out in the mirror, ran his fingers through his hair. He was looking *good.* But now what? He'd thought about it all through the ice cream, and there was no longer any doubt in his mind that Frank'd figured out what Rikki'd planned for him, and somehow beat him to the punch.

Newt was terrified. Rikki had been quick as a bolt of lightning, Newt the thunder that had followed in his wake. All noise, all noise. He had no illusions about what was next on Frank's agenda. The way Lulu had come on to him was a dead giveaway.

Newt softly opened the bathroom door. Lulu and Frank stopped talking and turned to look at him. He gave them a wan smile, adjusted his tie. "Guess I must've ate something didn't agree with me."

Frank said, "I tried the front desk, both restaurants and the bar. Nobody's seen him."

Lulu said, "Anybody in the mood for a swim?"

Frank smiled. He was pretty sure he knew what his baby had in mind – she wanted to bounce Newt's skull off the tiles, ease him into the deep end of the pool and hold him under until he'd run out of bubbles.

Lulu was staring at Newt. He shook his head, no. Where in a bathing suit could he hide such a big gun?

Lulu said, "Frank, you want to come along and keep me company?"

Newt caught the look that passed between them. What was going on, what were they up to?

He suddenly realized why Frank had been gone so long when he made the trip to the liquor store. Somehow, he'd done Rikki.

Newt pulled the Smith. He said, "Rikki's dead, ain't he?"

Frank looked surprised, but Lulu didn't. Newt said, "All I want is out. That's all. Out. Is it so much to ask, Frank, after all we've been through?"

Frank took Lulu's arm and started towards the door.

Newt said, "Hold it."

Frank waited.

Newt said, "I need somebody to drive me out to the airport."

"No problem."

"Not you, Frank. Her." Newt aimed the gun at a spot midway between Lulu's breasts. He said, "Just do me this small favor, Frank. Go stand by the TV and don't move an inch."

Frank said, "This is really dumb, Newt."

Newt waited until Frank had moved and then went over to Lulu and slipped an arm around her tiny waist. He opened the door. The corridor was empty. Newt said, "I ain't gonna hurt her. Just remember, the best thing you can do is to stay put."

Frank said, "I don't know where Rikki is or what happened to him."

Newt shut the door. He buried his nose in Lulu's ear and sniffed deeply. "I'm crazy about your perfume."

"Giorgio," said Lulu, pushing him away. She added, "Frank's going to kill you."

"I don't think so – why would he bother?"

"Because he loves me."

"Yeah, right."

It was no more than fifty feet down the hall to the bank of elevators, but by the time he got there, Newt was drenched in sweat, winded. He pushed a polished brass button. There was a faint rumbling noise, and then the maw of the closest elevator slowly opened wide. In they went, Newt dragging her all the way. He said, "Rikki made a move on Frank, didn't he?" Lulu kept silent. Newt said, "I know Frank. He isn't the kind of guy likes to swing first." The polished brass doors slid shut. Newt stabbed at the button for the lobby. The elevator twitched spasmodically as if awakened from a deep sleep.

Lulu tried to move away from Newt but he held her close, the gun pressing up against her, into the small of her back.

Could Frank catch up with them, using the stairs? She doubted it.

Newt said, "Gimme any trouble, I'll blow your brains out."

To underline his point, he tapped her gently on the skull with the barrel of his gun.

Lulu twisted towards Newt, as if to embrace him. She grabbed the gun and held on tight. The move was purely defensive, but

Newt thought she was trying to take the weapon away from him, and fought her for it. She kneed him in the groin. His legs buckled. She grunted and kneed him again. His eyes filled with water. All those sweaty calisthenics had made her so damn *strong*. He tried to shake loose but it was like trying to pull bark from a tree. Never had he been so intimately embraced.

Lulu worked a finger inside the trigger guard, tried to knee Newt again. His right thigh went numb. Their rate of descent slowed. The elevator doors slid open.

Newt saw that the lobby was full of cops – there were dozens of them, too many to count, guys in uniform and an ERT team in cammies, detectives with their badges clipped to their suits, the tightly packed mass of them waiting to get on the elevator. Tight, empty faces. The smell of sweat, gun oil. He spotted Phil Estrada, and Roger, both of them lurking in the background, squinty-eyed and empty-handed. His eyes locked on Claire Parker just at the moment Lulu chose to slide her teeth into his wrist, gnaw him mercilessly. He screamed, jerked away from her. The Smith's hammer fell in slow motion, struck and ignited the primer. The copper-jacketed hollow point ripped through Newt's soft tissue at a velocity of 975 fps.

Newt's gaping mouth filled with a white heat. His flushed cheeks ballooned comically. Smoke got in his eyes. Blood splashed across the burnished copper wall of the elevator. His eyes seemed to deflate, sink into his skull. His ruined head snapped back. A tooth glinted in the overhead lights.

Lulu held him tightly for a moment – just long enough to register the memory.

Then let him drop.

27

Inspector Homer Bradley flipped open the lid of the ornate Haida-carved cedar box his brand new ex-wife had given him on the courthouse steps so many years ago, as she'd kissed him goodbye for the very last time.

The box was empty. It was damn near inconceivable, but during the night somebody had strolled into his office and stolen over seventy dollars worth of the best cigars that Havana could make.

He flipped the lid shut and then quickly flipped it open again. Damn. He said, "You're absolutely sure you never saw the guy before last night?"

Parker said, "How could I forget somebody with a name like that? Rikki Acapulco. Inspector, how could *anybody* forget a name like that?"

Bradley had been up all night, and it was now pushing noon of the following day. Lack of sleep had left him in a somewhat spiky frame of mind. But he had to admit that Parker had a point. He said, "You faxed Rikki's pic and prints to LA?"

Parkler nodded, suppressed a yawn.

Willows said, "And Acapulco, and Mexico City, because of the tattoo."

"What tattoo?"

Bradley reached for Rikki's file. At the moment, it was flatter than his wallet, but he had a hunch that as soon as they got past Rikki Acapulco's AKA and found out who he really was, the file would assume the size of a telephone directory. Newt, of course, they already knew about.

"He had a tattoo on the inside of his upper thigh," Willows said.

Bradley couldn't help himself; he snuck a quick look at Parker.

Parker was ready for him. She said, "It wasn't all that artistic, basic pin-and-ink stuff."

"Yeah, but what did it say?"

"*Mexico City.*"

"In English?"

Willows said, "No, it was in Spanish."

Bradley leaned back. He felt vaguely disappointed, but wasn't sure why. He said, "Too early to get anything back, I suppose?"

Willows said, "From Mexico, yeah."

"You heard something from Los Angeles?"

Parker said, "They've been looking for Rikki. AKA Ricardo Montalban AKA Yves Montand AKA Thomas Gomez . . ."

"Wait a minute," said Bradley. "Montalban and Montand are actors, aren't they?"

"So's Gomez. He's probably best known for his work in *Key Largo* and *Beneath the Planet of the Apes.*"

"Great, but what's he done lately?"

"Nothing much," said Parker. "He died in nineteen-seventy-one."

"What was Rikki's real name, or does anybody know?"

"They *think* it's Emilio Fernandez, but they're not sure. Nobody is."

Willows said, "Rikki was the kind of guy who changed his name more often than he changed his socks. A human chameleon."

"What'd LA want him for?"

"Everything from shoplifting a case of toilet paper to first-degree murder. A couple of days before he and Newt flew up here, the body of young woman named Annette Mickleburgh was found in a vacant lot in Glendale. Newt had asked her out a few days before she was killed. She'd told her fellow employees all about it – Newt's Porsche and his house on the beach . . ."

"So why Rikki?"

"He left his fingerprints all over her neck."

Bradley turned to Parker. "And the way Frank Wright tells it, Newt and Rikki came up here to bump you off."

Parker nodded.

"Because you shot Newt."

"That's Frank's story," said Parker. "So far, he's sticking to it."

"Good motive, revenge."

Parker didn't say anything.

Bradley said, "You buy it?"

Parker shrugged. "There are a few holes. Nothing we could lead a prosecutor through."

Bradley said, "Share your thoughts with me, Jack."

"I think Newt hired Frank to hit Claire. Frank can't remember where he's spent the past couple of years, but I wouldn't be surprised if it was in California, working for Newt. Maybe Frank couldn't set things up to Newt's satisfaction, or maybe he decided he didn't want the job. Either way, I think that's why Newt and Rikki came to Vancouver."

"Barry Chapman, the gunshop owner?"

Willows said, "Chapman had a closed-circuit video camera – the same kind of setup used by the banks. We've got the whole thing on tape, from the moment Rikki walked in the door right through the bludgeoning, theft of the guns, everything."

Bradley smiled. "Rikki liked movie-star aliases, and then turned into a star himself, and didn't even notice." He checked the cigar box again. Still no magic. "What about the albino?"

"Lulu."

"Yeah."

"No priors, but I'd say she was working the hotel, met Frank sometime after he checked in."

"Love at first sight," said Bradley.

Parker said, "It happens."

Bradley said, "Yeah, I saw it on TV a couple of weeks ago." He used his index fingers to play a little tune on the cigar box. "The Joey Ngo inquest?"

"Scheduled to start next Tuesday."

"So, except for a little paperwork, you two've got a clean plate." He leaned forward. "You're unemployed!"

Parker glanced at Willows, looked away.

Bradley said, "The Japantown killings. Just between you and me, Kaplan and Wilkinson are in way over their heads, the case is almost twenty-four hours old and we've got nothing, zilch. I want you to take over, point them in the right direction."

Willows said, "Inspector, my kids are flying in from Toronto tomorrow, at noon."

"Sean and Annie?"

Willows nodded. "My vacation was supposed to start yesterday, at end of shift."

Bradley cocked an eyebrow. "You're letting them ride alone on the plane?"

"No, there'll be a pilot on board."

"Eddy's the comedian, Jack. How long are they gonna be in town?"

"Three weeks."

"*Three weeks!* You take 'em to the zoo, then what?"

"We're going over to the Island. I rented a cabin on Long Beach."

"Nice." Bradley turned to Parker. "You've got the next few weeks off too, right?"

"That's right, Inspector."

"And where exactly are *you* going to be spending your summer vacation?"

Parker glanced at Willows, quickly looked away.

Bradley grinned lasciviously. "You're going to have to tell me all about it when you get back."

"Not a chance," said Willows.

28

This is how it went with Joey.

The air was warm and soft. In the darkness, it moved across his body the way Emily had touched him, so gently, so sweetly.

He still couldn't believe he'd killed her. He knew he had done it, but somehow it didn't seem real. Or was it that nothing else was real?

He had thought his brother worked as a cook, but it turned out the restaurant where Cherry arranged to meet him had gone out of business. Cherry used the place to store and sell stolen cigarettes and that's why he wanted Joey there, to help him move a couple hundred cartons of Camel Filters. But first they walked up the street to the grocery store for the sweet potato. Back at the abandoned restaurant, Cherry had shown Joey how the sweet potato could be used for a silencer. Alone with his brother, Joey had wanted to tell him what he had done, confess his sins. But as they'd talked, it became clear that Cherry didn't give a damn about Emily. He believed the bullets that killed her had been meant for him. His only concern was finding out who had done the shooting, and why.

Joey wouldn't meet his brother's eyes. He stared at a picture of a water buffalo in a rice paddy, that was thumb-tacked to the wall.

Then Cherry put his hand on his shoulder and smiled into Joey's eyes as he'd told him that he'd seen him in the black Honda CRX, refused to believe it at first and then worked it all out, that Joey had intended to blast him, not Emily.

After that he had picked up the telephone and called the police, spoken to Claire Parker.

Joey's shame turned to rage. There was a struggle, another accident. It *was* an accident. As he sat there in the apple tree, he told himself over and over again that his brother's death could not have been anything but an accident – something he hadn't planned or expected and had no control over, that had simply happened.

In the days that followed, he phoned Claire Parker several times but always found himself unable to speak. Hoping it would be easier if he could talk directly to her, he'd gone all the way across town one night to her apartment. But then, as he stood on the sidewalk, she had come to the window and looked out, and he'd lost his nerve, slipped away and never gone back.

Now, sitting in the apple tree with darkness all around him, he unbuttoned his shirt and pressed his hand against his chest.

His heart fluttered beneath his skin.

The barrel of the .45 was cold. Shivering, he drew back the hammer. He had thought about this a great deal. He knew what he was going to do, but somehow could not believe that he was going to do it. His finger stroked the trigger. A light came on in the house where the old lady lived. He saw her in the kitchen window. Her head was bowed. In a moment she would look up, and see him. He held the sweet potato in his left hand. Its skin was smooth and firm. He willed the old lady to look out the window. If she would only look up, she was sure to see him.

As he waited, he slowly increased the pressure of his finger on the trigger.